*P*ower in the *B*lood

E. L. Wyrick

Power in
the Blood

St. Martin's Press
New York

MYSTERY
FICTION
WYRICK,
E.
1996

A THOMAS DUNNE BOOK.
An imprint of St. Martin's Press.

POWER IN THE BLOOD. Copyright © 1996 by E. L. Wyrick. All rights reserved.
Printed in the United States of America. No part of this book may be used or
reproduced in any manner whatsoever without written permission except in the
case of brief quotations embodied in critical articles or reviews. For information,
address St. Martin's Press, 175 Fifth Avenue, New York, N.Y. 10010.

Design by Ellen R. Sasahara

Library of Congress Cataloging-in-Publication Data

Wyrick, E. L.
    Power in the blood / by E. L. Wyrick.—1st ed.
        p.   cm.
    "A Thomas Dunne book."
    ISBN 0-312-13590-4
    1. Women lawyers—Georgia—Fiction.   2. Georgia—Fiction.
I. Title.
PS3573.Y68P69   1996
813'.54—dc20   95-4506
                                                                 CIP

First Edition: April 1996

10 9 8 7 6 5 4 3 2 1

34 4/29/96 22.95

For Forrest G. "Spec" Towns
in memoriam

An Olympic champion
and
A special friend.
Forever and ever,
Amen.

Acknowledgments

The author wishes to thank the following people for their invaluable help: Athens/Clark County Assistant District Attorney Rick Dickson; attorney Jenny Turner; Jackson County, Georgia, Sheriff Stan Evans; Gwinnett County, Georgia, policeman John Hobson; instructor of nursing Benna Cunningham; and Roscoe and Diana Foster for their special expertise.

Also, thanks to those who read and responded to the manuscript: Pete McCommons; Melissa and Johnny Blackstone; Bob Hall; Betsy Lindsey; Church Barrow Crow; Ann Dunn; my sister, Cathy Miller; and my parents, Ed and Lois Wyrick.

Particular appreciation is extended to the best nonprofessional responder to manuscripts that I have discovered to date. Her name is Emily Grace Blackstone, who was thirteen years old when she read this book.

Donna Wenzel, who proofed early versions of the manuscript, is a jewel.

I cannot imagine a better scenario than to have Robin Rue as my agent; and to be edited by Ruth Cavin, who is also a wonderful teacher.

Finally, and most importantly, I want my wife and children—Pat, Heather, Kalli, and Mariah—to know how much I appreciate their patience and support.

Chapter One

Something's happening.

My fear is diminishing. It hasn't gone away, but during the past few weeks there were times when I *should* have been afraid, but wasn't. Not for long, anyway.

Anger has replaced the fear and that *does* scare me. If the wrath keeps surfacing, someone who doesn't deserve it will be hurt badly someday.

That someone may be me.

Psychologist Josie Beam, who I've been seeing for more than a year, predicted the emotional shift. She didn't predict another change—one that's not so disagreeable.

Growing up in a small south Georgia town meant watching my role models be dependent on their men—their daddies, brothers, boyfriends, and husbands. Despite my awareness of that socialization process and my attempts to alter the preordained, it has been only during the last few months that I've begun to take care of myself without seeking a man's guiding hand. During the past few weeks, I believe that I have taken another step in that direction.

But, early experience isn't overcome easily. The fact is, the deep-seated reliance on men inspired by my upbringing was probably why I asked Mitch Griffith to accompany me on an unlikely mission in early October.

The mission was to meet a potential client who wanted to buy a town.

"Yassuh, Masser," Mitch said.

"Yassuh, Masser, what?"

"I don't know, Tammi. It's this place." Mitch slumped his shoulders and began shuffling again. "It be weird. I's jes feels it in my bones."

The place was Warrendale.

I stopped walking and Mitch stopped shuffling. We were standing in the middle of an empty parking lot that fronted the town's entire business district. In fact, it fronted just about all of Warrendale, period. I gazed at the row of red brick buildings ahead of us. Most were attached to those on either side, but had apparently been built at different times. The setting October sun reflected off a window of the Warren Furniture and Appliance Mart. Next to it was Warren Hardware, which in turn abutted the Warren Five and Dime. A small alley separated the group of buildings from the Warren Grocery.

To our right, across the narrow asphalt strip that was Georgia Highway 28, sat the Warrendale Baptist Church. Fire-Baptist is what I guessed. The singing of the Sunday evening congregation drifted across the road. I joined in:

> Take my life and let it be,
> consecrated, Lord, to Thee.

I stopped when I saw Mitch's look. "Just feel it in my bones."

Mitch said, "Like I said, this place be weird."

"I can't imagine why he wants to buy it."

"Gonna make it Hollywood East, I heard."

I shook my head. Strange things happen, but *that* was preposterous. "He said to meet him in the old mill." I looked to my left at a two-story brick building with a tin roof that stood perpendicular to the stores. There wasn't a sign, but because it was the only other structure in sight, I presumed that was it. "Come on."

"Yassuh, Mas—"

"Shut up, Mitch," I said before he could finish.

The mill sat next to a sharp bend of the Olkmolknee River. On that side of the building, a rotting waterwheel rested above a dry ditch that at one time must have had diverted water running through it. Above the shaft of the wheel, rows of cracked and broken windows that had been painted green ran the length of the structure. The front of the building had only a door, which wouldn't open.

"Are you sure this is where he said to meet?" Mitch asked. He looked back at my Yugo in the otherwise empty parking lot.

"Yeah. He called only a couple of hours ago. Meet him here at seven, he said." We stood still and looked around. "Let's try the other side." We walked the width of the building and turned the corner. "Bingo," I said. A bright red Miata was parked next to a door midway down the mill. The car's vanity tag read, N TUNE. The mill's windowed side door was ajar, but it was flush with the floor and took a good push to open it further.

We walked into the cavernous interior. Rusted machinery sat scattered across the concrete floor, casting shadows from the sunlight that filtered through the windows in the wall across the way. Cobwebs hung everywhere. Mitch walked to a huge spool sitting on a shaft that still held bailing twine. He ran his fingers across the twine. In a rich baritone, he sang:

> Nobody knows the trouble I've seen,
> Nobody knows but Jesus.

He stopped and said, "I don't like it here."

I didn't either. I wanted to take care of business and head home. I yelled, "Mr. Fletcher!"

Mitch jumped. "Jesus H. Christ," he exclaimed. "Give me some warning, will you?"

Our voices echoed through the mostly empty space.

"Sorry." I pointed to an area that appeared to be an office. "Maybe he's in there."

The partitioned space held nothing. As we walked back toward the side door, Mitch said, "I say yet again, this place be weird. Let's get out of here."

"I'd like to, but that's his car out there. He must be around here someplace."

"How do you know it's his car?"

"The tag. 'N TUNE.' His first big movie was *In Time, In Tune*."

"Never saw it."

I said, "Fore."

" 'For' what?"

"You asked for a warning," I said, then screamed, "Lawton Fletcher! Where are you?" Still, nothing but an echo. "Oh well, let's go."

"Great!" Mitch shot out the door.

I stopped to pull the door closed. It didn't want to come, so I stepped back inside to pull it with two hands. A shaft of sunlight reflected off the door's window and illuminated the area behind the spool of twine. I stopped pulling and said, "Mitch."

"Yeah?"

"Come here."

"Aww, Tammi," he said, but came back inside.

I felt his hand wrap around mine as we stared at the bloody body of Lawton Fletcher, movie star.

Chapter Two

T he public telephone next to the Warrendale Furniture Store was housed in a booth like those Superman used back when calls were a nickel. In fact, he may have used this very booth, because the sign still said calls were a nickel. Of course, calls cost more than a nickel and the phone didn't work.

I stepped from the booth and looked around. There was no urgency. Lawton Fletcher had no pulse, and the amount of blood spreading from the back of his head was a clear indication that attempting to resuscitate him would be useless. Despite that knowledge and despite its eternal state, death—especially violent death—creates an obligation to act fast. Plus, Mitch was keeping watch over the body and he didn't much like doing that.

From across the road I heard:

> Praise God from whom all blessings flow,
> Praise Him, all creatures here below,
> Praise Him above, ye heavenly host,
> Praise Father, Son, and Holy Ghost.

The doxology. If I hurried I might be able to catch a deacon before he sat down after collecting the offering.

The double front doors to the church were open, and I could see two deacons walking down the center aisle toward the rear. I quickened my pace to try to catch the eye of one, but that wasn't necessary. One of the men turned and disappeared, but the other kept going out the doors, then stopped and lit a cigarette. The deacon, who was dressed in a cheap suit that hung loosely on his sloping shoulders, saw me crossing the road and cupped the cigarette in his hand to hide it from me. I suspected he drank his beer on the back porch.

When I stepped on the bricked sidewalk, I asked the man if the church had a phone. He sniffed through his narrow nose and said, "Got one in Preacher's office." His hand, with the cigarette still cupped inside, moved up as if to point. The heel on one of my pumps caught on a cobblestone, and when I reached out to regain my balance, our hands collided.

"Goddamnit!" he exclaimed as he threw the cigarette down and waved his hand in pain. His shoulders slumped another couple of inches as he turned toward the church. Members of the congregation in the last rows had turned grim faces toward the foul intrusion into their Sunday evening worship.

"I'm sorry," I said, "Are you all right?"

The deacon was still waving his hand and hissed, "Sheeeit."

"Listen. I've got to use a phone. Is there one in the church?"

Apparently the pain had diminished because he quit waving and cursing. "Yeah, but you can't use it during the service. Preacher wouldn't like it."

"This is an emergency. I've got to call the police. A man's been killed." I waved across the road.

He squinted and looked toward the mill. "Killed? Who was killed?"

"Lawton Fletcher."

"Sheeeit." He lit another cigarette, inhaled deeply, and let the smoke out slowly. "Lawton Fletcher. I'll be goddamned." He spit on Highway 28 and looked at me. "Who are you?"

"My name's Tammi Randall. I'm an attorney from Patsboro."

He took another drag on his cigarette. "Lawton Fletcher. How 'bout that. Guess that means he won't be buying the town."

Quick thinker, I thought. "How about the phone?"

He wiggled his nose. Apparently that was part of his decision-making process. "Come on."

I followed him around the white frame church to the back where a set of dilapidated wooden steps led to a door. We went down a hallway to the preacher's office. When we entered, the preacher's voice could be heard plainly. He was alternately shouting and whispering and punctuated each sentence with a "hah."

"Does Warrendale have a police department?" I asked.

"Sheeeit. Got Donald Lee."

"Is he the chief?"

"He's the whole goddamned department."

"How do I get in touch with him?"

"Probably down at his beer store and pool hall."

"On Sunday?"

"Sheeeit. Being Sunday don't make no difference to Donald Lee."

I thought about teaching the deacon some new expletives, but instead said, "Do you know the phone number?"

He hesitated, then told me.

Lee was there, and I told him about Fletcher. By the time the deacon and I had stepped out the back door of the church, we could hear a siren screaming.

"Goddamn. Ol' Donald Lee loves this shit." At least his inflection had changed. When we rounded the church a police car with its lights flashing was parked next to my Yugo. The siren was still blaring. The deacon followed me across the street.

Lee got out of his car as we approached. "You Tammi Randall?" He was shouting, but I could barely hear him over the siren. After I nodded, he shouted, "Where is he?"

"Turn it off!" I screamed.

"What?" Lee shouted back.

"The frigging siren! Turn it off!"

Lee reached in the car and flipped a switch. My ears were still humming despite the silence. "Where is he?" Lee asked again.

Donald Lee looked to be in his thirties and was about an inch taller than my five eight. His belt looped just above his groin underneath a protruding belly. The buttons on his shirt were strained. His holstered gun dug into a roll of flab that surrounded his waist. A thick, black mustache sat above a pair of thick lips that matched his droopy cheeks and jowls.

I pointed toward the mill. "He's in there."

Lee got back into his car and said, "Get in."

He must have misunderstood, I thought. Again, I pointed to the mill, about a hundred feet away. "It's just right there."

"Get in," he repeated and turned on the siren.

"Lord Almighty, help me," I muttered, then walked around the car and saw that the congregation had gathered behind us. Through the church's open door, I could see Preacher gesticulating in front of empty pews, apparently unaware that his congregation had departed. I'd barely closed the door to the cruiser when Lee stomped on the accelerator and fishtailed toward the mill. I yelled that we needed to go around the building.

As we swerved around the corner of the mill, I screamed, "Look out!" Lee turned the wheel, barely missing Mitch, whose arms flew up as he jumped back. Lee jammed on the brakes, and I careened forward. My right forearm slammed against the dashboard, my head stopping an inch from the windshield. I watched as Donald Lee's cruiser slid into Lawton Fletcher's sports car. The siren suddenly stopped, apparently destroyed by the impact.

Lee jumped out and slammed his door. He walked to the front of the car and surveyed the damage. He came back to the open window on the driver's side and said across the seat, "Why the hell didn't you tell me there was a fucking car back here?"

I got out and slammed my door and glared at Lee through the flashing lights on the car's roof. "I was operating under the obviously mistaken assumption that you had driven before."

"Sheeeit," Lee said and slammed his palm on top of the car. He turned toward the mill's door. "Fletcher in here?"

"Yes." I walked behind the car to Mitch, who was sitting

against the mill's wall. He was still breathing hard. "Are you all right?" I asked.

Before he could answer, the congregation appeared and the deacon approached Mitch and me. The deacon's thin lips parted in a smile and his eyes fell to Mitch. "Looks like ol' Donald Lee just about got hisself a goddamned colored boy."

Mitch looked up and said in high-brow British, "By jove, that was a bloody close shave, wasn't it?"

The deacon's smile turned into a quizzical look as he stared at Mitch.

I heard the mill's door scrape, and turned to see Lee running to his car. I helped Mitch up and we joined him. Lee was talking over the radio to the Park County Sheriff's Department, telling them Lawton Fletcher'd been shot and killed. The woman radio operator replied that she'd contact the Georgia Bureau of Investigation and an ambulance. I was glad to hear it. I couldn't imagine Donald Lee investigating a case of jaywalking, much less a suspicious death. Lee threw the microphone on the seat and turned to me. "I need to ask you some questions."

"Why don't we wait for the GBI?"

Lee looped his thumb between his pistol's handle and the holster. "Lady, you're in my town. I'll ask questions when I want to."

I didn't want to go through it twice, and I knew I'd be talking to the GBI. "I'm still dazed from the crash. Can't remember much right now."

"Uh-huh." Lee looked at Mitch. "What about you? How'd you find him?"

Mitch reached out and grasped Lee's right arm and responded in something that sounded like Chinese.

Lee said, "Sheeeit" and pulled his arm away. He walked back into the mill.

Mitch and I leaned against the patrol car. He said, "Sure do feel comforted knowing Chief Lee's on the job."

I looked at Lee's mashed car and giggled.

Mitch said, "Sheeeit." He sounded just like Chief Lee.

That did it. I laughed and then he laughed. I howled. Tears were streaming down my cheeks. Slowly, the laughter subsided and I was able to get some air. I took a deep breath and looked up at the bright pink sky. I looked at the members of the congregation who were staring at Mitch and me. I tried to regain a solemn face.

Death isn't funny. But while earning an undergraduate degree in psychology, I'd learned that laughing and crying are closely related. I'd relearned that in my weekly sessions with Dr. Josie Beam, who I started seeing a little over a year ago, after I killed Buddy Crowe and Radar Gilstrap. I shot Crowe when he raped me. Gilstrap, who had sent Crowe to Patsboro, came later.

With Josie's help, I'd come to understand that it didn't matter whether you laughed or cried. What mattered was what you felt inside. I didn't know Lawton Fletcher, except to see him in his movies, but seeing his lifeless body produced a profound emptiness that I've felt with every death I've experienced. My father, elderly relatives . . . even Crowe and Gilstrap.

As I was thinking about all that, one of the few young members of the congregation approached us. She might have been out of her early teens, but not by much. She was wearing an ankle-length, white linen dress with tiny flowers embroidered across the front, above her breasts. Flaxen hair fell across her shoulders. She had the classic model's face—high cheek bones, blue eyes, full heart-shaped mouth, strong chin.

When she arrived, she shifted her baby from one arm to the other. "Is it really Lawton Fletcher?" After asking the question, her lips separated in a grimace. Two teeth were missing, several were discolored, and there appeared to be an extra tooth behind one of her incisors.

"Yes," I said.

The woman bit her lower lip and made a sound.

"Did you know him?"

She shook her head. "No. I just hoped if he bought this town, he'd make it better."

Before I could respond, an olive green sedan turned into the parking lot. The congregation parted and the car stopped in front of us. A woman in a blue windbreaker emerged from the sedan, then reached into her car to retrieve a notebook and a camera. Large yellow letters on the back of the windbreaker announced that she was GBI. She sauntered to Mitch and me. "Where's Lee?"

She was tall, over six feet, and solid. Her sandy hair was short, as if cut with the aid of a bowl. Straight bangs fell above brown eyes.

"He's in there," I said, pointing to the mill. "We found Fletcher. This is Mitch Griffith and I'm Tammi Randall."

She looked at Mitch and me, her eyes showing signs of recognition. Radar Gilstrap had been a GBI agent. "I'm Agent Malone," she said, then walked to the front of Lee's car and inspected the damage. She put her hand on the red Miata. "Is this Fletcher's car?"

As I said it was, Lee came out of the mill. The GBI agent looked at him. "Great job, Lee. It's always good to cream the evidence."

I already liked this woman.

Lee pushed a finger in his shirt and scratched his belly button. "That's *Chief* Lee, Molly."

Malone smiled. "Okay, *Chief*. Have you got your men inside searching for clues?" Warrendale's only policeman dug deeper into his navel. The GBI agent glanced at the congregation. "How about interviewing some citizens? One of them might have seen something."

Lee removed his finger from his shirt. "This is my town, Molly. You're here by invitation."

"Sure," Malone said equably. She looked at her watch and said, "Considering who you got in there, I'd give it an hour before the reporters arrive." She headed toward her sedan. "Have fun."

The implications were obvious, even to Lee. "Wait a minute," he said.

Malone stopped and turned, her expression sanguine.

"Sheeeit," Lee said and walked to the congregation.

Malone regarded Mitch and me. "Y'all mind coming with me?"

We followed her into the mill. With the sun setting, it was darker than before. She tried a bank of switches next to the door to no avail. "A lab team's on its way from Atlanta. They'll have lights," she said more to herself than to us. She pulled her camera off her shoulder and began taking pictures of the body.

Two young men in jumpsuits with patches reading Park County Rescue entered. One was in his twenties, the other was younger. They squatted next to Fletcher's body, then stood. The older EMT said to Malone, "In my opinion he's deader'n a door nail."

"Thanks for the confirmation," Malone said, then added, "How about waiting outside?" The two men shrugged and left.

When she was through taking pictures, the agent said she needed to ask us some questions. We moved to an area in the mill where the sun afforded some light.

In response to her questions, I told her I was an attorney for the Teal County Legal Aid Society, my age was twenty-eight, and I was single. Mitch explained he owned a chain of appliance stores, was twenty-seven and single, too. When he mentioned his stores, Agent Malone said she'd thought he looked familiar. She'd seen his advertisements on cable TV. "I love the Bill Clinton one," she said. Mitch's uncanny ability to imitate voices had helped his stores become wildly successful.

When Malone asked how we had come to find Fletcher's body, I told her about the phone call I'd received a week ago from Professor Gatlin. While in law school at Catledge University in Patsboro, I'd been in the professor's contracts class. Now he was a visiting professor at Harvard. On the phone, he explained that he'd received a call from Lawton Fletcher's agent, who Professor Gatlin knew from his college days. The agent said Fletcher was interested in buying Warrendale and wanted an attorney whom he could trust, and who wouldn't use involvement in the sale to produce publicity. Professor Gatlin asked me if I would do it.

I didn't tell Agent Malone that my initial response was to decline the offer. My limited experience consisted mostly of defending indigents who'd been charged with small crimes and misdemeanors, along with an occasional civil case involving things like failure to pay loans to finance companies. But Professor Gatlin had insisted I could do it. He'd said I was the best contract law student he'd taught.

The professor also said he assumed that I could use the fee that a seven-million-dollar sale would bring, given my limited salary from the society. He said even though a large amount of money was involved, the sale was relatively straightforward and that he would be happy to provide advice if needed. He was right about my being able to use the money. The next day I called him back and accepted.

I did tell Malone that Fletcher had contacted me earlier that day. He said he wanted to meet and show me the property. Mitch and I had arrived at the appointed time, and found Fletcher's body in the mill. Malone wanted to know why Mitch was there. I explained that I'd asked him to come. I thought his entrepreneurial acumen might be helpful, and in the last two years, he'd bought a lot of property.

Malone pursed her lips. She asked if we'd seen anybody or anything else. Mitch shook his head and so did I. We hadn't seen anything but Fletcher's body. At that moment, Lee appeared.

"I got him," Lee said.

"Got who?" Malone asked.

"The perp. He's out in my car."

Malone, Mitch, and I followed Lee out the door. His car was now sitting well away from Fletcher's. It was nearly dark, but a figure of a hulking man could be seen in the back seat.

Malone looked at Lee and said, "What's the deal?"

"That's Freddy Meadows," Lee said. He pointed to the congregation. "Deacon Bell saw him over here this evening before church started. Meadows is a mean son of a bitch. I went over to his house and got him."

"For questioning?" Malone asked.

Lee hooked his thumbs in his gun belt. "Hell, no. I arrested him."

Malone shook her head and opened the car door. She said, "Are you Freddy Meadows?"

Meadows nodded.

"Did you kill somebody tonight?"

Meadows shook his head.

Malone closed the door. "Since he's apparently not confessing, Lee, you wouldn't happen to have anything on this guy would you? Stuff like, you know, evidence?"

"He was placed at the scene and is known to be violent," Lee said defensively, a hint of whine in his voice.

He started to say something else, but the *whop, whop* of a helicopter interrupted him. Suddenly, the parking lot was lit by a powerful searchlight. We all looked up, then the congregation scattered as the helicopter landed. On its side was written 11 Alive News.

I said, "Chief Lee, as an attorney I advise you to let that gentleman go. Lots of headlines could be made by some lawyer wanting to make a name for himself. Wrongful arrest is a cinch in this case."

Lee said, "Sheeeit," but opened the back door of his patrol car and took the handcuffs off Meadows, who then started to leave.

"Hold on, there," Malone said. "I still want to talk to you."

I said, "Do you need us anymore? I'd just as soon not get involved with them." I nodded toward the helicopter.

"You can go," Malone said. "We'll be in touch though."

Mitch and I edged around the crowd and climbed into my Yugo. Soon we were driving through the dark countryside toward Patsboro.

Mitch said, "That was an interesting way to spend a Sunday evening."

"Yeah," I said.

After a few minutes of silence, Mitch mused, "Molly Malone." He started humming a familiar tune. Suddenly he sang:

> As she wheeled her wheelbarrow,
> Through streets broad and narrow,

I joined him:

> Crying, cockles and mussels,
> Alive, alive oh!

"You're not going to get involved in this are you?" Mitch asked. "I mean, if Lee pursues that Meadows guy. He looked like he'd qualify for the society's services."

I shook my head. "We've applied for a grant to become a regional center. If that happens, we'd serve Park County. We don't now though."

I glanced at Mitch. He was nodding.

I said, "If we were involved with Park County, I'd ask Bernard to do this one. He's had a bunch of experience in this sort of thing."

Mitch was still nodding.

"To tell you the truth, I've been . . . uneasy about even handling this sale. I mean, a whole town, Mitch. Even with Professor Gatlin's help, I'd—"

A deer appeared at the side of the road. I slowed down to get by it. The buck stood and stared as we passed.

"At about two o'clock this morning, when I couldn't sleep from worrying about representing Fletcher in this deal, I promised myself I wouldn't get involved with anything else that was over my head. Defending the accused murderer of a movie star would be over my head."

"Uh-huh," Mitch said.

"I mean it. I promised myself and that's it."

That promise lasted less than twenty-four hours.

Chapter Three

The knife whisked within inches of my belly. A quick step back had saved me, but that option was running out. I was trapped.

The man called Chico laughed. My stomach tightened reflexively as I stared into his slitted eyes. In my peripheral vision I could see the knife in his left hand. Chico's flimsy brown hair was matted on his forehead, stuck there by sweat. His thin lips curled in a snarl. In a reedy voice he said, "Come on, baby. Come to Chico."

I moved to my left, keeping my feet spaced for balance. When Chico turned with me, his hairless chest became visible. It rose and fell evenly as he breathed, making the sailing ship tattooed above his nipples expand and contract.

I wiggled my fingers and took a deep breath. A quick kick to the groin would end it, but if I missed he'd have me. There was *no* way he was going to have me. My concentration wavered as the vision of Buddy Crowe captured my consciousness. He was kneeling between my legs and pricking my inner thighs with his razor-sharp knife. The image was so clear, I could even smell his rancid odor.

I shook my head slightly, clearing Crowe's horror from my mind.

Never again.

Patience Tammi, I thought. Wait for him . . . wait. Stay with it—concentrate. Stay loose. Be ready. Chico threw the knife from his left to his right hand. That's what I was waiting for. When he used his right, he jabbed rather than swung.

"Hey, sweetheart. You ain't going nowhere," he said. In a falsetto voice he sang, "No where to run, no where to hide. No where to run, no where to hide." Then he laughed and took a step forward. I took a half step back. I needed to be a little closer. Another full step back and I'd be against the wall anyway.

He did it. A short jab with his right hand. I took a quick step to the left, being sure to keep my balance. I moved swiftly and encircled his wrist with my right hand. Immediately, I swung my left forearm up, midway between his underarm and elbow, providing a fulcrum. He grunted when I snapped his wrist downward. The knife fell soundlessly onto the floor.

There was no time to think. I knew Chico's slight stature was deceiving. He had amazing strength. With his wrist still in my hand, I stepped back and kicked the front of his leg, between knee and groin, with my right heel. He expelled air and collapsed. I raised my foot again, this time to finish it with a kick to the groin.

"Whoa, Tammi," Chico said from his prone position. "I'm wearing a cup, but let's not take any chances."

Clapping and cheering filled the air as the other nine women in Chico's self-defense class expressed their approval. Chico stood and we bowed to each other. When I retrieved his rubber knife and gave it to him, he was rubbing his leg. "You know, in here we try to hold back a little bit," he said.

"I'm sorry. I guess I got into it. Are you okay?"

"Yeah. I'm just glad I stopped you before the finale." His phone rang and he went to answer it.

In the past year I'd become an early riser. On Monday morning, I attended Chico's self-defense class for working women. I swam laps at Catledge University's indoor pool on Tuesday, Thursday, and Saturday. Wednesday mornings were spent at Jackson's Indoor Shooting Range with my daddy's Smith & Wesson, Model 58. Friday was reserved for breakfast at Shoney's restaurant with Mitch Griffith and Dan Bushnell, though for the past couple of months, Dan hadn't come. On Sundays, I slept in. Chico called me to the phone. "It's Mr. Fuchs," he said.

Bernard Fuchs was another attorney at the Legal Aid Society. He was supposed to be semiretired from a lucrative practice in Atlanta, working part time with us and raising horses on his farm outside Patsboro. The society's board had asked him to become our director, and he'd finally agreed. Old habits die hard, and he usually arrived at work early.

"I hope I did not interrupt your training," he said.

"No problem."

"I would like to speak with you when you arrive here. Something has come up that may be of interest to you."

"Okay," I said, waiting. I knew he hadn't called just to tell me that.

"I understand you were involved in a discovery last evening."

"Yes."

"I would like to hear about it. Unfortunately, others would also. The phone is ringing incessantly and two reporters from Atlanta have bivouacked in the waiting room. I thought I should warn you. You may wish to avoid the front entrance."

"Yes, I would."

"I will ensure that the window is unlocked."

I thanked him and hung up. A year ago, my name had figured prominently in the news. I didn't like it and Bernard knew it.

Chico's studio was only a few minutes from the society's offices, which were located on the second floor of a building in downtown Patsboro. The entrance was a door leading to steps that separated Chuck's Pizzaria from Belmont Men's Store. This morning I parked a block away, bought a copy of the *Patsboro Herald* from a machine, and made my way through an alley to the back of the building. A metal fire escape hung on the wall. It ended at a window that provided light for the room where we had a microwave, refrigerator, and coffee maker.

I felt foolish crawling through the window until I peeked out the door of the break room. Two men were slouched in chairs facing the normal entrance. I poured a cup of coffee, slipped out, moved down the hall to my office, and closed the door behind me. After calling Bernard on the phone system to let him know I'd arrived, I sipped and read.

The headline was huge. LAWTON FLETCHER FOUND DEAD was spread across the top of the page. Underneath, a subheadline in smaller type read FOUL PLAY IS SUSPECTED. The large type wasn't surprising. Patsboro is still a small southern town, albeit separated from the norm by the presence of Catledge University. A movie star's slaying in the vicinity would be big news in any event, and Fletcher's being from Patsboro added another quarter inch to the headline. The people here felt a proprietary attachment to him. Even the transient university students claimed him as one of their own because he'd attended Catledge for a semester before heading west.

The article contained little I didn't already know. It mentioned that Mitch and I had found Fletcher's body and added that I'd played a part in uncovering Gerald "Jink" Jarvis's smuggling ring five years ago, and the more recent incident involving Radar Gilstrap and Michael Hutcheson. I wish they hadn't included my past, but Mitch would be happy at the mention of his stores and his renown for his cable television advertisements. He'd probably make a few sales on that. Donald Lee was quoted as saying, "We're on the perp's trail. We'll get him." They must have edited out the "sheeeits." The one new piece of information was that the GBI's initial investigation appeared to rule out suicide.

There was a soft knock on the door. I started to say "Come in" but thought better of it. I opened the door slightly, and saw that it was Bernard. He slipped in and I locked the door behind him.

"Good morning," he said as he moved to the chair in front of my desk. He would never sit before I did.

"No court today?" I asked needlessly. He was wearing an open western shirt with a plain bolo tie and he had on leather boots. If he were appearing in court, he'd be wearing a stoned bolo and his alligator "court" boots.

He shook his full face. "My presence is not required. One case was scheduled, however the district attorney had a change of heart on Friday and dropped all charges."

"Good," I said and took another sip of coffee. The DA had learned that his case better be airtight if Bernard was involved in the defense. I held up the newspaper with its blaring headlines. "Thanks for the warning."

"You had expressed your displeasure with the fourth estate previously."

"It would just be nice if they'd be more careful." Aside from my own involvement in a couple of cases, I was interviewed frequently regarding my clients. As often as not, my remarks were taken out of context. The result usually made me look like an idiot.

"May I make a suggestion?" Bernard asked.

"Of course."

"As you know, from time to time in the past I have been involved in rather high-profile cases. My experience suggests that those reporters"—he nodded toward the lobby—"will not depart until they have received something for their efforts." The phone had been ringing constantly since I'd arrived, and at that moment its faint chirping could be heard again from Mrs. Thompson's reception desk in the waiting room. "Additionally, others, not quite so dedicated as the two out there, will continue to call until you speak to them. It will not end."

"Great."

"It would be provident, I think, to announce a news conference and meet their needs simultaneously."

"A news conference? I don't know anything, except that I was supposed to meet Fletcher but found him dead."

Bernard arched his bushy eyebrows. "Then tell them that and be done with it. I know you will be happier, and you may very well extend Mrs. Thompson's sanity, such as it is."

I chuckled. Our secretary, Alva Thompson, was somewhere in her seventies, descended from an old-time Patsburg family. Though she came from the poor side, she held considerable influence with the political structure of Patsboro and Teal County. We'd taken her from the mayor in exchange for his continued support for funding the society. That allowed him to hire another secretary who could transfer phone calls without cutting people off, take messages reliably, and type. Mrs. Thompson had great difficulty with those tasks.

As a result, we did our own typing and tried to answer the phones when we could. That left Mrs. Thompson free to read the Bible and spread gossip. She loved her job. This morning, she had to be miserable.

"Okay," I said. "I'll speak to them en masse this afternoon. They *will* be disappointed, though."

Bernard nodded as he pulled a pink message slip from his shirt pocket. "Before Mrs. Thompson arrived, I was answering the phones. Most of the calls were from reporters, of course. I thought you might want to know of this one, though." He leaned forward and handed me the slip.

Bernard spoke precisely on all occasions, but his handwriting was indecipherable. "What's his name?" I asked.

"I am sorry. Her name is Charlotte Perry."

"You must know her."

"Not until this morning. She said she was Lawton Fletcher's sister. She wishes to speak to you."

"Why?"

Bernard shrugged. "She did not say."

There was a knock on the door. Bernard and I sat quietly, but the knock became louder. Bernard stood and pulled the door open carefully, then opened it wide enough for Mrs. Thompson to slip in. "I thought I heard voices in here," she snapped as she pushed her cat-eye glasses up her nose. "How'd you get in here, Miss Randall?"

From behind her, Bernard said, "We all have our ways, Mrs.

Thompson. We all have our ways." Even Bernard never called her Alva.

Her lips curled. "Miss Randall, you *must* do something about all these reporters. It's absolute madness. I haven't been able to get a thing done." What she meant was she hadn't had time to gossip about the most famous death she'd ever been around. Nothing thrilled Mrs. Thompson like spreading news of death.

"The media will be taken care of shortly," I said.

"Good," she said and turned to leave. As Bernard moved away from the door, she said to him, "Eddie is still waiting to hear from you, Bernard."

"Yes."

Mrs. Thompson pursed her lips and exited.

"Where are we on that?" I asked. The other attorney in the society, Peter Landry, had recently vacated his position. His father had secured a position for him on the California governor's staff. Landry wanted to be in politics and had decided that his idea about coming to Georgia, where he thought anybody could get elected, was not fortuitous. Like a lot of people, he had equated the southern accent with stupidity. Bernard had been looking for a replacement.

Eddie Thompson was Mrs. Thompson's nephew. He'd graduated from law school a year ago, but hadn't found a job.

Bernard responded to my question, "There are two excellent candidates. I will make my decision this week."

"Is Eddie one of them?"

"No," he said and furrowed his brow. "I am always amazed that an individual can complete a rigorous academic program, such as law school, and still not have . . ."

"A lick of sense."

"Precisely."

"Mrs. Thompson will not be happy."

"Yes," Bernard said. "Indeed."

Bernard left my office, leaving the door open. He told Mrs. Thompson and the reporters in the waiting room that a news conference would be held at one o'clock that afternoon.

I found his announcement to be embarrassing. It would undoubtedly be the shortest press conference in history. How long could it take to tell them that I didn't know anything?

Chapter Four

Two hours later I was on my way to Charlotte Perry's house. On the phone, she'd said only that she wished to talk to me and would rather do it in person, but she wouldn't elaborate. I explained that I knew little of the circumstances surrounding her brother's death, but she said that didn't matter. She still wanted to meet.

Charlotte Perry's house was a blond brick ranch on a half-acre lot in a neighborhood called Forest Glen. The name was a misnomer, for the area had few trees and was neither secluded nor in a valley. I suppose the developers liked the sound of it. I parked my Yugo on the street and went to the door.

As is common in moviedom, a large part of Lawton Fletcher's appeal had been his good looks. Unfortunately, that couldn't be said of his sister.

Charlotte Perry would not be considered attractive in any culture. She lacked a chin and her wide mouth featured an upper lip that protruded well over her lower. Her eyes were narrowly spaced, giving her face the appearance of a pear. Her body, too, was pear-shaped, and the knit pants and tucked-in blouse accentuated the effect. Fletcher had been taller than six feet. His sister was barely five. She appeared to be in her forties, which would make her ten years older than her actor brother.

"Please come in," she said. I followed her through a small foyer to a living room that favored a bowling alley. The long, narrow room had hardwood floors and a fireplace at the far end. The furniture was nice, but aged, as though it had been inherited. It was worn in all the right places. I was impressed by the piano that stood against the wall on the far end of the room, adjacent to the fireplace. It was rosewood. I knew that only because a friend at college had been a music major and lusted for a rare rosewood piano.

Charlotte sat on the edge of the sofa and I sat in a wing chair across the narrow room. Moments passed as I waited for her to begin. She didn't. Eventually, I said, "I'm sorry for your loss."

Charlotte nodded her head.

Silence ensued. Finally, I asked, "How can I help you?"

"That's what I would like."

"What?" I asked, puzzled.

"Your help."

"Oh." Again, we sat quietly. Again, I said, "How can I help you?"

"Yes," she said. "That's it."

I knew her brother had been killed the night before, but I wanted to get a look at her pupils. This lady had to be on something. I tried, "Exactly what kind of help do you want?"

"To find out," she said.

I waited, but I couldn't stand it. "Find out . . . ?"

"Yes."

I was beginning to understand how to do this. I said, "What exactly do you want me to find out?"

"About Lawton."

I was about to say, "About Lawton, what?" Instead I said, "What exactly do you want me to find out about Lawton?"

"What he was doing." Her voice became a whisper. "Why he changed."

I leaned forward. "I don't think you understand. I'm an attorney. It sounds like you want a private investigator. Or better yet, just talk to the police. They are investigating those things." Except maybe why Lawton had changed, I thought. I wondered what she meant.

She shook her head, reached under the coffee table sitting in front of her, and retrieved a book. She held it up for me to see. It was a copy of *Triple Threat*.

The book was about a true crime—the Jarvis episode that Mitch, Dan, and I had uncovered. Lucas Anderson, a detective in the Patsboro Police Department, had written it. It had sold well locally, but hadn't elsewhere.

I said, "My part in that wasn't much. I just happened to be there when Dan Bushnell got involved with Jarvis while he was trying to help a student find his father. I was working part-time while I was in law school, and Dan was my boss. I was a minor player. As I said, I'm an attorney for the Legal Aid Society, not an investigator."

She nodded.

Good, I thought, she understands.

She said, "I was very impressed. I'll pay you. You really need to go to Los Angeles. He was out there when he started changing. I'll also pay expenses."

I sighed, crossed my legs, and leaned back, slouching on the chair. She just didn't understand. "I'm afraid my duties at the society would make that difficult." Despite my protestations, I *was* wondering how Lawton Fletcher had changed.

She stood, walked to the fireplace, took down a framed picture, and returned to the sofa. She looked at the picture and said, "After Lawton left for Hollywood, we rarely heard from him. Three years ago, Father died. Mother had a heart attack and died two months later. Lawton was making a movie in Europe. He didn't come for the funerals."

I decided to hear her out. I was raised to be polite. "When did you see him last?"

"Years ago. But he was supposed to stay here last night, after he saw Warrendale."

"So he had been in touch with you."

"He called a year ago. Out of the blue. He said I'd be getting something in the mail. He said to enjoy it." She continued to stare at the picture.

"What was it?"

"A check. For ten thousand dollars. He also started calling almost every week. Just to see how I was doing. He'd never done that before. Each month after that he sent another check. I told him he didn't have to give me any money." She glanced toward two portraits hanging next to each other on the wall above the fireplace's mantel. "Mother and Father left me well taken care of." She stood, moved to a small secretary, and opened a drawer. She held up a handful of checks. "He told me to save them just in case, but I have few needs."

I nodded.

"That's when he told me he'd heard about Warrendale being for sale. He said he wanted to buy it."

I sat straight again. "But he didn't say why?"

She shook her head. "I want you to understand," and handed me the picture. It was an eight-by-ten of a boy, about ten, a girl in her late teens, and an older couple.

"That's us," she said.

Looking at the image, it was obvious Lawton's genes had skipped a generation. Charlotte Perry looked just like her mother. The father shared his wife and daughter's lack of good looks. Lawton, even at that early age, was already striking.

"He was adopted," Charlotte said. "My parents kept foster children. Lawton came when he was eight. We were his twelfth foster home. They adopted him when he was ten, just before that picture was taken."

"Twelfth," I said, shaking my head. I suppose his being a foster child and an adopted child had been mentioned in the magazines that feature celebrities. I never read them.

"He had behavior problems. My parents persevered. He got better. Much better."

"He was lucky," I said. "You must have had good parents."

"Yes," she said. "They tried very hard. But he reverted when he went to Hollywood. He started using his old last name."

I tried to be helpful. "Perhaps he was searching for his roots. But, from what you said, he changed back for the better."

"Yes. I need to know about that. It's important to me. My parents didn't get to see it. That's why I want you to go out there and find out what happened."

Again, silence settled in the room. I checked my watch. This had become interesting, despite the weird beginning, but the news conference, so to speak, would be starting soon. And the truth was I didn't know how I could help her.

I stood, gave the picture back to her, and said, "I appreciate your faith in me, but I'm afraid I just can't help you. It happened in Park County. The society does not serve Park County and, even if it did, we have no money for investigators. The truth is, that's not the sort of thing we do." She held the picture against her chest. "Why don't you call the GBI? There's an office here in town. Ask for Agent Malone. She's investigating your brother's case. She might be able to help you."

Charlotte shook her head.

"Well, as I said, I'm not an investigator." I moved toward the door and said, "It was good to meet you."

As I was shutting the door, I glanced back at Charlotte. She had *Triple Threat* on her lap and was flipping through the pages.

"Was the blood around his head in a little pool, or was it spread out all over the floor?"

I looked at the reporter through the microphones in front of me. "That's an absolutely asinine question."

The press conference was being held in the courthouse, a block away from the society's offices, because we had no room large enough to hold reporters from the Atlanta television stations, their cameras, and twenty-some members of the print media. Bernard had known what was likely to happen, so he'd made the arrangements. I'd called Mitch and had invited him to join me. He was excited at the prospect. He said the reporters were killing his sales with their constant calls.

As I anticipated, I felt silly sitting in the mayor's chair in the city council room. I'd read my statement, which included everything I knew. It took one minute. The blood question was the first asked after I was finished.

"Could you describe how the body was lying?"

"No."

"Did he have a gun?"

"I don't know."

"Did you see any drugs?"

"No."

"How about you?" one asked Mitch.

In a guttural voice, Mitch said something that sounded like "Nyet."

"What?" the reporter asked.

Mitch shook his head quickly, and puffed out his cheeks, making a sound like a machine on its last legs. Then he repeated, "Nyet."

"Good strategy," I said under my breath.

He stared straight ahead, blinked slowly, and smiled.

The questions continued. A transcript of my side of the news conference would read like this: No; I don't know; No; No. One time I threw in a "You got me." The reporters were getting impatient. I didn't care.

That changed when a woman in the back of the room said, "Do you have a comment regarding the arrest that was made this morning?"

"What arrest?"

"A man was arrested early this morning and charged with the murder. It's been on radio and television."

"I've been busy," I said.

She flipped a page on her notebook. "They arrested a guy named Freddy Meadows."

"Oh, Lord," Mitch said quietly.

"Did Chief Lee arrest him?" I asked.

The reporter shrugged. "I don't know who arrested him."

The reporter who asked about the blood and had remained silent since said, "You look surprised. Do you know anything about him?"

I shook my head. "Ladies and gentlemen, I told you all I know in my statement. My desire is to stop being called and visited upon so that we can continue our work at the Legal Aid Society. That's why I am here. You have heard it all."

Mitch and I stood and left the room. As we walked down the concrete stairs in front of the courthouse, he said, "You're going to Warrendale, aren't you?"

"It had to be Donald Lee who arrested Meadows. As soon as Agent Malone and I left, he went on and did his thing. I have to be sure the kid's properly represented."

"Ah haaa!" Mitch screeched. "I knew it. I just *knew* it!"

"Knew what?"

"That you'd get involved in this thing." He shook his finger at me. "And you promised, young lady."

"Promised what?"

"Last night. On the way back from Warrendale. You said you promised yourself that you wouldn't get involved."

"I'm not getting involved. I'm just going to find out what's going on and be sure Freddy Meadows gets the representation he deserves." I looked at Mitch. "By somebody up there."

Mitch shook his head. "My momma always told me," he said, "that God don't like it when you break a promise."

Chapter Five

The new black asphalt contrasted sharply with the bright white and yellow lines on the road to Warrendale. A year ago, this highway had been destined for destruction. Its path lay across what was to have been a second Atlanta airport that was planned for Teal County. I'd volunteered to represent a group of small farmers trying to fight it. I'd like to say our efforts stopped the airport, but I can't. Our group was but a gnat in the eye of the Atlanta power structure. However, even that behemoth couldn't alter the effects of two airline bankruptcies. A month before grading was to begin, the project was canceled.

As I drove past woods of pines, maples, and oaks, broken occasionally by a pasture fronted by ill-kept fences, I considered why I was sitting in my Yugo as it whined toward Warrendale. When I asked Bernard if I could spend the remainder of the day in Park County, I told him what I had told Mitch, but I knew there was more to it.

The first reason was just plain curiosity. What had Chief Lee found on Freddy Meadows, if anything? Had he lost his fear of wrongful arrest overnight and arrested Meadows with no more evidence than Deacon Bell's saying he had seen Meadows in the vicinity around the time of the murder? In Park County, that might be enough.

Even though last night had been only the second time I'd been there, I knew Park County. I grew up in Maytown in south Georgia. Although the two places are hundreds of miles apart geographically, I suspected they were political twins. I'd chosen to work for a legal aid society after watching what happened to poor folks in Maytown. Often enough, it suited the powerful few to overlook a little thing like lack of evidence if it would interfere with a conviction. That was the second reason I was on that road.

The third was Charlotte Perry. Lawton Fletcher's adoptive sister was a little strange, but her concern about what had happened to him seemed genuine. It wouldn't hurt to check it out for her.

Curiosity, concern, compassion. I wondered which was number one.

The woods thickened on either side of the road before I crossed over the Olkmolknee. The river was down, as most are in Georgia during the fall when the rains usually stop. After crossing the bridge, I knew I was in Park County. There was no sign announcing it, but I could tell. The road turned into one of compressed gravel and tar with only a faded white line in its center to control traffic. Patsboro and Teal County were growing, thanks to Catledge University's attraction to industry. Park County was not.

Twenty minutes later I was back in Warrendale. The parking lot that had been empty the night before was now half full. I parked and approached a group of men, all at least seventy, who were playing checkers in front of the grocery. There were five of them. Four were sitting on a bench in pairs with a board between them. One was standing and watching. They laughed when I asked for directions to the city hall.

One of them, dressed in overalls that covered a red-and-black checked flannel shirt, jerked his thumb over his shoulder and said, "Wilbur's office is in there, behind the meat counter. He's the mayor. Took over when Pete Warren got hisself and his brother killed in that jet airplane."

"Actually, I was looking for Chief Lee."

The man who was watching the checkers games said, "Ol'

Donald Lee'd be down at the beer store." The one in the overalls moved a checker and hissed laughter through a smile. "Sheeeit," he said at the same time.

The store was just beyond the town's center, on the right side of the road. Pickups filled the small, graveled parking lot that sat in front of the red brick building. Its only sign was hanging above the door. It said General Lee Surrendered, I Didn't. A Confederate flag hung to the sign's left. Was Donald Lee a descendant? Surely not. Robert E. Lee was known to be a gentleman with grace.

Because of the full parking lot, I drove past the store, found a spot to stop just off the road, and walked back. I went through the glass door that was front and center in the building. A counter with a cash register was to my left, and a row of refrigerated display cases filled with beer stood against the left wall. To the right were three pool tables with a dim fluorescent light hanging over each one. Men of assorted ages, dressed in jeans and boots, were playing. Donald Lee was leaning across the far table, lining up a shot.

As I walked across the concrete floor toward him, the men at the tables quieted. I could feel twenty pairs of eyes on me. After I went by the first table, I could hear little clucks and soft whistles. I was wearing a conservative knee-length dress with a jacket, but I felt naked. All the men had stopped playing but Lee, who was concentrating on his shot. When he hit the cue ball, it jumped a foot, then bounced off the table. He said, "Sheeeit." Then he looked up and saw me.

He leaned on his cue stick and hooked his thumb under his gun's handle. In the silence of the room, his leather boots and gun belt squeaked loudly when he moved. He smiled and said, "Well, well. If it ain't the lady lawyer."

"I was wondering if I could speak with you." I tried to add "Chief," but couldn't.

He looked at the men in the room, who were still staring at me. He winked, made the sound with his tongue that a squirrel makes when it's agitated, and said, "Sure, honey."

A momentary flash of heat flew through me. I took a step forward. It was okay now to say it. "Chief, you do that again and it'll take a pound of Ex-Lax to get that stick you're holding out of you." The boys hooted and slapped their hands on the pool tables. I said to Lee, "Come with me" and walked out the door.

Behind me, one of the boys said, "Go on, Chief. She wants you." More hooting followed.

I was leaning against the spotless tailgate of a black Toyota pickup that was jacked up at least two feet off the axles when Lee came out the door. He stopped several feet in front of me. "What you want?"

"I heard you arrested Freddy Meadows again. I was wondering if you'd found something that caused you to do that."

The day was bright. Lee took his sunglasses from his shirt pocket and put them on. "I don't have to tell you nothin'."

I stared into my image that was reflected off his Ray-Bans. "That's true. Of course, it won't be hard to find out from somebody else."

He shifted. It was obvious that he was proud of himself. He couldn't *not* tell me about it. "I caught that boy speeding just as he come past the city limits."

I'd noticed that the city limits to Warrendale started about five miles from the town, and that the speed limit dropped at that point. I'd seen it before in small towns. You'd be driving along in the countryside, when all of a sudden the limit became twenty-five. That served to increase a lot of towns' treasuries.

"And you happened to be there," I said.

"Just doing my duty."

"What happened?"

"He started smart-mouthing me. I had to arrest him for that. Found Fletcher's wallet when I searched his Bronco."

"Did the GBI find anything at the scene implicating him?"

"Not yet," Lee said. "Don't matter though. I got the wallet."

I pushed away from the truck. "Seems kind of stupid to me. Speeding into town and carrying the wallet of the guy who you killed the night before."

Lee nodded his head. "Ain't nobody ever claimed Freddy Meadows was a genius."

"Where is he?"

"County jail. In Braxton." Park County had two towns. Warrendale and the county seat, Braxton.

A boy who should have been in school stuck his head out the door and said, "Chief Lee, you got a call."

As I watched his broad rear end as he waddled away, I knew that my threat to impale him with his cue stick had been only rhetorical.

Chapter Six

The road to Braxton was narrow and full of curves through the foothills of the Appalachians. I took my time, enjoying the unusual circumstance of being away from the office and court-rooms on a Monday afternoon. I rolled down the window, turned on the radio, and tried not to think about the stack of files sitting on my desk. I'd been with the society for four years and had taken an aggregate of four days off. And this wasn't exactly what you'd call a vacation.

The radio station I listened to played oldies, mostly from the late sixties and seventies. I enjoyed them because they reminded me of my childhood. I started listening to the radio when I was eight. We could pick up two stations in Maytown during the day. One played country. I avoided that one like the plague. The one I did listen to played a variety of music: an hour of blues, an hour of gospel, an hour of folk songs—like "Molly Malone." At night, I'd search the dial for rock. When Fort Wayne faded, I turned to Chicago. I'd wear headphones and hum gospel while I listened, which was tricky, but I had to do that in case Mama walked by. Mama knew that rock music led you straight to the devil.

I stopped at a roadside stand in front of an orchard and bought an apple. It was crisp and tart and looked real, which is to say the skin was faded and flawed. The air was fresh-looking under a bright blue sky. WFOX played John Denver's "Sunshine on My Shoulders" and I reveled in the pleasantness of it all.

The Park County jail was not pleasant. It smelled of stale cigarettes, unwashed people, and urine. The two-story box of a building held the sheriff's office in the front, on the first floor. Sheriff Cox wasn't in, and it took some talking before I could get the deputy on duty to let me see Freddy Meadows. The deputy led me through a room that held a table covered by overflowing ashtrays, half-filled coffee cups, and empty Coke cans. We went through a metal door to a room that had five cells. The space was dark, dimly lit by a low-watt bare bulb in front of each cell. The cell on the far end had sheets hanging from the bars, and I could hear a female voice singing softly. Meadows was in the cell to the far left. The deputy let me in and then stood in front of the bars. I told him he could go. It appeared that he didn't want to, but he did.

The three cells between Meadows and the woman each held three or four men. Meadows was by himself. That meant one of two things. Either he was considered too dangerous to have roommates or he was privileged for some reason. He was sitting on the bottom one of the cell's tier of bunks, leaning against the wall. The shadow from the top bunk cut the weak light off at his waist. From the shadow, he said, "Whoa, honey. I don't mind staying here for a while if you're part of the deal."

"I'm an attorney, Mr. Meadows. I'd like to talk to you about last night."

He swung his legs off the cot and sat on the edge. He had long blond hair that was tied into a ponytail. His shoulders were broad and his arms muscular. His stomach protruded slightly, showing the fat that athletes often develop when their activity slows down. Despite that, Meadows's fat looked hard.

He said, "Don't need no lawyer. But, if I did, you'd be a sight better than Carl White."

Carl White was the only lawyer who practiced in Park

County, other than the district attorney. I presumed that Meadows's attorney would be court-appointed, which would mean it would be White. I'd seen him in action once when he represented a Park County man on a charge of solicitation in Patsboro. After watching Carl White in that case, I had been surprised when his client wasn't sent to the chair. Fortunately for the client, the maximum sentence was a few months in jail and that's all he got. The judge seemed extremely disappointed that he couldn't do more.

Meadows swung his legs off the bunk, stood, and moved toward me. He was wearing a dingy T-shirt and jeans. He stood in front of me and said, "But, like I said, I won't be needing no lawyers." He put his hands on either side of me and gripped the bars. His face was six inches from mine. He moved his right hand off the bar and rubbed his finger across my cheek.

It was instinct born from anger. I lifted my leg slightly, then smashed the heel of my shoe on Meadows's stockinged right foot. He cried out and shifted his weight to the other. My right knee came up and caught him square in his groin. He gasped, sucking in air, and bent over. His weight was mostly on his uninjured foot, and when I popped his forehead with the heel of my hand, he tumbled backward and fell on the toilet.

The door to the front slammed and the deputy appeared outside the cell. He looked at Meadows, who was sitting on the toilet with his head between his knees, then at me. "It's all right, Deputy," I said.

He cocked his head and looked beyond me to Meadows. Through a slight smile he said, "Let me know if you need anything."

After the deputy left, I said, "Meadows, never, *never,* touch me again without my permission."

His head came up. His pained expression turned to one of anger. "Get the hell out of here, lady."

I took a deep breath. This guy wasn't the first jerk I'd worked with. When you work for Legal Aid, you don't often deal with the genteel. I said, "You need to pay attention to this. We're not talking about your typical Park County stuff here. Lawton Fletcher was famous and he's dead and you've been charged with his murder. People outside of this county are interested. You better start realizing that."

I said that with conviction because I believed it. That was before I knew how quickly fame and public interest can fade.

"They'll take care of me."

"Who?"

He didn't respond.

"Did you kill him?"

"No," he said. His tone of voice had changed. Maybe he'd talk to me now, I thought.

"How'd you get his wallet?"

I fully expected him to say Lee had planted it. Lee had been with the body by himself before Agent Malone showed up. It wouldn't have been a surprise to me if he had taken it, just on general principles, then planted it in Meadows's Bronco so he could look good after his embarrassment last night.

That wasn't what Meadows said.

"I found it. In the parking lot in Warrendale." He was sitting up now, still on the toilet.

"When?"

"Last night."

"What time?"

"I don't know. Sometime after six."

"Why'd you take it?"

I leaned back against the bars. He stood, and I straightened, becoming balanced. He moved to the bunk and grunted when he sat. He said, "Because it was there."

"Why were you there?"

"I'd been hunting and stopped to make a phone call and there it was."

"So . . . you had a gun?"

He shook his head. "Bow and arrow."

One thing I knew for sure was that Fletcher wasn't killed by a bow and arrow. "What phone were you going to use?"

"The pay phone. The one in the parking lot."

The one that was broken when I tried to use it a little after seven, I thought.

"Who'd you want to call?"

He was staring across the cell. He turned and looked at me. "None of your goddamn business."

I let that go. I was interested in something else. "Did you make the call?"

"Yeah," he said. He's lying, I thought.

"Did you get through?"

"No. The goddamn phone was broken."

He wasn't lying. "Why did you still have the wallet this morning? After last night, you must have known the trouble it'd cause you."

He shrugged. "Forgot about it, I guess."

"You forgot about it? You're carrying a murder victim's wallet around with you, you've been arrested for the murder once and let go, and you *forgot* about it?"

"Hey, I was busy. All right?"

From behind me, I heard, "Time's up." I turned to find the deputy in the hall behind me.

I looked at Freddy Meadows. "I'm going to talk to Carl White. See what he plans to do. If his answers aren't satisfactory, I'll be sure you get adequate representation."

"Go to hell," Meadows said and lay back on his bunk.

Chapter Seven

In front of the jail, a bench sat under a tree on a square patch of grass that was about as big as Freddy Meadows's cell. A natural wood sign that stood behind the bench had "Pendleton Park" etched on it. I settled on the bench and breathed deeply, trying to get the remnants of the rancid air from the cells out of my lungs.

Braxton was nestled in a valley surrounded by small, rounded mountains. It was a strip town that lined both sides of the highway for a quarter of a mile. I watched farmers going in and out of the feed and seed store across the street.

I thought about my attack on Freddy Meadows.

Chico had warned us that he was teaching self-defense. He had said that no matter what you know, bigger usually wins and our best strategy to avoid being molested was to stay out of situations inviting danger and to run if possible. Freddy Meadows was definitely bigger than me. I'd been able to stop him because I surprised him.

I'd reacted violently to his manner and touch automatically. No thought was involved, and that bothered me. I hate violence. I'd done the same thing, verbally, to Donald Lee earlier that day.

I decided to talk to Dr. Beam about that in our next session.

The deputy on duty had told me where Carl White's office was. I stood and headed uphill on the cracked sidewalk.

White's office turned out to be one half of a building that had been a gas station. The half that was once the garage area now held a videotape rental store. Metal blinds on the door clanked as I entered a small reception area. A woman, maybe eighteen, was behind a desk talking on the phone. Light brown hair fell half over her face. She wore long false black eyelashes and red lipstick so bright it almost hurt to look at it. She also had the biggest boobs I'd ever seen in my life. I don't normally say "boobs," but these were *boobs*. Almost half of them was visible above her low-cut blouse.

She said, "Hold on a minute," cupped her hand over the phone, and said to me, "Can I help you?" I said I wanted to see Mr. White. Putting her phone on hold, she asked for my name, then announced me on the intercom.

I tried to thank her, but she was already back on the phone. There were two doors along the cheaply paneled back wall. Figuring I had a fifty-fifty chance of guessing right, I picked one and opened it. It was a closet. That's why I don't gamble. The second door opened to White's office.

The room still looked like a gas station's office. The walls were painted concrete and the room was lit by hanging fluorescent lamps. Pictures of fishing scenes in cheap plastic frames adorned the walls. Behind the desk, hanging from a nail that had been pounded into the masonry, was a calendar featuring Miss October as chosen by the Billups Bolt and Nut Company. The scantily clad woman was wearing a necklace of large metal wing nuts that covered her strategically.

Carl White stood up behind a shabby gray metal desk and extended his hand. "Miss Randall, it's good to see you."

"I'm surprised you would remember me."

"Oh, no problem there," he said, then winked. I checked the seat he indicated before I sat. The office had a greasy feel to it and my clothing budget is limited. I didn't want to ruin anything.

White slumped in his chair and picked up a cigarette from an ashtray that featured a drawing of a bare-breasted woman in cowboy gear. His brown hair was curly and was puffed into an Afro. His skin was pasty white. When he smiled, a gold tooth glimmered. He was wearing a white shirt with rolled-up sleeves and a loosened floral tie. I kept expecting him to make an offer on my car.

The attorney took a drag from his cigarette and blew it out slowly through his nose. He tapped an ash on the cowgirl's breasts, then asked, "What can I do for you?"

I crossed my legs, saw him glance down, and uncrossed them carefully while pulling my skirt down. "I presume you'll be representing Freddy Meadows."

" 'Fraid so. Probably be pro bono. For a while anyway. The county's defense fund is tapped out until more property taxes come in. They're due later this month. Might get paid something then."

I nodded, showing sympathetic understanding, but I was questioning his priorities. "What have you found out?"

His eyes blinked from cigarette smoke. "What's your interest?"

I shrugged. "I found Fletcher's body last night and was there when Chief Lee brought Meadows in the first time. Just curious, I guess."

"You came all the way up here out of curiosity?" He asked the question with a tone of disbelief.

"It seemed to me that Lee was acting precipitously last night. I wondered what had changed."

"You work for Legal Aid in Patsboro, don't you?"

I nodded.

He leaned his chair back and looked at me through narrow eyes. "You're young, but not that young. I distrust noble motives."

I sighed inwardly. Play the game, I thought. I said, "I may have a client apart from the Legal Aid Society. I'm just checking some things out to see if I've got anything to work with."

That seemed to satisfy him. "You're welcome to Meadows. He's a nasty son of a bitch and, like I said, if I ever get anything from it, it won't be enough."

"You misunderstand. I'm not looking to represent him."

"Who's your possible client?"

I shook my head.

"Okay. I understand. Big shot like Fletcher gets killed. I understand."

I was glad he did. I didn't have a clue. "So, what have you discovered?"

He stubbed his cigarette out on the cowgirl's stomach and pulled another from the pack on his desk. The pack was white. The only thing on it was the word CIGARETTES written in block letters. He put his lighter on the desk in front of me. Deliberately. It had a picture of a woman and a man whose clothing began to disappear slowly. "Not much," he said. "Lee found Fletcher's wallet in Meadows's car. Meadows says he saw it lying on the ground and took it."

I tried to keep my eyes off the lighter. "What are you going to do?"

White shrugged, then ran a hand through his curly hair. "In the best interest of my client, I'll suggest he plead guilty and hope they don't fry him, I guess." He paused. "I had one go to the chair not long ago. The idiots in Jackson didn't get it right and it took two or three jolts to finish him off."

I remembered the incident. I hadn't known White was his attorney. "You believe he's guilty? Meadows, I mean."

White shrugged again. "That 'in the best interest of my client' bullshit was for the bar should I ever need it. This next thing, I never said. If Meadows ain't guilty of murdering Fletcher, he's guilty of something else. The county'll be better off without him is all I know."

Curiosity, concern, compassion. I was moving from curiosity to concern. What chance did Meadows have with this guy defending him? Even if Meadows is rotten to the core, he's a citizen of the United States and deserves the best defense possible.

To fail him is to fail everybody. I believe that.

Maybe I am too young.

"Are you sure you don't have a conflict of interest here?" I hinted.

He startled me by slapping his hand on the desk. "I knew it." He sucked on his cigarette again. "There's no problem coming up with a conflict. You're welcome to him."

I was treading on thin ethical ice. Once an attorney is assigned an indigent case by a judge, he's usually stuck with it. Conflict of interest is one cause for a recusal. I stood. "I don't know yet. I've got to talk to my boss at the society."

"Bernard Fuchs?"

"Yes."

White swiveled in his chair. "Now that's a guy who did it right. I've seen him in action a couple of times. Wish I could talk to a jury like he can."

It takes some soul, I thought. I said, "He has a talent." I headed toward the door. "I'll let you know."

As I walked through the reception area, I heard White call his secretary. The young woman stood, revealing a tight skirt that ended well above her knees. I stepped out the door and thought about the men I'd met so far in Park County: Donald Lee, the deacon, Freddy Meadows, and Carl White.

Poor girl, I thought.

Chapter Eight

I jerked my hand away from the steam escaping from the aluminum foil packet.

"Hurt yourself?" Molly Malone asked.

"Mmm," I said as I sucked a finger. "I'll be glad when I learn to cook without maiming myself."

The GBI agent nodded in agreement.

I pulled the foil apart farther and used tongs to pick up and move a chicken breast to a plate. With a spoon I scooped up the rice and onion slices that were covered with undiluted cream of mushroom soup. I repeated the process with the second packet, this time avoiding the steam. Two stalks of buttered steamed broccoli completed each plate. I put the plates on the table along with the biscuits and sugared iced tea that was already there.

"This looks great," Malone said.

I sat across the table from her. "The recipe came from *The College Kid's Cookbook*. The biscuits came from a can. There's not much to making it, but it looks fancy."

Molly took a bite of the chicken. "Tastes great, too." She was sitting in my kitchen because of our telephone conversation earlier that day. After returning from Park County, I'd called her to get the details on Freddy Meadows's arrest. The conversation led to my inviting her for dinner.

"This is a neat old house," Molly said.

"It belongs to Professor Gatlin and his wife. He was the law professor I was telling you about last night. The one who asked me to handle the sale of Warrendale." I took a bite of the broccoli and chewed before continuing. "They bought the house right before he was offered a visiting professorship at Harvard. It had been converted to a boarding house and they planned to reconvert it. The professor asked me to house-sit while he and his wife are away. Given my finances, I jumped at the offer." I spread butter on a biscuit. "Professor Gatlin was supposed to be at Harvard for a year originally, but he was asked back. So here I remain."

"You ever get nervous being in this big old house alone?" Molly asked, then looked as though she wished she hadn't. Buddy Crowe's attacking me was not public knowledge, but with her being in the GBI and serving Patsboro, I figured she knew.

"Dan Bushnell, a friend of mine, installed some pretty secure locks after . . ." I couldn't finish the sentence.

Molly's soft brown eyes were on me. She nodded.

"I feel safe enough."

We ate in silence for a while before beginning the ritual of discovering each other's pasts. I told her I was raised in the tiny community of Maytown in south Georgia. I told her about my father, who died when I was in high school from drinking too much, and about my mother and her Congregational Holiness fixation.

Molly Malone didn't pull punches. "Must have been weird being raised by a fundamentalist Christian and a drunk."

"Yes," I said. "The strange thing is that my daddy taught me how to be kind, understanding, caring . . . that sort of thing. He never stepped foot in a church. Mama, on the other hand, operates on the principle of guilt and judgement."

"Original sin."

"I guess. Only she'd never talk about it that way." I took a sip of iced tea. "We get along okay now, though. I've learned to ignore that part." Most of the time, anyway, I thought.

"Never been married?"

"Not even close," I said. "How about you?"

"For three years. My mother made me when I got pregnant."

"You have a child?"

"Misty is fifteen."

"You have a fifteen-year-old daughter?" I said with incredulity. Molly appeared to be close to my age, but my knowledge of human physiology escaped me momentarily. I don't know why. I've represented twelve-year-olds who've had children.

"I was fifteen when she was born."

We continued to reveal our pasts while we ate and while she helped me wash dishes, then we sat at the table again. The only other room in the house that had furniture was my bedroom, and that consisted of a full-size bed, a chest of drawers, and a rocker that I'd inherited from my Aunt Ouida. I seldom had visitors.

"Tell me about Freddy Meadows," I said.

She ran her fingers through her short, dirty blond hair. "Not much to tell. Ol' Donald Lee, as they say in Park, found Fletcher's wallet and arrested him."

"Y'all, the GBI, I mean, didn't find anything else?"

Molly shook her head. "Not a scrap. There were footprints in the dust on the floor of the mill, but that won't help. There were too many."

"Mitch and I walked around quite a bit."

"That didn't matter. The place hadn't been cleaned since it was closed."

"Any hypothesis on how Fletcher was killed?"

"We won't get the written report of the autopsy for a month, and that's if we're lucky. Arthur Ramsey, agent-in-charge here in Patsboro, called the lab and asked about the cause of death. No need for hypothesis on that. Gunshot to the base of the skull. Found a thirty-eight-caliber bullet."

"That's a start," I said.

"More than a start. The rifling marks on the bullet indicate it came from a gun manufactured around the turn of the century.

When we find that gun, we've found the murderer."

"Have you searched Freddy's place?"

"Yeah. He lives in a trailer—surprise, surprise—a few miles from Warrendale."

I nodded. "There does seem to be an inordinate number of mobile homes up there."

Molly laughed. "Ramsey says you have to obtain a zoning variance in Park County if your house doesn't have wheels."

I chuckled and so did she.

"It appears Fletcher was in the far end of the mill, the end away from the road, when he was shot, then was dragged behind that spool of twine where you found him."

That surprised me. "How do you know? I didn't see any evidence of that."

"It was getting pretty dark when you were there. Once we got the lights up we found a pool of blood on the far end. Streaks led to the body where the blood pooled again."

I shuddered involuntarily. "I don't know how you look at that kind of thing all the time."

Molly shrugged. "Like anything else, you get used to it."

"I suppose," I said, not convinced. "You know, one thing I noticed is that Fletcher didn't look too good when I saw him."

"Yeah, well. Getting the back of your head blown away doesn't do much for your appearance."

"I guess you're right. It just seemed he looked sort of drawn . . . or something. But I've only seen three people who've been shot." It wasn't necessary for me to add that I'd shot two of them. She knew. We sat in silence for a moment. "So what do you do now?"

"The lab's comparing the bullet they found to others on file to see if it might match another homicide. Other than that, that's about it for us."

"You're not investigating more?"

"Sheriff Cox says he'll handle the rest. He and Donald Lee. Lee was right last night. We investigate by invitation."

My thoughts went to Charlotte Perry and what she'd told

me. I told Molly about that conversation and her job offer. I said, "What kind of motive would Freddy Meadows have for killing Lawton Fletcher?"

"The sheriff says robbery, but . . ."

"What?" I prodded.

"Rural crime just doesn't happen that way. There's not much random killing to get a wallet. The vast majority of homicides are domestic. Like a case I handled last month when one old guy killed his lifelong friend while they were arguing over whether to cook their steak medium or well done." She stroked her eyebrow with her finger. "Freddy killing Fletcher doesn't fit the normal homicidal intent in Park County. I tend to wonder about things that are contrary to the statistical norm."

"Fletcher's sister, or rather his adopted sister, says Fletcher had changed. I wonder if his murder could have anything to do with something going on in California?"

Malone half nodded and half shook her head. You got me, was the message.

"Will anybody go out there and investigate?"

"I doubt it." She thought a moment. "I'll amend that. There ain't no way. They got Freddy Meadows and that's it. The most that might happen would be a phone call to LA, but I doubt it'll even go that far."

I snapped my fingers. "I almost forgot. You want some dessert? Pecan pie made with nuts from the backyard."

"Sounds good," Molly said.

"Coffee, too? It's decaf."

Molly nodded. As I set about making the coffee she said, "Are you going to accept the job? Charlotte Perry, I mean."

I shook my head. "I can't. I've got a regular job." The coffeepot was gurgling and I began slicing the pie. "I'd feel better, though, if somebody other than Carl White was representing Meadows. With White's track record as a defense lawyer, Meadows could be hung on a lot less evidence than possession of a wallet."

Molly laughed. "White's a district attorney's dream."

I put the plates holding the pieces of pie on the table. The smell of brewing coffee was filling the room. Molly took a bite of pie. "This is great."

I never have learned how to respond to praise. Mama never gave me any and Daddy taught me modesty. I poured coffee with an awkward nod.

I was still thinking about who else, besides Carl White, could represent Meadows. I said, "We've applied for a grant that would give us funds to become a regional center, but we won't hear from that for a while. I'm afraid Meadows is stuck with White."

Molly said, "I guess if you *could* represent Meadows, I'd have to watch what I say. You and I would be on opposite sides."

"Depends on how you look at it," I said. "If the line's drawn at who wants the truth, I suspect we're teammates."

"Touché."

We moved back to personal talk and I enjoyed it immensely. In my counseling sessions with Dr. Beam, I was working on how to drop the iron barrier I usually hold before me. Mitch and Dan Bushnell and Dan's wife, Meg, were the only people who'd gotten through it.

Molly was easy to be with. She listened well and her stories were interesting. We also discovered that we had a lot in common. Neither of us watched much television. We both liked mysteries and read many of the same authors. We both listened to a wide variety of music. We had similar experiences with men. The difference is she got pregnant during her teenage indiscretion and I didn't. She had more experience in that regard in later years than I did, which wouldn't be hard because I'd had exactly one voluntary sexual experience since high school and the man ended up shooting himself in the head. That was part of the reason I was seeing Josie Beam.

Molly was telling me that she and her daughter had to find a new place to live because her duplex had been sold and the rent was being increased beyond her means, when I glanced at the clock hanging on the kitchen wall. The time had flown. It was almost eleven thirty.

She must have seen me look at the clock. "I'm sorry," she said. "I've kept you up. I didn't realize how late it was. Misty will be worried."

"Don't be sorry. I've enjoyed the evening."

I never make decisions impulsively.

Never.

Now I did.

"Where are you going to live?" I asked.

She shrugged. "I don't know yet. The rents around Patsboro have skyrocketed." She laughed. "Probably end up in one of those trailers in Park County."

"Why don't y'all move in here? There's plenty of room. An army could live in this place. And the rent should be to your liking. There isn't any."

Molly stared at me. "You realize," she said, "Misty is fifteen. Have you ever lived with a teenager?"

"It can't be that bad," I said. "We were all teenagers once."

"Take it from me. You forget."

We sat in silence. Molly was giving me a chance to reverse my impulse. I liked that. I liked her. I was tired of being alone.

"The offer stands," I said.

"Accepted," she said.

We sat in silence.

I broke it by asking, "Misty does have headphones, doesn't she?"

Chapter Nine

I am afraid that I have distressing news." Bernard was sitting ramrod straight in the wooden chair behind his desk. His jowly chin was tucked against his chest as he stared at me over the half-moon reading glasses resting on the tip of his nose. I was leaning forward in the vinyl covered chair opposite him. After my regular Tuesday morning swim, the hair dryer that I kept in a locker at the university had developed emphysema and wouldn't blow. The dampness was seeping through my dress to the skin between my shoulder blades.

"What distressing news?" I asked.

"Late yesterday afternoon I received a telephone call from Dr. Crawford. He serves as president of Catledge University."

"I know," I said, wondering what bad news Dr. Crawford could provide.

"It seems the vacancy on our staff had come to his attention and he indicated a wish to provide input for our decision as to whom we might employ."

The Legal Aid Society was jointly funded by the university and the city of Patsboro. Dr. Crawford's input would be significant.

"Who does he want us to hire?" I asked.

Bernard laced his fingers and rested them on his belly. "I am afraid he is advocating Eddie Thompson's candidacy."

"No. Not . . . you're kidding? Please say you're kidding?"

Bernard opened a drawer on the right side of his desk and retrieved a pipe. He filled it with tobacco from a pigskin pouch he'd had made from the hide of a wild boar he shot near Hudson Bay a year ago. Bernard smoked his pipe only on rare occasions, like when a jury was out on a case in which his client faced the death penalty. Hiring Eddie Thompson would be an appropriate cause for firing it up.

When the pipe was lit, he blew smoke, then said, "It seems, according to Dr. Crawford, that James Robert Thompson, better known as Jim Bob, received a phone call from his poor relation Alva." He nodded toward his door, indicating the reception area where Mrs. Thompson was now sitting reading her morning devotional. "Jim Bob relayed to Dr. Crawford that his cousin"—he nodded toward his door again—"was concerned that the 'newcomers' were prejudiced toward those that have roots in Patsboro and Teal County. She seems to believe some sort of conspiracy is afoot."

"I've heard the speech. A hundred times."

"Yes," Bernard said. "It seems that Jim Bob Thompson is a major contributor of funds that help ensure the Catledge Cats' continuing good fortune on the playing field."

"King Football," I said while shaking my head.

"It was my distinct impression that President Crawford believes strongly that his mission to continue building the academic integrity of his university is directly related to the accomplishments of those young men of fall Saturday afternoons. He does not wish to jeopardize his mission on such a trivial matter as who is employed to assist the indigent patrons of our society in their legal travails."

I leaned forward. "In other words, the president of Catledge University doesn't give a flip about Eddie's ability to help our clients, so long as Jim Bob Thompson keeps providing the grease to stay in the top ten."

"Precisely."

"What are you going to do?"

"Soon after Dr. Crawford spoke to me, the mayor called. It

seems Mrs. Thompson enlisted his aid as well." Bernard relit his pipe. "I believe Kenny Rogers put it in as succinct a manner as possible, 'Sometimes you have to hold them, sometimes you have to fold them'." Bernard blew smoke. "With our present hand, I am afraid we must fold them."

I blew air and shook my head. "This is going to be a nightmare. What are we going to do?"

Bernard set his pipe in an ashtray on his desk and interlaced his fingers, then leaned forward while resting his hands palm down on his desk. "The answer may be found in the grant application."

"To become a regional center?"

"Precisely. We would be able to hire two additional attorneys. Eddie could be assigned cases that do not require . . . an ability to think in the abstract."

I nodded. "Things like dealing with loan companies."

"Yes. Those cases that must be done, but that require little but time and effort. Someone like Eddie Thompson could actually be an asset. It would free the others we may hire to utilize their talents more fully."

"Assuming Mrs. Thompson doesn't have any more nephews."

We sat in silence.

Then it hit me.

"The decision on the grant's going to be made next month, right?"

Bernard nodded.

"It occurs to me that it might be helpful to demonstrate the need for our being a regional center in a more concrete manner than the statistics we included in the application. Something high profile."

Bernard leaned back in his chair. "What do you have in mind?" Before I could respond he held up his hand. "You are thinking of the Lawton Fletcher case?" Bernard had no problem with abstract thinking.

"Right."

Bernard stroked his chin and puffed on his pipe. "You did say Carl White has already been assigned to defend that fellow who has been charged?"

"Yes."

"It would have been good if he had not been appointed as yet."

"That may not be a problem. He thinks he may have a conflict of interest."

"Really?" Bernard said, skepticism heavy in his voice.

"Like you said about the cards, sometimes you have to fold them. Even with ethics."

"Sad, but true."

After a moment of silence, I said, "Of course, President Crawford and the mayor might not like our using the society's time in Park County on their money."

"I believe I may have been premature in laying down my hand. A trade may be in order."

"We take Eddie. They allow us to defend Meadows."

"Yes."

I crossed my legs at the knees and rearranged my shirt dress. "When would Eddie start?"

"Immediately, I suppose," Bernard said. "He is ready to commence his career and I suspect our offer of a job to him will not face competition."

"Good. He can take over the piddling stuff, and I'll take your cases."

"My cases?"

"Of course. You'll be handling Meadows's defense."

Bernard shook his head. "I have not given up my retirement completely. I have enjoyed the routine nature of this position. I am able to continue to be active in my chosen profession, yet be home every afternoon in time to participate in my equine pastime. From what you have told me, the Lawton Fletcher murder is far from resolved. There is an investigation to be done, and that is much better suited for the young not only in spirit, but also in body."

We stared at each other. "You want me to defend Meadows?"

"Yes."

"As you said, this case requires investigating. That's over my head."

"You sell yourself short."

"No, I don't. I'm realistic. Besides, there will be publicity. You're used to that. I'm not. I don't like it."

"You will become accustomed to it. If this thing is to be done, you must do it."

We stared at each other again. I broke it and looked out the window past Bernard. The city of Patsboro sat on a hill, and from this vantage point on a clear day like today, the foothills of the Appalachians were visible. Park County lay in that direction. "I'll need your help."

"I will be available to discuss your findings, as usual. However, I wish you to know that I am fully confident of your capabilities."

I looked at him again. "I wish I shared your confidence."

Bernard stood. "Now, I must call President Crawford and the mayor. Then I must inform Mrs. Thompson of our decision."

"She will gloat," I said.

"Yes," Bernard said sadly.

Chapter Ten

Back in my office, I sat in the leather desk chair that Dan Bushnell had given me years ago. When I first met Dan, he was directing a federally funded program for Teal County schools. He told me the federal program director's mission in life was to garner the biggest budget she could. In spite of his objections, she had bought the chair. None of the furniture or equipment had been inventoried, and after federal education funds were cut and the program ended, Dan gave the chair to me. He reasoned that a Legal Aid Society attorney deserved to receive the fruits of government largesse as much, if not more, than the assistant superintendent who had lusted after the chair. My having it was without doubt an illegal diversion of tax monies, but that is one ethical dilemma I avoid thinking about. It is truly a fine chair.

I rocked and absently twirled a lock of hair and thought about the task that lay ahead, assuming, of course, that Bernard played his hand well. And I was sure he would.

I realized my thoughts were jumping around randomly, so I retrieved a legal pad from my desk and made a list of things to do:

- Contact Carl White. See if he's discovered a conflict of interest that would be sufficient cause to be removed from the case.

- Call Charlotte Perry and let her know what I've discovered (not much).
- Call Mitch.
- Call Dan.

I wanted to let Mitch know what was going on because I knew he would want to know. He was already in on this. I wanted to talk to Dan because . . . he helped me to get organized. He was a clear thinker and had an ability to put events in a logical perspective. I was only just learning how to do that.

The call to Dan would have to be long distance. He was somewhere in southern Indiana participating in an educators' exchange program. He and a school counselor from there had temporarily swapped places. When I learned of his plans, I was surprised that he'd leave Meg and his kids to do that. Dan had said only that he needed to become revitalized in his profession. His demeanor sugested that there was more to it than that, but I didn't pry.

One thing that I felt certain about was that nothing bad was going on between Dan and Meg. She'd called shortly after he left and had given me his new phone number. If their relationship was in trouble, I believe she would have talked to me about it. She and I had a strong relationship and she was always very open.

I'd call him tonight, I decided.

Carl White wasn't in when I called. His secretary said that Freddy Meadows's first appearance was scheduled for ten o'clock this morning and that White would probably go there before coming to the office. During the conversation she said perhaps five sentences, but it took five minutes for her to say them. I'd hear a muted chirping, then she'd say, "Hold on." I couldn't believe Carl White received that many phone calls. I suspected she spent a lot of her working hours talking to her friends. Remembering her short skirt and low-cut blouse, I suspected White didn't care.

Forty-five minutes later I walked into the courthouse in Braxton. It was packed. The dingy hardwood floor squeaked as I made my way up the aisle to the front row, where a small space was vacant. To get to it, I had to step around a shiny brass spittoon that I hoped was there for ambience. Carl White and Freddy Meadows sat in front of me at a large wooden table on the other side of a picketed rail that ran from the jury box on my left to the wall on my right. An empty table holding an opened briefcase was to the right.

A man, who I assumed was the district attorney, was standing behind a podium set between the tables. Above the podium, a ceiling fan revolved slowly. I assumed he was the district attorney because he was suggesting to the judge that Freddy Meadows was a danger to the community and was asking that substantial bail be set. He did not suggest an amount, but continually emphasized the word *substantial.*

I didn't notice what the DA was wearing because I was too busy looking at Carl White. I couldn't believe what I was seeing. White was dressed in a white turtleneck shirt adorned with three gold necklaces. That courtwear was a poor enough choice, but was boundlessly overshadowed by his coat. At age eight, about the time I started listening to the radio, I became interested in fashion, mainly to spite my mother and the Congregational Holiness, and from way back then the history of the flash-in-the-pan Nehru jacket made its way through my memory banks.

My consternation was interrupted by a sound from the end seat across the aisle to my right. I turned in time to see a brown mass hit the inside top of the spittoon and felt a splash of residue fall on my pantyhose. I understood now why the seat I occupied was still available despite the crowded courtroom. I glanced at the spitter, who was wiping the back of his hand across his bearded face. Lovely.

The DA ended his presentation and the judge removed his horn-rimmed glasses from his puffy, pink face. He asked Carl White to respond.

White stood, walked to the podium and proceeded to plead on behalf of his client. His entire presentation was: "Your honor, I do believe you ought to go easy on the boy." Then he sat down. Meadows, who was wearing the same jeans and shirt he had on three days previously, stared at White, then nodded at the judge.

The judge's lips flapped as he blew air. Then he announced that Meadows's bond was set for a thousand dollars.

The district attorney stood immediately. "Your honor, I *must* approach the bench." He and White stood before the judge and talked quietly. White shrugged, then both lawyers returned to their respective tables.

The judge's eyes were cast down on the papers in front of him. Occasionally he would look at the now silent courtroom, first to the left, then to the right, then down to the papers again. I looked around to see who, or what, he was looking at. The packed courtroom offered no clues. Finally he said, "After further consideration, perhaps my original decision was . . . imprudent. Bail is set at a million dollars." He pounded his gavel, left his paperwork on the bench, and bounded out a door to his left.

There was a beat of stunned silence in the courtroom before it exploded with noise. White and the DA were immediately surrounded by reporters. I took advantage of the now empty pew to slide away from the spittoon and waited for the journalists to finish. Fifteen minutes later, I walked to the railing as White was picking up the briefcase he had never opened.

"What happened?" I asked.

White winked at me. "Good to see you, darling."

I ignored that. "What did he say to the judge?" I asked. "Big difference between a thousand-dollar and a million-dollar bond."

Meadows tugged on White's Nehru. The attorney pulled his arm away and told Meadows he'd be in touch. He turned away as Meadows was led from the courtroom by a deputy. White pulled the swinging gate toward him and walked down the courtroom aisle. I followed. He said, "The DA just provided the judge with some additional information that he found enlightening."

"Like what?"

"Let's just say he presented a syllogism the judge found hard to ignore. Personally, I think he made a mistake. There's got to be more than one interested party in this case, and he ought to know that."

We were walking down the steps of the courthouse when I tugged on the Nehru as Meadows had done earlier. Only this time White didn't pull away, but looked at my hand on his arm and raised his eyebrows twice. I dropped my hand quickly. "What are you talking about?" I asked.

White pulled out a generic and lit it, blew smoke through his nose, and shook his head. He took another drag from the cigarette.

It bothered me that the smell reminded me of my father. Daddy had his faults, but he wasn't a slug.

"Like I already told you, I never wanted this." He looked in my eyes. "You want this one, you got it."

"It's not that easy."

"Yes it is. Wait here."

Ten minutes later White reappeared and handed me a document. "Done."

"What's the conflict?"

White wheezed a laugh. "Don't ask. Judge Gee didn't." He lit a cigarette. "Listen, like I said, you're welcome to Meadows. I'll follow Georgia Superior Court rules and notify the bastard . . . in writing and in person." He looked up toward the mountains that surrounded Braxton and grimaced. "His Honor is spooked on this one."

"Who was in there? In the courtroom? The judge kept looking around."

White shook his head slightly and made a grunting sound that had a touch of irony to it. "That, little lady, you'll have to find out yourself. I'm out of it."

I watched White moving away from me, not knowing what to think.

Meadows needed defending, and it appeared somebody wanted him put away. The society needed the grant, and Charlotte Perry needed to know who had killed her adopted brother. Defending Meadows was the right thing to do on all counts.

And, I knew the politics of rural Georgia counties.

"Sheeeit," I said to myself as I headed toward the Park County jail. It was time to visit Freddy Meadows once again and explain the facts of life to him.

Chapter Eleven

Dan sounded breathless when he answered the phone.

"Are you all right?" I asked.

A pause followed as he took a deep breath. "Yeah. Just came in from a run around the cornfield." After another heavy inhale and exhale, he said, "Trying to get back into shape. Let that slip lately." A briefer pause this time. "So, how you doing? Other than finding dead bodies and stuff."

"You know about that?"

"Sure. Meg told me about it, so I paid closer attention than normal. Saw you and Mitch on CNN, too. They had a small clip of your press conference. Mitch appeared to be in his usual fine form."

"Yeah. He was a big help."

"I liked what you said. About the asinine question particularly."

"I've been worried about that."

"I knew you would be. It was fine. Even necessary. It was nice to see somebody challenge one of their dumb questions. I think you're probably the hero of everyday, normal Americans."

"Thanks, Dan." I'd seen it time and again. Dan's perception of people is uncanny. He hones in on the nitty-gritty quickly, gently, and helpfully. "I've gotten involved a little more. Actually, a lot more. I'm representing the guy they arrested for Fletcher's murder."

"Why am I not surprised?"

"Can I run some things past you? You're good at organizing thoughts. You see things I miss."

"You're too kind."

"Really, I mean that."

"Thanks. Okay, go ahead."

I went through the whole thing. After I told him about my conversation with Carl White, and my agreeing to take Freddy Meadows's case, he said, "Considering your description of the first meeting, I expect Freddy Meadows was real excited to see you again."

"The second time I stayed outside the cell. I think, though, that it's finally beginning to dawn on him that he might be in trouble. The judge setting the bail at a million dollars sent him a message. Despite that, he was still resisting my help, but at least he knows he needs some."

"You think he's innocent?"

I breathed deeply before answering. "I know he's innocent until proven guilty. I don't know enough about this thing to have an opinion, and I don't wish to form one. All they've got is a wallet and a witness who saw him in Warrendale shortly before we found Fletcher's body. I do know that Freddy Meadows is a jerk."

"I know what you said about the Legal Aid Society's grant, but I'm not sure that's enough reason to take this on if you don't have to."

The words flashed through my mind: Compassion, concern, curiosity. "The society's grant *is* important. But there's Charlotte Perry's stuff too. And, there's Freddy Meadows himself, damn it."

Dan knew I rarely swore. "You have a hard time with that one."

"He's a slug."

"You've defended slugs before." He paused. "Charlotte Perry is right. If you're determined to defend him, you need to go to Los Angeles. Check it out, at least. Take one thing at a time and eliminate it, or prove it. It makes sense that Fletcher might have been involved with something there that followed him to Warrendale."

"Yeah," I said.

"You don't need anybody's permission to do that, you know."

Once again, Dan's perception was on target. I *was* looking for some kind of permission, or . . . validation of my instinct.

He added, "Take Mitch with you."

My hackles rose. "I can take care of myself."

"I know that. You made that clear with Radar Gilstrap. But Mitch knows big cities. You don't."

"He knows inner-city Newark. We're talking Beverly Hills."

"Principles are the same. Just different methods. Besides, I think he'd like it."

I allowed my hackles to fall. "It may be a moot point anyway. Charlotte Perry offered to pay my way, but I can't take her money. Not if I'm defending the accused murderer of her brother, and I don't think the society could afford it."

"My guess is that you'll find a way."

"Yeah, well . . . anyway, enough of that. Have you learned lots of new things up there?"

A pause. "I've learned what I came up here to learn. Don't know that it's new. Just a confirmation."

"Oh?"

He didn't elaborate. "I've got another couple of weeks to go up here. Might take a week of annual leave after that. There're some things that I want to check out. I'll call you when I get back."

After hanging up, I moved to the veranda and sat on the porch swing, enjoying the crisp fall air. Thoughts about Lawton

Fletcher and Freddy Meadows kept being pushed away by my concern about Dan.

Through the magnolias and water oaks, I could see the brightly shining stars. I said aloud to them, "What's going on with him?"

Chapter Twelve

I hate this part."

I lifted my head from the newspaper and looked at Mitch. He was standing at the floor to ceiling window that faced the cockpit of the jet that we were due to board in twenty minutes. He was wearing a shirt on which enormous flowers alternated with Hawaiian hula dancers. Baggy shorts fell to just above his knobby knees. Sandals completed the outfit.

"What part?" I asked.

He turned away from the window and glanced around the waiting area of Gate 4, Concourse B of Atlanta's Hartsfield International Airport. "I always think of those movies. The ones where the plane crashes and they show the victims getting ready to go. At home with their kids, fighting with their wives, worrying about their jobs." He walked to me and said in a powerfully deep voice, "As the passengers readied for their flight, little did they know that"—he affected three flawless drumbeats—"fate . . . is . . . the hunter."

I buried my head in the paper. "I don't need this, Mitch." And I didn't. I'd only flown once before. That was when Dan and I went to New Orleans. I knew the statistics. Our odds of dying were far greater during the drive from Patsboro to the airport than during the flight to Los Angeles. I also knew from my course work in psychology that phobia knows no reason.

It had been three busy days since I'd talked to Dan. Bernard had found enough money in the society's budget to pay my way to LA. At least that's what he said. I suspected he might have found some of his own money, but I didn't argue about it.

Charlotte Perry was pleased to learn that I was going to California and immediately started to write a check. I told her I couldn't take the money now that I had been appointed to represent Freddy Meadows, the accused killer of her adopted brother. She insisted on making the check out to the society. When I refused to take it, she said she'd mail it instead. She also gave me a set of keys from Lawton Fletcher's personal effects that the GBI had turned over to her, and reiterated her desire to know why her brother had changed.

When I asked Mitch about going, he'd said that he'd been considering exporting his chain of appliance stores out of Georgia and figured he might as well start on the other end of the country and work toward the middle. When I expressed doubt, he said that would sound good to the IRS anyway. He could write off his expenses.

I'd spent yesterday with Mrs. Thompson's nephew. Bernard had been right about his being able to start immediately. I went over the files of the cases he was being assigned. They were all straightforward issues that took little cerebral effort. After spending a day with him, I fully understood Bernard's hesitancy in hiring him. The grant making us a regional center that would allow adding additional staff became imperative.

Now it was Friday morning and our flight was due to depart at seven fifty, which would put us in LA at eight fifty, their time. I'd called Lawton Fletcher's agent as a starting place. We were to meet him at eleven forty-five.

But first we had to get there. The choice of seats in the plane had been limited because of the late reservation. We were able to find two seats together, but they were in the middle of the center section. As it happened, we were surrounded by two families with young children. If I go to hell when I die, the devil will put me on an airplane with children for eternity.

The two-year-old in front of me did go to sleep. Unfortunately, that occurred a minute before the captain came on the intercom saying, "Ladies and Gentlemen, we are now beginning our descent into Los Angeles." The little girl did nothing but scream for the other three hours and forty-five minutes of the flight.

The five-year-old sitting next to Mitch settled down sooner. Taking advantage of the boy's mother's trip to the bathroom, Mitch had turned to the boy and, in a voice that incredibly included an echo-like tone, said, "Little boy, I am God. I command you to sit still and be quiet." The kid sat in terrorized silence for the next two hours.

For the first time in a long time, I appreciated my childlessness.

I said a prayer of thanksgiving as we deplaned. That lasted until we hit the car rental agency. It took almost as long to rent a car as it did to fly across the country. At least it seemed that way. Actually, we pulled away from the LA airport with an hour to spare before the appointment with Fletcher's agent.

"You should've let me rent the car," Mitch said as I followed the map leading us to the Four-oh-five, as the car rental agent had called it. I glanced at Mitch. He was a couple of inches shorter than my five feet eight inches, but his legs were disproportionately long. His bare knees were resting on the glove compartment of the Honda Civic I'd rented. "Like I said, it's deductible."

"Now you tell me," I said. "I have to be careful about spending the society's money." I glanced again at Mitch, "I need to tell you, I'm not too sure about the hotel. We're sort of talking one star . . . maybe."

"Tammi," Mitch said.

"Yes," I said.

"I grew up in a ghetto in Newark."

"I know. The facilities don't really matter to you, I guess."

"I made reservations."

"Where?"

"L'Ermitage. Beverly Hills. Five diamonds."

"Oh," I said. "Mine's somewhat south of Beverly Hills, I think."

"I booked a suite. Two bedrooms with a Jacuzzi. I would have booked two, but that's all they had left." He pointed to a sign directing the way to the 405.

"I see it," I said as I wound around the single lane leading to the freeway. "Yours sounds somewhat better than mine."

"Cancel yours," Mitch said. "Mine has, as I said, two bedrooms and nobody in Patsboro will know anyway."

"Jesus Christ!" I exclaimed. I had been raised to avoid taking the Lord's name in vain, but couldn't help myself. We were suddenly on the 405 along with a million other cars on at least eight lanes of traffic. I didn't have any idea how I even got on it and was too terrified to count. All of the lanes were packed solid. I threw the map at Mitch. *"This* is midmorning traffic?" I screamed.

"Calm down," Mitch said. His voice was strained and I wasn't sure if he was talking to me or himself.

Fletcher's agent's office was on Beverly Boulevard, and we were looking for the Santa Monica Boulevard exit. We crossed Interstate 10 and Mitch counted down until we reached our goal. I'd stayed in the middle lanes as much as possible, and, I hate to say it, closed my eyes while changing lanes to exit the 405. As soon as I was able, I turned into a parking lot and stopped.

"I thought you said his office was on Beverly Boulevard," Mitch said. "Why are you stopping?"

"It is. I need the rest." I laid my head back on the headrest and closed my eyes. "These people are nuts,"

Mitch nodded in agreement and looked at the map. "Looks like we can go to San Vicente. Beverly appears to dead end onto that.

"Want to drive?"

"Nuh-uh," he said.

"No guts," I said and pulled back onto Santa Monica Boulevard. Being off the freeway and back in traffic made for normal human beings allowed me to relax and think about why we were in Southern California, braving bratty children and kamikaze freeways. We needed to find out if Lawton Fletcher was caught up in something out here that followed him to Warrendale, Georgia. Or at least the hint of something. I had no intention of investigating possible criminal activity in Los Angeles. If we found anything that might hint at it, I'd let Molly Malone know.

Chapter Thirteen

I didn't know what to expect of a Hollywood agent, but whatever vague notion had laid in the back of my mind, Cal Adamson wasn't it. Everything about him was rail thin except for a bowling-ball potbelly and thick lips that surrounded a mouth too wide for his face. Age spots covered the top of his head, which was surrounded by mostly gray hair that was cut short. He was wearing a white shirt with the sleeves rolled up to his elbows and a loosened thin, solid navy tie.

We were sitting across the room from Adamson's desk. Mitch and I sat in pleated black leather chairs that faced a matching sofa in which Adamson lounged. Above his head, pictures of actors and actresses hung on the wall. I recognized several, but Lawton Fletcher's was the centerpiece. Adamson noticed that I was staring at it. "I guess I'll have to do something about that," he said, flipping his head upward.

I nodded, not knowing what to say, so I let it pass. I said, "Mr. Adamson . . ."

"Cal. Call me Cal."

"Okay." I probably wouldn't, though. I never used first names with my elders unless I knew them well. That's the way I was raised. "As I told you on the phone, I'm trying to figure out why Lawton Fletcher was killed. I . . . find myself in an unusual position, though." Adamson nodded, but said nothing.

"You see, I'm defending Mr. Fletcher's accused murderer, but I also—"

"Charlotte Perry called me. I am aware of the situation."

"Good," I said, then noticed Adamson looking at Mitch. "Mitch and I found Lawton Fletcher's body."

"I see." He returned his eyes to mine. "How can I help?"

"Charlotte told me Lawton had changed."

Adamson nodded.

"From what she said, it sounded like a change for the better. But . . ."

"Yes?" Adamson prodded.

"Any kind of change makes one wonder. He started sending her money after years of hardly paying attention to her or anybody else in his family."

"He did change. For better or worse, I don't know. I haven't seen him in two years."

"Two years? Why not?"

Adamson uncrossed his legs, stretched them in front of him, and placed his hands behind his head. "I don't know much. It started during the final days of shooting *Perfect Places.*"

"His last movie," Mitch said.

Adamson nodded. "There were days when he didn't show. And when he did, he wasn't at his best. Kerplan, the director, called to complain. Angie Flabert, who produced the movie, called too. When I called Lawton, he didn't want to talk about it."

"That was unusual? That kind of behavior, I mean?"

Adamson looked at me. "Not in his personal life. Unusual for the set though. He got serious during the shooting."

"I saw *Perfect Places*. I liked it."

"They worked around him enough to get it done."

"What happened after that?"

"Nothing."

"What do you mean, 'nothing'?"

Adamson sat straight and shrugged. "Nothing. He, in essence, disappeared. I never saw him again. We talked on the phone; the last time was about his interest in buying Warrendale. I sent him some scripts. He'd send them back, all but one, anyway. First the scripts would be returned with an explanation of his problems with them. After a while, he started to just write 'Sorry' across the cover."

"He kept one?"

"One he asked for. Some obscure thing. I don't even remember the title. I think *Dawn* was in it though."

We sat in silence for a moment. I broke it to recapitulate. "So you haven't seen him for a couple of years. You have no idea what was going on with him."

"Not much. I know he sold his house in Malibu. Moved down south. From the address, it was anything but an upwardly mobile move."

"Was he having money problems?" Mitch asked.

"Not at all. He partied, but he also invested wisely. No problems there."

"That you were aware of," Mitch said.

"Well," Adamson said while uncrossing and recrossing his legs, "I was reasonably knowledgeable about that. In addition to being his agent, I was also his attorney and our firm managed his finances."

"You're a lawyer?" I said, surprised.

"Mainly that's what I am. Adamson Associates is primarily a law firm." He put his hands behind his head again. "I have a few clients for whom I act as an agent. What an agent does is make contacts, know the industry, and negotiate contracts. Most of our legal work is with the entertainment industry. I had the contacts, so having a few clients sort of evolved. I don't seek them, though."

"So you drew his will."

"Finally, I drew his will. I'd been on his case to have one, but like most young people, he wasn't interested. Changed his mind a year ago."

"So, who inherits?" I asked.

Adamson shook his head. "It hasn't been read."

"I am an officer of the court, defending a client accused of murder. I'm investigating. I need to know."

Adamson looked at his watch, stood, and moved toward a door at the back of the room. "Would you like something to drink? A pop . . . or something stronger?"

"Co-cola'd be good," Mitch said.

"Co-cola," Adamson said slowly. "All right. How about you, Tammi?"

"Nothing, thank you."

When he disappeared, I looked at Mitch. "Co-cola? What happened to *soda?*"

He pursed his lips and drawled, "Ah am, my deah, a truly born-again southernah. The *dis*gusting whuds *soda* and *pop* will nevuh cross these lips again."

Adamson returned with a can of Coke for Mitch and had a tumbler of something stronger for himself. Noon had come. He sat on the sofa again and took a sip. He appeared relieved. "I have a question for you, Tammi. Why are *you* doing the investigating?"

"I work for a Legal Aid Society in a small southern town. My hourly pay works out to a few dollars more than minimum wage when you consider total time spent on the job. We simply can't afford an investigator."

Adamson pursed his lips and nodded.

"Now, it would be very helpful for us to know who benefited from Fletcher's death, as I'm sure you can imagine."

Adamson drained his glass. "His estate goes to two people. Charlotte Perry gets half. The other half goes to a woman named Florina Harvey. The address that we have is in Miami, but it appears she's moved. We're looking for her."

"Mr. Adamson—"

"Cal."

"Charlotte Perry gave me Fletcher's address. Can you tell us how to get there?"

"I can't tell you exactly, but I can get you in the vicinity. I checked a map when I first got his address after he moved from

Malibu. It's just on the other side of town."

"Good. I don't want to drive far in that devil traffic," I said in relief.

"This time of day, should make it in a couple of hours."

"A couple of hours!" I exclaimed.

"LA is a rather . . . expansive place," Adamson said dryly.

"Great," I said.

"Com'on Tammi, it's not that bad," Mitch said.

"Want to drive?" I asked.

"Nuh-uh."

I started to rise, then stopped. "Oh, I've got one other question. Who else could we talk to? Somebody close to him."

Adamson shook his head. "I have no idea. I've been calling his friends, that I know of anyway, for the past year. They're as baffled as I am."

"Do you think, Mr. Adam—" I stopped and raised my hand in surrender. ". . . Cal, that he became involved in something illegal? Something that would get him killed?"

"I wouldn't think so," he responded. His lips pursed. "You just never know, though, do you?"

Chapter Fourteen

Mitch and I left Cal Adamson's office and found the L'Ermitage. Hoping to defeat the jet lag, I took a nap. I don't know what Mitch did.

The meeting with Cal Adamson had produced more questions than answers. What could have caused a successful actor to suddenly drop out? Why would somebody with a substantial bank account move to a down part of town?

I wanted to see his apartment, but I also wanted to talk to Fletcher's neighbors, so I decided to arrive there around seven, figuring more of them would likely be home at that hour. I forced the car onto the 101 for a short trip to Chinatown for dinner. That was Mitch's idea. I would just as soon have had a Big Mac. Afterwards, as we reached the I-5 and headed toward Orange County, Mitch said, "Tammi, I need some water. I'm dying."

"Its the MSG," I said. "I'm *not* getting off this frigging freeway until we get to Orange County."

"How much longer?"

I grabbed the map that had been sitting on the seat next to me and threw it at him. "I don't know, Mitchy. Figure it out." The traffic was getting to me.

Mitch whined only occasionally after that until we found the exit that led to Fletcher's apartment building. It was a two-story stucco in a part of town that, according to Adamson, had once been de rigueur but was now in the process of disintegration. Fletcher's building fit that description. The decor appeared to be well done, but the paint was now peeling and flaking. We walked through glass doors in which one pane had been replaced by plywood. There was a small lobby that led to another set of doors that opened to a courtyard containing a swimming pool half filled with filthy water. The grounds surrounding the pool were barren, save for one palm tree that was threatening to fall on what had once served as a bathhouse. Entrances to the apartments were from walkways on the first and second story. It looked like a Holiday Inn that had gone decrepit.

We found Fletcher's apartment on the bottom floor, used the key Charlotte Perry had given me, and walked into the terrazzoed entrance. The air was thick and stuffy. I left the door open and moved onto the worn beige carpeting of the living room, which contained a set of pine furniture. It was the kind that costs a couple of hundred dollars at furniture stores that go out of business every other month. The walls were dirty, except for splotches of white where pictures had hung at one time. Now they were bare.

Mitch immediately moved to the galley kitchen in the efficiency apartment and drank water from his cupped hands under the faucet. I looked at the nearly empty living room. The rough-hewn coffee table held one magazine—*Boys Life*. "Not much here," I said to Mitch after he turned off the faucet.

Mitch wiped excess water from his chin with the back of his hand. "Not exactly the picture you get when you think about a rich movie star."

A doorless opening to the right of the sink led to the bedroom, which was even more austere than the living room: a twin-bed size mattress sitting on the floor, a three-drawer chest, and a Parsons table that held a reading lamp, a telephone, and a manila folder. Mitch raced through a door to the left of the bedroom entrance and soon I heard water running again. "Don't blow yourself up," I said.

The water stopped. "What?"

"Excess in anything is harmful."

Mitch reentered the bedroom, patting his stomach, which I could see was beginning to protrude despite his loose-fitting shirt. "I'm dying either way. Aren't you thirsty?"

"Not yet." I flipped through the pages of the folder that was on the table. It was the script Adamson had said Fletcher had asked for. The title was *New Dawn*. I'm no expert, but a quick glance wasn't impressive. The dialogue seemed stiff and unreal. I threw it back on the table and opened a sliding door to the closet. Three shirts and a couple of pairs of pants hung from the rail. A worn pair of New Balance running shoes sat on the closet floor.

Mitch was opening the drawers in the chest. "Anything?" I asked.

"Some underwear, socks, T-shirts," Mitch said and opened the second drawer. He pulled out a couple of knit shirts. "Nothing," he said.

"He adopted an ascetic lifestyle," I said.

"An ascetic with a few million in the bank," Mitch responded.

The bottom drawer was filled with books and pamphlets. Mitch and I pulled them out, examining titles. The pamphlets were mostly religious tracts that ranged from the Catholic church to mainstream Protestant denominations to more unusual groups like the Church of the Followers of the Mystic Mountain. The books were an eclectic collection of nonfiction, with no definable pattern except that there was nothing light. There were several philosophical works and a lot of books on the occult. I closed the drawer.

"Some kind of religious thing," I offered.

"According to Adamson, he hasn't given his money away yet," Mitch said.

I looked around the room. What was going on? What had happened to this movie star to cause him to move into this space? I sat down on the mattress. Clearly, he had some kind of interest in religion and philosophy. It could even be called a fixation. That drawer was filled with tracts. But there was no indication of his being involved in any particular one. There was no indication of drug use, which often causes significant lifestyle changes. Some kind of mental illness? When he talked to me on the phone to set up our meeting in Warrendale, he sounded . . . happy. He seemed excited about buying the town, but his happiness was normal, not the excitement one would expect from a manic-depressive on a high. I looked over the room again. This time, from my vantage point close to the floor, I saw a drawer on the front of the Parsons table, just under the top of the table that extended over its legs.

I pushed myself up and opened the drawer. It contained three envelopes addressed to Fletcher. The return address on each indicated the writer had been a woman named Florina Harvey. The address on the envelope was in New Orleans.

Florina Harvey was the woman who would inherit half of Fletcher's estate. I pulled the letters out and read them. They were short and apparently responses to letters Fletcher had sent her. All three were less than a page and each started with a paragraph expressing her pleasure that Fletcher was doing well. The other passages just said she thought he was doing the right thing.

I felt Mitch's presence over my shoulder. "What 'right thing'?" he asked.

I shrugged. "I'm going to take these." Maybe holding onto them would osmose some meaning that wasn't readily apparent. "Let's talk to some neighbors."

"What about his other stuff?"

I glanced around the room. "Leave it. I'll make sure Adamson takes care of it." I locked the door and we went to find some neighbors.

The first was a woman in a housecoat. A baby was screaming behind her. "I knew it was him, I just knew it! I kept telling Harold, 'That's man's Lawton Fletcher!' He'd say, 'Get real, Bev.' I knew it! I knew it!"

"Did you ever talk to Fletcher?" I asked.

She shook her head. "Who talks to anybody around here?"

I thought of Maytown, where I grew up in south Georgia. Not to speak would have been cause for comment. I couldn't imagine living next door to someone and not at least saying hello.

The woman kept gushing about Lawton Fletcher and I nodded politely. She asked if I knew him. I said I'd only talked to him on the phone. That was good enough for her. She invited us to come inside.

I was shaking my head and beginning to decline when Mitch said, "You mind if I get a drink of water?" I looked at him. "Just take a minute," he said as he charged through the door.

None of the other neighbors knew anything about Lawton Fletcher. Ninety minutes later I drove the Civic out of the parking lot and headed through the darkness toward I-5.

Mitch squirmed in his seat. "What next?"

"Talk to his friends, I guess." I turned right, following a sign pointing to the interstate. "And the police. See if Fletcher had any kind of problems with them. I'll call Adamson in the morning and see if he'll make arrangements." Another interstate sign appeared directing me to angle to the left.

I glanced at my watch. "At least it's late. The traffic ought to be better."

Wrong.

The interstate appeared quickly and, having no other choice, I charged into the right lane, praying somebody would get out of the way. "My God! It's *ten thirty* at *night!*" I screamed. The traffic hadn't abated an iota since seven o'clock. If anything it was worse.

Mitch said, "It's Friday night. Even the traffic in Patsboro's pretty crazy on Friday nights."

I was too busy panicking to respond. My peripheral vision began to blur and my ears roared as I squeezed the steering wheel. The next entrance ramp appeared with a line of cars dashing onto my lane. Got to get over, I thought. A glance in the side mirror revealed a solid line of cars in the lane to my left.

I wanted to squeeze my eyes shut as we approached the ramp, but didn't. Instead I stared straight ahead, kept the speed at a steady fifty-five and whispered, "Please, please, please . . ."

Somehow we made it by the entrance ramp without getting creamed. I haven't a clue as to how that happened. When I glanced in the side mirror again, a miraculous gap was apparent in the traffic. A quick move to the left got the Civic out of harm's way of traffic entering the freeway. I took a deep breath and wiggled my fingers on the wheel to loosen my hands, which had rigored from terror. The L'Ermitage was ninety minutes away, but now I could drive steady and straight and let the crazies who were constantly changing lanes worry about avoiding me.

Mitch squirmed again, turned on the radio, and found a station broadcasting an old radio show. I recognized George Burns and vaguely remembered that his wife's name had been Gracie. The show was entertaining, but just as I was beginning to relax a tiny bit, it ended and the eleven o'clock news came on. I don't know why, but I couldn't believe it. The first story was a traffic report, something about a doghouse and a bunk bed that had fallen on "the One-oh-one." "These people are crazy," I said again.

Mitch had remained unusually quiet during the ride. Now he said, "Uh, Tammi . . ."

"Yes?"

When he didn't respond I took a chance and glanced at him. His hands were intertwined between his legs and he was leaning forward, rocking slightly.

I looked ahead again. "Are you all right?"

He breathed deeply. "I don't think so."

"What's the matter?"

"Tammi . . . I've got to go."

A beat passed before the horror of what he was saying hit me. My hands tightened on the steering wheel. My voice was low and harsh when I said, "What?"

"I thought I could wait." He rocked harder. "I can't."

"Yes you can."

His voice was strained. Through clenched teeth he said, "No. I've *got* to go. *Now.*"

I stared straight ahead and whispered, "Sheeeit!"

Chapter Fifteen

Three exits passed before I managed to move into the right lane. As the next opportunity to get off the interstate approached, I looked for signs indicating establishments that might have public bathrooms, like a Burger King or Motel 6, but saw nothing. I considered going on, but Mitch's breathing intruded on that thought. He sounded like he was deep into Lamaze. When I was in law school, I had been the coach for a pregnant student whose husband was in the navy. Mitch had progressed into the pant-breath mode. Not a good sign. I took the next exit despite there being nothing to indicate a public bathroom.

The exit dead-ended onto a narrow, darkened street. Old apartment buildings that had the look of public housing lined the street in front of us. To our left was an abandoned gas station whose windows and doors were long gone. On the corner to our right was a restaurant that appeared to have once been a Kentucky Fried Chicken. The writing on the plywood that covered the former windows read, "Bea's Eats." The door was open.

I pulled to the side of the building and Mitch bounded out before I was completely stopped. I planned to lock the doors and remain in the car, but then I decided to take the opportunity myself to be sure we didn't have to stop again.

Music blared from the restaurant, loud enough to hurt my ears when I walked in. The dimly lit eating area was nearly empty, but three men were hunched over a table against the back wall. As I approached, I saw they were watching two other men play some kind of board game, one I'd never seen before. Marbles fit into indentations on the board, reminiscent of Chinese checkers, but not quite. The men had an Asian look, but didn't appear Chinese or Japanese. Perhaps Vietnamese or Thai. Maybe even Filipino. I couldn't tell. Maytown's ethnic diversity was limited to whites and African-Americans, and Georgia Southern College wasn't much different. Catledge University had a large contingent of foreign students, but they were mostly in math, science, or engineering—not in law school.

I approached the men and asked if I could use the ladies' room. The man with his back to the wall glanced up at me and nodded toward a corridor to my right. His eyes returned immediately to the game board.

The hall was dark and covered with water that deepened as I moved toward the doors to its rear. The letters "WO" were on the first door and I presumed that one was for me. I stopped short when I opened the door. A horrific stench flowed from the room and I gagged reflexively. I peeked in. A toilet covered with grime, and who knows what else, was against the wall and was flanked by a sink that was half hanging off the wall. A brown ooze dripped from the unattached drain beneath it. Getting off the freeway in case of an emergency suddenly became less daunting. I closed the door and walked out of the restaurant.

I walked quickly past the men who were playing the game and out the door to my car. I was about to slide the key into the car door's lock when I heard a sound behind me.

"Hey, babeee. What's happening?"

I jerked around. A featureless figure was silhouetted against the light that hung over the restaurant door. His hands were in the pocket of a jacket that he wore despite the warm air. I didn't recognize the accent.

More sounds. I looked around to find six or seven others surrounding me and the car. One said, "Man, Kong, look at that." They were teenagers, and had the same kind of Asian features as the men inside the restaurant.

The jacketed one nodded. "Yeah, man, I see it."

I pointed beyond Kong, who stood between me and the restaurant door. My face was numb and I had to concentrate to make my mouth move. "My friend's in there using the bathroom. He'll be out anytime."

Kong laughed. "You mean the midget nigger? Watch me shake, lady."

The others laughed. I glanced around to see them begin to move toward me. My eyes scanned behind them. The street was empty. No one was in sight around the apartments across the street. The music continued to roar from the door of the restaurant. No way Mitch or the men inside would hear me if I screamed.

"Y'all need to go on. Leave me alone."

"Oooh, listen to the way she talks," Kong said. "Say something else, lady. I like that." He stepped toward me.

My stomach tightened and my vision blurred. I turned and tried to unlock the door.

They were on me. Two boys grabbed my wrists and pulled them up above my head. A hand pushed my head against the top of the Civic, then twisted my face so that my cheek was pressed against the roof. I felt a body press against mine from behind.

A voice I recognized as Kong's said, "Let go of her." As soon as the boys released my wrists, Kong's strong grip replaced theirs.

When the hand that was holding my head moved, I pulled it up. Kong's face was next to mine, cheek to cheek. His breath smelled of unknown spices.

"Heeey, relax, lady. Chill out. I know you're gonna like it."

A slight snap in my mind. Enough to begin thinking again. The Civic's key was still in my left hand. I moved it so that it stuck out between my fingers.

Kong tightened against me. I could feel him against my buttocks. He began moving his hips.

Never again!

It was automatic. Practice makes perfect. I flexed my right wrist and jerked it toward the ground. Simultaneously, I kicked backward with my right foot and caught Kong on his shin with the heel of my shoe. That cost him his balance. I found his right wrist and spun, my left hand jerking away from his grip. Immediately, I was behind him pushing his right arm toward the back of his neck. My left arm went around him and underneath his jacket. The key struck against his ribs, which were covered now only by a T-shirt. I slammed him against the car, where I had been a moment before.

He swung back at me with his left arm and the other boys jumped toward me. I jabbed the key against Kong's ribs. His scream stopped the others in their tracks.

I said into Kong's ear, "Tell them to move away."

He growled in response and twisted to his left. I jerked his right arm up and jabbed harder with the key. He screamed again, then yelled to the other boys, *"Back the fuck up!"*

I glanced around to see that the others were slowly moving backward. After a few steps, they stopped.

I tried to look back toward the door of the restaurant. Where was Mitch? There was one of me and a bunch of them. I'd surprised Kong, but this couldn't last forever.

I looked across the roof of the Civic. A figure appeared from the darkness behind the restaurant wearing a raincoat and a floppy hat. The man was singing as he approached the boys who still stood on the other side of the car. He grabbed one of the boy's arms and said, "Hey, buddy, how you doing?"

The boy jerked his arm away.

"Hey, man, you got some dollars I could borrow? I sure could use some help right now. Know what I mean? I need some stuff. Bad, man."

The boy he'd grabbed pushed the derelict away. "Get the fuck out of here you stinking nigger."

The push caused the man's hat to flop up momentarily. It was Mitch. Kong moved slightly and I jabbed him again.

Mitch went to another boy. "Come on, man, help me out. How about it?"

"Get away from me, asshole."

"Asshole?" Mitch said in a high-pitched, feminine voice. "You want asshole, you got it. Yeah, all'a you got it. I just need some stuff." He grabbed his crotch. "I don't mind working for it. Looks like you boys need it bad, any which way you can."

The boy closest to Mitch screamed something in a language I didn't recognize and grabbed for him. Mitch ducked and backed away. The other boys started toward him and Mitch turned and ran. All of the others chased him around the corner of the restaurant.

I was left with Kong. I said slowly and clearly, "I'm going to let you go. But I want you to understand something. When I do, you run." I jabbed the key hard into his ribs. He screamed, then slumped on the car. "You don't run, and I'll kill you. I've done it before, and I'll do it again. You made a major mistake tonight. Do you *understand* that?" I jerked his right arm up a notch.

Kong grunted and nodded.

I pressed the key into his ribs. "What?"

"I'm gonna run, lady. Just like you say."

I let him go.

He ran.

I unlocked the car, jumped in, then locked both doors. I shoved the key into the ignition, turned it, and grabbed the steering wheel.

Mitch!

What do I do? Sit and wait? Find a phone and call the police? I looked around. No sign of him. Call the police, I decided. The spoken language was different, but Mitch knew the language of the streets. I figured the teenagers didn't have a chance of catching him.

I put the car in reverse and spun the steering wheel. The moment I put the Civic in drive, I heard a pounding on the roof. It startled me enough to release the accelerator. Mitch's face appeared in front of the windshield.

"Let me in!"

I unlocked the doors and he bounded across the hood and dived into the Civic. "Get the hell out of here!"

For the first time in my life, I laid rubber and wheeled out of the parking lot, ran a red light, and reentered the interstate. I didn't even look for other cars, which is probably, I decided, how you need to drive out here anyway.

We were silent as I maneuvered into an interior lane. My mind was numbed, but thoughts and feelings soon returned.

I glanced at Mitch. "That boy was right. You stink." I rolled down my window.

"Used what I had. Saw what was going on, then retreated to the kitchen." He held up the hat. "Found this stuff and some kind of rotgut liquor. Poured it over me and did my thing." He threw the hat in the back seat. "Just like old times in Newark."

Part of the feeling that had returned was anger. "Mitch."

"Yes?"

"Tomorrow."

"Yes?"

"When we head off to who knows where."

"Yes?"

"Wear a diaper!"

Chapter Sixteen

An hour later Mitch and I were in the suite at the L'Ermitage. I called 911 and reported the attack by the boys. The woman said I needed to go to the precinct where the attack occurred and began giving me directions.

"Never mind," I said and hung up. First, there was no way I was getting back in the traffic that night. Second, even if Kong and his friends were found, it would be a case of their word against Mitch and mine's. And if California's juvenile justice system was anything like Georgia's, the most that would happen in any case would be a probation extension for the teenagers.

Meaningless.

I dialed Adamson's number, hoping he had a machine or an answering service. It was a service. I left my name and number and asked him to call in the morning.

Mitch was sitting in the huge Jacuzzi in the corner of the suite's living room. Water bubbled just under his chin. "Want to get in?"

I took off my shoes and lay on the sofa. "Didn't bring my suit."

"Too bad. This is great."

"Just as well. I'd probably fall asleep and drown." It was midnight in California, but 3:00 A.M. body time. I was approaching twenty-four hours since sleeping last and my body was withdrawing from the shot of adrenaline provided by the attack. My eyes rumbled as they shut.

"So what's next?"

"Adamson, again," I mumbled. "Police . . . check out Fletcher with them." I was floating.

"Tammi, you think it was worth coming out here?"

I wanted to respond, or, at least, shrug, but couldn't. Then I was gone.

The doorbell was ringing. But that didn't make sense because I don't have a doorbell. Must be something outside, I thought, and turned over. Suddenly, I was falling.

The fall was short. I opened my eyes, trying to figure out what was going on.

Ding-dong, ding-dong.

Using the glass-topped coffee table to my left and the sofa to my right for leverage, I pulled myself up, looked around, and realized I wasn't at home in Patsboro.

Still in a fog, I moved to the door and opened it without looking through the peephole. Nobody was there.

Ding-dong. Ding-dong.

I yawned and coughed at the same time. Another door somewhere? This was a big place and I had only been in this living room and my bedroom.

Mitch appeared through the door to his bedroom, still wearing his pajamas. "Somebody here?"

I shrugged. "Not at the door." I pointed to it. "Not this one, anyway."

Ding-dong. Ding-dong.

"That's the only one. Except to the balcony."

We stood silently for a moment, then both focused on the far corner of the room. "Telephone," we said at the same time and moved toward it.

Ding-dong. Ding . . . It stopped.

"Nuts," I said.

"What kind of phones go ding-dong?" He imitated the sound of the phone flawlessly.

"California phones." At that moment, the red message light began flashing. I called the desk and was given Cal Adamson's home phone number.

"I was afraid I'd missed you," Adamson said after I identified myself.

"We had a hard time finding the phone," I said.

Mitch said, "Ask him if his phone ding-dongs too."

I waved at Mitch to be quiet and said to Adamson, "Thanks for returning my call."

"I was going to call anyway."

"Really? Why?"

"I've made arrangements for you to talk to somebody who might help. Emily Jackson."

"The actress?"

"Yes. Of the group Lawton ran with, she was probably the one closest to him. In terms of friendship, I mean."

"That would help. Where and when?"

"My house in Westlake Village. Around three this afternoon. Is that okay?"

I agreed and he gave me directions. Amazingly, he added that the trip would take only about forty minutes. I was relieved when he said the traffic should be light on a Saturday afternoon. When Adamson asked me why I had called him, I told him he'd already anticipated one of my needs with Emily Jackson. I wanted to talk to somebody who was a friend of Fletcher's. I also wanted to find out if he knew anybody on the police force who would help.

"I don't deal much with the police. My practice doesn't involve that sort of thing, except for small stuff . . . like when a client runs a stop sign or something."

"I understand."

"But, wait." After a pause, he said, "Martin Macleod. I used to be an adjunct professor for the Benjamin Franklin School of Law in Encino. It operated at night. Martin was a student. I ran into him the other day and he said he's still with LAPD, Holly-wood division. He's a sharp guy. You can call him and mention my name."

I expressed my thanks and hung up.

"Emily Jackson?" Mitch said after I hung up.

"We're meeting with her at Mr. Adamson's house this after-noon . . . about three."

Mitch jumped around the room, clapping and chanting, "Oh, goody, goody, goody. Oh, goody, goody, goody."

"Gee whiz, Mitch, are we excited?"

Mitch tried to stop in midjump, but couldn't. He did stop in midclap. "Sure. She's an Oscar winner. Aren't you just a wee bit aroused by the thought of meeting her?"

The fact was, I was excited about meeting a movie star. Why couldn't I admit it? The only other one I'd met was dead at the time.

Oh, what the hell.

I started to imitate Mitch's "Oh, goody, goody, goody," but I stopped. "It just doesn't work for me, Mitch."

"I think," Mitch said, "that you have to find your own way."

"Stop, Tammi."

"What?"

"Pull in there." Mitch pointed to an empty parking space.

I slowed. "Why?"

"Please?" he said in a plaintive voice.

We were on our way to meet with Martin Macleod, the po-lice official Cal Adamson knew. I'd called him earlier. He hap-pened to be on duty that morning and, at the mention of Cal Adamson's name, agreed immediately to meet with Mitch and me. He gave me directions that kept us off the freeway, thank God. Now Mitch wanted to make things difficult.

I executed the parallel-parking task using the technique my high school driver education instructor had taught me. As usual, it didn't work. Cars backed up behind me as I tried again. This time I ended up only two feet from the curve. Good enough, I thought. I looked at Mitch. "I thought I told you to go before we left."

Mitch opened his door. "That's not it."

As I climbed out of the Civic, I asked, "What is it then?" Mitch was already moving across the sidewalk. I followed him down the street, catching up just as he turned into an appliance store.

The moment we entered, a heavyset man approached us. He said, "Now you are two lucky people. Everything in the store's on sale. Twenty percent off the list price. Every dadblamed thing in the store, yes sir."

Mitch looked around the store. Refrigerators lined the wall to the left. To the right were washing machines, dryers, and dishwashers. Video and audio wares filled the center. Mitch lifted the price tag on an Etonik television. "This the sale price? Four hundred ninety-nine dollars?"

"Yes siree bob. Great price, isn't it?"

"That's a model AS-Six hundred. The list price is four eighty-five. Check the sheet."

The salesman's smile faded and his eyes squinched slightly.

"You the owner?" Mitch asked.

"No. I manage the store, though."

"Think the owner wants to sell?"

"Sell what?"

Mitch swept a hand in front of him. "The store. Do you think he would sell the store?"

The man shrugged. "I don't know. I doubt it."

"Okay," Mitch said. "Thanks." To me, he said, "Let's go."

We were back in the car and I was struggling to de-parallel-park. "What was that all about?"

Mitch grinned and raised his eyebrows. "IRS. This trip is now *de*ductable."

"Hope you have a good attorney." I looked again at the directions Macleod had given me, and realized we were almost at the police station.

"Not only do I have a good lawyer, she's a good friend."

"I mean a tax attorney, Mitch. A *real* good tax attorney."

The police station appeared as advertised, and the lot across the street was only half full. Within minutes, we were sitting across Detective Martin Macleod's desk.

During the introductory conversation, Macleod said he had given up law school because it was taking too much time away from his family. That didn't surprise me because, somehow, he had that family man look. His suit and tie were neat, but not flashy. His black hair was groomed conservatively and topped a face featuring strong cheeks and a square jaw. He had an endearing crooked smile that seemed to come easily.

Probably, though, my intuition about his being a family man was helped by the two framed picture collections that hung on the wall behind Macleod's desk. They were filled with pictures of his wife and children.

I told Macleod of the circumstances and principals surrounding Lawton Fletcher's murder, including my client, Freddy Meadows and Charlotte Perry.

"So you're representing the accused murderer and working for the woman whose brother he killed. Seems . . . odd."

"I'm not working for her. Our interests just happen to coincide, but . . . odd would not be an inaccurate way of describing Ms. Perry," I said. I mentioned her fixation with Lucas Anderson's book, *Triple Threat*.

"I've read it."

"You have?" I said in surprise. "Lucas said it didn't do too well nationally."

"My brother-in-law is a regional manager for B. Dalton books in Santa Monica. He goes over the catalogs for books about true crime and lets me know." The detective leaned forward, placing his elbows on his desk. "I've been trying to remember where I've heard your name." He shifted his gaze. "And you're Mitch. Should have put that together before now."

Mitch smiled.

Macleod looked back at me, "So, how can I help?"

"I need to find out if Lawton Fletcher was into anything out here that followed him to a tiny town in northeast Georgia."

"Could have done that on the phone."

I nodded. "I could have. But I've found it's often more productive to see things and meet people firsthand. But you're right. The fact is I feel like I'm wasting the society's money, and there's not much to waste."

"No, *you're* right. You never know what you'll find." The detective lifted a sheet of green bar computer paper. "After you called, I ran this on Fletcher. There's not much. A couple of speeding tickets and an arrest, but no conviction, on possession of a small amount of marijuana. That was seven years ago."

I clucked my tongue. "You're right, not much."

Macleod raised his hand, holding a finger up. "But, I checked around. Turns out Fletcher did come to the attention of the drug enforcement people. A friend of mine over there checked the files. They were investigating a guy who Fletcher knew. Because of that, they became aware of Fletcher's travels. Seems he made several trips into Mexico, and a couple after that to the Caribbean within the past year." He leaned back again. "That's all they got, though. The file was thin. Either they decided Fletcher wasn't up to anything, or they just couldn't find anything. Fletcher's friend was arrested and convicted and that was that."

"Would the file indicate who had investigated?"

"Probably. I'll check. How long do you plan to stay out here?"

"We're leaving tomorrow."

"Short trip."

"As I said, our money is limited."

"Tell you what, I'll follow up on this and let you know if anything develops."

After warning him about Mrs. Thompson's propensity for disconnecting people, I gave him the phone number for the Legal Aid Society and my home.

When I thanked him, Macleod said it was fun meeting Tammi Randall and Mitch Griffith. He asked how Dan was doing, and I said he was doing fine, without conviction. He asked about Jarvis and if Crowe had been found yet.

It had been a year since Crowe attacked me, but my stomach tightened at the question.

Sensing my discomfort, Mitch said, "Yes. He was found. He's not a problem anymore."

Chapter Seventeen

We were heading toward I-5. According to Cal Adamson, to get to Westlake Village, we were to go north on the interstate, then travel west on Highway 101.

We were at a stoplight when Mitch said, "I'm getting out. Circle the block and pick me up."

"What?"

"Been thinking about what you said about the IRS. You're probably right. I won't be long." Mitch jumped out of the car and headed across the street.

I hollered, "Mitch!" but he didn't respond. Cars honked behind me when the light turned green. "Circle the block? What block?" I said aloud. Apparently Newark-raised Mitch hadn't noticed that most of LA, at least the part we'd been in, didn't have blocks. I wandered around, negotiating one-way streets and no-right turns, fighting panic all the way, until I finally found myself back at the stoplight where Mitch had bailed out. I didn't see him, and cars honked again when the light turned green again. "You are a dead man, Mitch," I said to myself as I drove slowly up the street.

Then, I saw him emerge from a store ahead. The sign above the door read Bill's Refrigeration. After I braked, causing another round of honking, Mitch jumped in the car. He said, "I offered to buy the store and the idiot actually wanted to negotiate. I gave him my card and told him I'd call him." In response to my hard look, he said, "IRS insurance."

I started to tell him to stay in the car from now on, but I didn't have to. By then we were on the entrance ramp to I-5. A couple of seconds later I said something I'd never said before in my life. In fact, I screamed it. *"This* is *fuck*ing light Saturday afternoon traffic?"

"Tammi!" Mitch said, shocked.

"Get over it," I said through clenched teeth.

Following Cal Adamson's directions, I exited Highway 101 at the Westlake Village exit and turned left. After about a mile, the road began climbing, then veered left and flattened out. The houses were large, but spaced, it seemed, about five feet apart. We found Adamson's and parked in the driveway behind a Jaguar.

A young, attractive Hispanic woman opened the door and motioned us in. Mitch and I entered a tiled foyer with stairs to the left that rose to a balcony that apparently led to bedrooms. To the right was a living room with a fireplace. I stopped for a moment and looked around. I don't know much about square footage, but this was a big house. It seemed to be about the size of the ones in McCarty's Creek, a subdivision in Teal County where houses sold for between two and three hundred thousand dollars. I was impressed.

The woman, who I presumed was the housekeeper, led us through a den, and out French doors. Now I was more than impressed, I was awestruck. A pool sat ten feet behind the house, and beyond that was a valley with mountains on the other side.

These mountains were different from the Appalachians. They were covered with brush, with only an occasional bush sticking up here and there. At the bottom of the valley, about a half mile down, was a stand of trees that ran its length. Somehow, the lack of vegetation added to the sense of vastness.

The view, incongruously, had both dulled and heightened my senses, and I was startled when Adamson said hello. He was neck deep in the pool. Next to him, also neck deep, was a woman whom I recognized from the movies and Oscar night on television.

Adamson said, "I'm sorry, I should have told you to bring your suits." He moved to the shallow end and climbed the stairs out of the pool. "But I might have some that would fit you two."

Emily Jackson said, "You and I are about the same size. I've got another one in my bag." She was moving toward the steps.

Mitch said, "I don't know. You're probably taller than me."

"I meant her, silly," Emily said as she came out of the pool. She was about my height, five foot eight, but her bottom half was thinner than mine. *Much* thinner. It was easy to tell because her thong covered next to nothing. She opened a bag and pulled out another suit and held it up. Another thong.

"Ummmm," Mitch said.

I gave Mitch a look that said, I don't think so. I actually said, "Thanks, Miss Jackson, but I'd better pass on swimming."

"Oh, pooh," she said.

Mitch looked at me and mouthed, "Pooh?"

"And call me Emily, please."

Somehow, I didn't think I'd have a problem calling her by her first name, although we'd just met. The rule didn't apply to children, and Emily seemed very childlike.

"How about you, Mitch?" Adamson said.

"You know, I think I'll just sit out here and work on my tan." He reclined in a lounge chair and pulled up his shorts.

Adamson was standing by a portable bar. "Care for anything?"

"Maybe," Mitch said as he looked across the narrow valley, "a frozen tequila sunrise."

"Can't do that out here, but it's no problem." He turned and called. "Esperanza?"

"I was just kidding," Mitch said, "The ambience got to me."

Esperanza, the housekeeper, arrived. Adamson spoke to her in Spanish.

"Really, I was just kidding," Mitch reiterated.

"It'll be out here in a minute." Adamson looked at me.

"Just some water, please."

"Booze would be cheaper, but if you insist." He poured water into a glass filled with ice, made a drink for himself and Emily, then invited me to sit. He settled in a chair next to me. Emily sat by the pool, one leg dragging through the water.

"I like your place," I said.

Adamson nodded. "I've enjoyed it, but I should have sold last year."

"Why?"

"Real estate's bottomed out. Really, worse than that. It's dropping. Should have taken the offer of three I had last year. I probably can't get two for it now."

I looked at the scenery. "A couple of hundred thousand would be a bargain for this place."

"Uh . . . actually that was million."

"Million?" Mitch said.

"Yes," Adamson said.

Three million? Two million? I couldn't comprehend it. The place was nice, but millions?

Mitch's drink had arrived. He slouched, took a sip, inhaled deeply, and said, "I think I could get used to this."

We sat for a moment in silence. I broke it by saying, "I appreciate your willingness to see us, Emily."

The actress hugged her knees and rested her chin on them.

"You were close to Lawton Fletcher?" I asked.

"For a while we were very close. Very, very, *very* close."

"How long ago was that?"

Emily squeezed her eyes shut. "Oh-h-h, I don't know. Five, six years ago. For a while after that we were just close, you know?" When she looked up at me, I nodded. "Then, we weren't close at all."

"What happened?"

Emily shrugged. "He changed. Quit coming to parties." She unwrapped her arms, stretched her legs in front of her, and leaned back on her elbows. "Really, he just disappeared. I hardly ever saw him."

"When did that start?"

"A couple of years ago."

"When did you see him last?"

"When we finished *Perfect Places*. I was really mad at him. We'd be set to do a scene and he'd be late. Toward the end he wouldn't even show sometimes." She sipped her drink. "I think he was on some heavy-duty stuff."

"Stuff?"

"Yeah. Sometimes at parties we'd do some coke or grass. Just a little bit, you know? Not enough to hurt anything. I thought he was too smart to really get into it."

Mitch said, "Smart don't matter when it comes to that."

I said, "Was there anything else he did that made you think he was into drugs? Other than being late, or not showing."

Emily rolled over and slipped back in the pool. "He'd forget his lines." She paused. "Well, really, he wouldn't exactly forget them. We'd be doing a scene and he'd stop. Sort of stare out into space, you know? Every time it happened, Gary got real mad."

"Gary?"

"Gary Kerplan, the director. Anyway, when Gary yelled at him, Lawton would say he was sorry and then he'd do it perfect."

"So he knew the lines, he just . . ."

Emily said, "Zoned out, you know?"

"Uh-huh. Anything else?"

"Let me think."

"Uh-oh," Mitch said softly.

"There was another thing. It was the last scene we did. He'd zoned a couple of times and Gary was getting really mad, you know? Then Lawton was supposed to pick up a glass and I was supposed to pick up a glass and we were supposed to clink them together. You know, like a . . ."

"Toast," I said.

"Yeah, like that. Lawton kept dropping his glass. I mean,

he'd pick it up, then his hand would start shaking, then he'd drop it. That's when Gary got really, really, *really* mad and he called Lawton a junkie. That's when I figured out what was wrong with him. That was the last time I saw him."

"That was almost two years ago?"

Emily nodded.

"Who's he been hanging around with?"

Emily shrugged.

Mitch asked, "Did he mention his religious beliefs to you?"

Emily shook her head.

Cal Adamson said, "I checked around with some other people from his old crowd. Nobody'd seen him or knew what he was doing."

"Didn't anybody try to see him? I mean, if they were friends . . ."

Adamson looked at Emily, who had pushed away and was backstroking across the pool. "These folks"—he nodded toward Emily—"tend to be here-and-now kind of people. Besides, Lawton wouldn't see even me. I doubt that he would have responded to anybody."

I stood. "Mr. Adamson—" He raised his hand, and before he could protest, I said, "Cal, I appreciate your arranging this." I looked at Mitch, who was sipping on his drink and watching Emily swim toward us. "Time to go Mitch," I said.

Before he could respond, Emily said, "Are you leaving? You just got here."

"Our flight leaves early tomorrow morning and I'm exhausted. Didn't get much sleep last night. At least, it doesn't feel like it."

"Jet lag," Adamson said.

Emily was at the side of the pool, resting her chin on her crossed arms. "Where are you from?"

"Georgia."

"What state is that in?"

"Atlanta," I tried.

"Oh yeah. That's in the South, isn't it?"

"Yes."

A self-satisfied look crossed Emily's face. "I thought so. I love your accent." She concentrated for a moment, then said, "I'm up for a part in a movie that's set in the South. Ohio, I think. Maybe you could coach me."

I heard Mitch grunt. I said, "Ohio's in a different part of the South. I don't think I could help you."

Emily nodded in an understanding manner.

We were in the middle lane of the 101. I'd figured out that's the best thing to do. Cruise in the middle lane and let everybody else weave around you.

Mitch said, "Do you think we've learned anything worthwhile?"

I shrugged. "We haven't learned much of anything. But sometimes seemingly insignificant things become significant later." I glanced at Mitch. "What did you think of Emily?"

It was his turn to shrug.

"What happened to 'Oh, goody, goody, goody'?"

"It was diminishing, but not gone, until Ohio joined the Confederacy."

"Ditz."

"Ditz City, honey." Mitch said.

"Yeah. Makes you wonder how she can memorize lines. Anyway, I think coming out here made some sense, because I believe Macleod is more motivated to investigate than if I'd just called."

"Agreed."

"It's apparent we know as much about Lawton Fletcher as we're going to know unless we stay a month, and we can't do that."

"Ditto."

"And I can tell Charlotte Perry that I tried."

"Guiltless."

Like Dan, Mitch had a way of honing in on the main point.

Yes. Guiltless. At least I knew I had made the effort. "From what Emily said, it sounds like Fletcher had the shakes. Drugs, you think?" I'd seen similar symptoms with clients who I *knew* were users.

"Makes sense, sort of."

"Yeah. Sort of. But it doesn't make sense, too."

"I know what you mean."

"Adamson, who should know, says Fletcher was, and still is, worth millions. We're not talking about somebody who spent everything he had to stay high. Why did he go low rent?"

"Good question."

Nothing was said while I negotiated the I-5 interchange. When we were safely back in the middle lane, I said, "According to Macleod, Fletcher'd traveled to Mexico and the Caribbean."

"Pipelines?"

"But if he had millions, why bother with smuggling drugs to make more? What's the point?"

"Believe it or not, for some people, enough's not enough."

"I know that. But he was giving it away, Mitch. Why risk prison for money when you're going to pass it along to your long-lost sister?"

"She wasn't exactly lost."

"You know what I mean."

"Yeah." Mitch agreed.

"Besides, zillions of people vacation down there. If he'd been involved in anything like that, my guess is that the drug enforcement people's file on him would be thicker.

"And why was he trying to buy Warrendale? What could that have to do with drugs?" I asked.

Mitch shrugged. "Maybe a distribution point. I mean if you own the town, it'd be easier to manipulate things."

I shook my head. "That's just dumb. How more high-profile could you get?"

"Doesn't hurt to brainstorm, Tammi."

A tractor trailer pulled in front of us, missing by inches. Mitch said, "Jesus, please save our poor souls." We were both silent for a moment.

I said, "That makes more sense."

"What?"

"Jesus, or some religious thing. Koresh had a compound in Waco. Imagine having a town. Controlling its government, law enforcement . . . everything."

"Something to think about. Maybe a combination. A cult that's into drugs," Mitch said. "What about Florina Harvey?"

"I've been thinking about her, too."

"I think she's a clue," Mitch said.

"I wonder how much more it would cost to change the tickets for a stopover in New Orleans."

"It's on the way. Shouldn't be much."

The exit that led to our hotel was approaching. I looked in the side mirror in preparation for moving to the right lane and saw a solid line of cars. I turned on my blinker, squinched my eyes, and moved over. I was just beginning to relax again when Mitch screamed, "Look out!"

I swerved just in time to miss a sofa that fell off the pickup truck in front of us. The car behind us wasn't so lucky.

When I could breathe again I said, "New Orleans has *got* to be better than this."

Mitch's head was cocked back against the headrest on his seat. "Yes. It's got to be really, really, *really* better than this."

Chapter Eighteen

This isn't better," I said. The traffic was solid on I-10 as we headed away from New Orleans International Airport.

"No," Mitch agreed, "it's not." A map of New Orleans that Avis provided was spread across his lap and he pointed to it. "Maybe it's because this big old city is stuck between the Mississippi River and . . . uh, Lake Pontchartrain. It looks like there's nowhere else to go but on I-ten."

I said, "Remind me where we're getting off?"

Mitch looked at an envelope that had Florina Harvey's address. "We're looking for David Drive, shortly before you get to Metairie."

"Oh, great," I said.

"What?"

"We passed that exit a minute ago."

"Get off at the next exit, then. We'll head back and try again."

"Wonderful," I said.

We'd left LA at ten that morning, which was noon New Orleans time. The flight took three hours. It'd taken an hour and a half to get our luggage, rent a car, and check into adjoining rooms at the Hilton across from the airport. I took a few minutes to freshen up. Mitch took the time to change clothes. He'd switched from the flowered shirts and shorts of LA to leather pants and a velour shirt. He had added wrap-around sunglasses to his costume. "Just gettin' in the mood," he'd said in response to my raised eyebrows when he'd emerged from his room.

By the time we found Florina Harvey's apartment building, it was approaching six. There was no answer at the door, so we tried her neighbors. Nobody had seen Florina for over a week, but the guy whose apartment was across the hall from hers said that wasn't unusual. He did tell us where she worked. She worked at Chealsea's on Bourbon Street. After some prodding, he told us she was a stripper.

Now we were back on I-10. "You sure you want to go there?" Mitch asked.

"I am absolutely sure I *don't* want to go there," I said.

"But we're going there anyway."

"Yes."

He still had the map. "Then get off at the Superdome exit. Looks like we can go down Canal Street to get there."

When we found Bourbon Street, I felt like an alien from another planet.

For one thing, it was Sunday evening and the bars were open. In Maytown and Patsboro, the Sabbath was still the Sabbath. It was kept holy. Except for K-Mart. It opened at ten on Sunday mornings.

Bourbon Street was not holy. The street was alive with music that was heavy on bass from the strip joints. Yet, Bourbon Street felt dead too. So much sin in one place. No matter what my brain said, I couldn't forget my lessons from the Congregational Holiness.

We approached a pair of legs in fishnet stockings that were swinging out of a hole in the wall above a window. At first, I thought it was a mannequin, but I soon realized the legs were attached to a real woman. I said, "I think, if there is a hell, this is what it's like."

"Hell's not supposed to be this much fun," Mitch said.

Chealsea's was at the far end of Bourbon Street. The cold that poured from the open door felt good against the warm, humid October air of New Orleans.

Mitch entered the strip joint and I followed. The place was bigger than it looked from the front. A bar extended along the right side. The other three sides had long runways along the entire length of the walls. A large revolving ball hung from the ceiling emitting random patterns of light. Lights in the base of the runways highlighted three dancers. Each was wearing a garter belt with dollar bills hanging from it. In the sunken center of the room were about twenty small tables, two of which had dancers gyrating on them. Mitch and I stood, taking in the scene.

"So?" Mitch asked.

"So, we find whoever's in charge. Find Florina Harvey."

A man approached us. "We're here to talk to somebody," I said. "Florina Harvey. I believe she works here."

The greeter ran a hand through his puffy hair and blew air. "I knew it. What's she into? You two police?"

"No. Not police. I just want to talk to her about a mutual friend."

"Lady, nobody here can help you."

Mitch still had his sunglasses on. He might have looked intimidating, except for the fact he stood five foot six. But he sounded intimidating when he said in a demanding voice, "Hey. We needs to rap with the young lady." He included a bit of the echo effect that had scared the bejesus out of that kid on the plane. It had worked on the kid and now it appeared to work on the man at Chealsea's. He backed away.

"Hey, no problem, but she's not here. Florina came in two weeks ago, picked up her paycheck, and quit."

I asked, "Did you talk to her?"

"Yeah. I do the payroll."

"Did she say anything? Like why she was leaving?"

"Nah. But that's not unusual or anything. The girls come and go in here . . . except for the regulars. Bambi wasn't a regular."

"Bambi?"

"Her stage name. What she went by in here." He ran his hand through his hair again. "I mean, whose gonna tip somebody named Florina? Know what I mean?"

I didn't respond because I didn't know what he meant. I had no idea what men did in places like this. Florina sounded okay to me. In fact, it sounded a whole lot better than Bambi, for heaven's sake.

Mitch said, without the echo, "Anybody in here who might know where she be at? Friends, or like that?"

"You got me," the greeter said. "I don't keep up with these girls' personal lives."

"Then, pray tell, who might know Miss Florina's plans, my man?"

"Try Theresa. She'd probably know. She handles the girls."

Mitch moved his mouth to the man's ear. "Where's Theresa?"

"Over there. By herself. On the runway." He scurried away.

We moved to a table that was adjacent to the runway that Theresa was dancing on. A waitress wearing what looked like underwear took my order for a Coke and Mitch's for a Miller Lite. After she left, I turned in my chair and watched Theresa. She was wearing gray-and-white striped seersucker short shorts, a halter of the same material, and patent-leather high heels. She was tall and lithesome—much more attractive than I would have thought. My only other experience with strippers were the hoochy-coochy shows that came to the county fair each fall in Maytown. I never went in, but the women would appear in front of the tent before their shows. *Attractive* was not a word that occurred to me when I watched them.

Theresa was well tanned, with light brown hair that reached midway down her back. Her stomach was flat and her legs were smooth, but muscled. Considering the energy she was expending on the dance, I figured that must keep her in shape.

When the song came to an end, there was scattered applause from the sparse crowd. Theresa walked to the end of the runway, reached behind her back, and unsnapped her halter. The music started again and she dropped the halter, baring her breasts. Just like that.

That wasn't the way I imagined it would be. This was supposed to be a striptease, but there was no tease involved. It was . . . mechanical.

When the next song started, Theresa removed her shorts. Except for the high heels and garter belt, she was totally nude as she danced in front of the men surrounding the bar.

I glanced at Mitch, who was staring at her. "Do you find this . . . sensual?"

Mitch half nodded and half shook his head. I wanted to ask what he meant, but decided not to.

The song ended and another dancer replaced Theresa as she moved to the end of the runway and put her outfit back on. Mitch and I stood and watched while she individually thanked each of the men who had contributed to her garter belt. She was about to disappear into a door in the rear when we caught up with her.

When I told her my name and Mitch's, she glanced at Mitch, who had replaced his sunglasses, then looked at me appraisingly, focusing on my legs. "Have you danced before?"

I don't think I'm stupid, but it took a beat before I realized why she was asking.

Mitch said to me, "You might want to consider it. Probably double your income."

"I do have an opening," Theresa said as she stepped to the side and looked at my backside. "Nice butt. Of course, I can't really tell for sure with that dress on."

Before I knew what I was doing, I said, "My legs are too fat."

Theresa looked down again. "No they're not. They're fine."

I wanted to argue with her until I realized what I was doing. And to be honest, I was relieved by her appraisal.

"I'm not looking for a job. We want to ask you about Florina Harvey," I said.

"You police?" she asked.

"No. I'm an attorney from Patsboro, Georgia. Mitch is a businessman there."

"You're a lawyer?" she said, surprised.

"Yes. I'm defending a man accused of the murder of Lawton Fletcher."

"Lawton Fletcher? I've heard the name . . . somewhere."

"He was an actor. Movie star."

"Oh, yeah. I don't go to movies much. Too much sex and violence."

"Too much sex?" I said reflexively.

A questioning look crossed her face, then she said, "Oh. You're surprised because of this?" She nodded toward the dancing women. "This isn't about sex. It's about money. Listen, honey, I've got a bachelor's in social work. Went on to earn a master's. After five years working at the mental health center, I was making less than a beginning teacher. But, you were asking about Florina."

"Yes. We'd like to talk to her."

"So would I."

"You don't know where she is?"

"No idea. She left me a note saying she had to leave and I haven't seen her since."

"Did the note say why she was leaving?"

"Nope. She obviously felt bad about not telling me. She was apologetic, and just said she had something to do. I've worried that she's gotten into something."

"Why? Not just from what she wrote?"

"Mainly, I guess, because she didn't explain. She could have talked to me, or at the very least said more in the note. But she didn't."

"Why would she owe you an explanation? I would think women come and go from here pretty regularly."

"Sure they do. All the time. But Florina was different. She was older. Midthirties, and she had some flab. Not a lot, but more than we usually accept. The thing is, she was nice, and I felt sorry for her so I took a chance. And it worked out. She didn't get the tips the other girls do, but she developed a following. Really, the men who seemed to enjoy her the most appeared to be the nicest guys." Theresa thought for a moment. "Maybe they felt sorry for her too." She paused again. "We developed a pretty close relationship. At least, close for in here. She knew that most of the places on Bourbon wouldn't hire her, and she appreciated the job. But, to answer your question, she didn't *owe* me an explanation. It's just that, knowing her as I do, I would have expected one. Anyway, why do you want to talk to her?"

"We just came from Los Angeles and we think that she may have information that would help my client. Lawton Fletcher had some letters in his apartment from Florina. They were short letters and didn't say much. Mostly she was thanking him for something, but whatever it was he did for her was not mentioned."

"Florina knew a movie star?"

"Apparently."

"Hmmm," Theresa said thoughtfully. "A couple of times, Florina mentioned a friend who was having some kind of difficulty. At least, she was worried about him."

"Did she say what she was concerned about?"

Theresa shook her head. "It was like she wanted to talk about it, but couldn't."

"Do you know where she's from?"

"Here, there, everywhere."

"I mean, do you have a place of birth, the name of a relative, or previous employers? You know, the kind of thing most places ask for when they hire somebody."

"This place is different. Most of the girls would lie anyway. What's the point? We get a social security number and make sure they don't have fresh tracks in their arms or legs. That's about it." Theresa stood. "That's all I know, except she did say something about working in Miami before. Listen, I need to get back to work."

I gave her my card. "If you hear from Florina, will you call me?"

"Sure. I wouldn't be surprised if she showed up again. That's usually how it works. They come and go . . . back and forth, up and down."

"Except you," I said.

"Yeah. The difference is, I know what I'm doing." She turned and disappeared through a door.

"Interesting lady," Mitch said.

"Yes," I said.

Before we left, we asked the greeter for a picture of Florina Harvey and received two publicity shots. I put them in my purse.

The sharp rays of the early morning sun reflected off the top of the clouds as the 727 emerged from the goop that had covered New Orleans. Up here, the air looked crisp and clean, the sky a deep blue.

"Other than to satisfy Charlotte Perry, was this trip worth it?" I asked.

Mitch laid the *Gentlemen's Quarterly* he was reading on his lap. "Seems to me it was."

"What did we learn?"

"We learned that something was going on with Fletcher out there. More than you knew before."

"But what?" I asked.

"Finding Florina would really help."

"Yes."

"Considering her relationship with Fletcher, maybe she moved north. Like Atlanta, or its environs," Mitch suggested.

"If that's what she did, what do you think she'd be doing?"

"What she does best. What she knows how to do."

"She'd probably be working in Atlanta."

"One would think."

"Would you mind?"

"In the evenings would be okay. I do need to attend to business."

"I know. I ask a lot. But, I'm not real wild about hanging around those kind of places. You know?"

"Yes, Tammi. I know. I don't mind. I'll look for her."

"You're a good friend."

Mitch laughed. "How hard can it be? You're asking me to spend my evenings with a bunch of naked women for a noble cause. Even my mama might approve."

"From what you've told me about her, I doubt it. In a lot of ways, strange ways, your mama and mine sound a lot alike."

Mitch picked up the *GQ*. "I've met your mother. I think yours is harder."

Chapter Nineteen

It was nearly ten when I arrived home and was surprised to find my front door unlocked. Music was blasting from inside the house.

Then I remembered. Molly Malone and her daughter were moving in while I was gone over the weekend. I put my suitcase in my bedroom, which is just to the right of the front door, and went up the stairs, hollering "Hello" as I climbed, but knew that calling was useless considering the volume of the music.

The last time I'd been upstairs was when my mother and Big Jack Pelham, who had since become my stepfather, visited a year ago. The stairs bisected a hall that had two bedrooms to the left and two to the right, with a bathroom in between. The sounds of R.E.M. were pouring from an open door at the end of the hall to the left of the landing. The bedroom door to the right of the bathroom was open too, and I stuck my head in it. Molly was busy unpacking boxes of clothes and putting them in a chest of drawers.

"Hi," I said.

She didn't respond.

I said, "Hi" again, louder.

Still no response.

Giving up, I walked in and tapped Molly on the shoulder. She flinched and turned. "Oh. Hey, Tammi. Hold on a minute." She stuck her head out the door and screamed, "Misty!"

"What?" Misty hollered back.

"Off!"

"Why?"

"Off!" Molly yelled again. *"Now!"* Suddenly there was silence. The GBI agent turned to me. "Sorry. I didn't know when to expect you."

"That's okay," I said.

"What's the matter . . . Oh, hi." Misty was standing at the bedroom door. She was wearing Guess jeans, topped by a long-sleeved teal Gap shirt, and Asics tennis shoes. She had Molly's facial features, but her hair was a gorgeous auburn, tied in a ponytail that hung midway down her back. Considering what Molly had told me regarding her finances, I wondered how she could afford those clothes for her daughter.

Molly said, "This is Tammi, Misty. I thought it would be good if she didn't kick us out before we got unpacked."

Misty made her own apology. "I'll wear my headphones from now on."

Good, I thought. I said, "I'm happy to meet you."

"Same here."

Her mother cleared her throat.

Misty said, "It's really nice of you to let us live here."

I shrugged off the thanks. "It'll be good to have some company."

"Get back to it," Molly said to Misty. The teenager turned and left. Molly said, "You must be wondering about her clothes. They're yard-sale stuff. From McCarty's Creek subdivision. It's amazing how quickly those people lose interest in their possessions."

I sat on Molly's bed. "Let's clarify something now. You never have to explain to me what you do or why."

"Thanks. I guess I feel funny moving in and not paying rent."

"I don't pay rent either. I talked to Dr. Gatlin, and he's glad to have somebody else live here. He figures another tenant will add to the security."

"Okay. That's done then."

"Done." As Molly began unpacking again, I asked, "Misty take the day off from school?"

"We both took the day off. I'd hoped to be finished with this over the weekend, but I had to work a dead body they found up in Park County on Saturday."

"Another one?"

"Yeah. Seventeen-year-old kid named Robert Estafan. Found him in some woods outside of Warrendale."

"Migrant?" I asked. Apple picking season had begun, and the workers, mostly Hispanic, would be up there in full force.

"No. But I understand that he was the progeny of one. And, to answer your question before you ask, there doesn't appear to be any connection to Fletcher. Definitely a murder, but a completely different deal. Different cause of death."

"How'd he die?"

"His throat was cut. Sliced by a real sharp knife. But that wasn't the bad part."

"Sounds bad enough."

"He was found by a couple of kids who were playing in the woods. He was covered with blood."

"That makes sense to me. I'd think it'd be natural, considering the artery that runs through the neck."

"I talked to the lab yesterday. When I said covered with blood, I meant it. He was covered from his head to his toes. Some of the blood was his. Most of it wasn't."

"What type?" Despite Molly's insistence that this murder was unrelated to Fletcher's, I was remembering all the blood on the floor of the mill.

"It wasn't human blood."

"What?"

"It wasn't human. It was animal blood. They'll be running antigen tests to find out what kind, but there's no telling how long that'll take. The lab's chronically backed up."

"How long had the body been there?" It had been over a week since Lawton Fletcher was murdered.

Molly shrugged. "Hard to tell. The whole thing is weird. It appears the kid had been frozen."

"Frozen?"

Molly nodded. "Ice crystals had formed internally. He hadn't thawed totally when he was found."

I stood and moved to the window that faced the overgrown backyard. "That *is* weird."

"It's a first for me, that's for sure."

The apples on a tree just behind the house were turning red. Blood red.

The body was covered by animal blood. I thought of the books on the occult that Mitch and I had found in Lawton Fletcher's apartment. I turned to Molly and said, "I don't know much about it, but isn't animal blood a big part of satanic rituals?"

Molly was trying to open a drawer that was stuck. She put a foot under it, yanked hard, and flew back on the bed when it popped open. "Yard-sale chest of drawers," she said as she moved the drawer off her lap. "I don't know much about satanism either, but that came immediately to mind. We've got a guy at the bureau who focuses on cults, so we called him. He was real interested and came up yesterday from Atlanta. He wasn't in Park an hour before six people had told him about a kid named Joe Coulter. Seems to have a reputation that suggests he might be into satanic stuff."

"Listen, Molly. They could be connected. Fletcher and Estafan, I mean."

Molly had replaced the drawer and was filling it with underwear. "What makes you think that?"

I told her about what we found in LA.

Molly said, "Do you think Fletcher was involved in some kind of cult or drugs?"

I shrugged. "I don't know what to think. There certainly wasn't anything concrete in his apartment to support the drug thing. That came from his change in behavior and the actress's description of Fletcher's shakes on the set."

"His behavior sounds typical of a user, though."

"Yeah, except his lifestyle change doesn't compute with his healthy bank account. That doesn't follow the usual pattern of a life ruined by drug abuse. The money usually goes first."

"True."

"Hopefully, Macleod will find more for us to go on than a drawer full of books and pamphlets. But Fletcher's early life was hard. He was moved from foster home to foster home. It would make sense that he had some kind of deep-seated problems that might emerge no matter how successful he'd become. Deep-seated problems cause one to look for solutions somewhere. Sometimes, anywhere."

Molly had stopped unpacking her panties and bras. "I never could figure why'd he want to buy Warrendale. I mean, there's nothing there but some old stores, a bank, and that abandoned mill."

"But if you own a town—the land, buildings, and businesses anyway—you'd be in a position to establish a—"

Molly finished my sentence. "A cult. With his money, Fletcher could have created a situation where the locals wouldn't complain no matter what he did. Particularly considering the depressed nature of Warrendale and the area around it. The need to eat and stay warm often supersedes other concerns."

"Like satanism?" I suggested, thinking of a dead body covered with some kind of animal blood.

"Even that. Even in the middle of the Bible Belt."

I stood. "Are you investigating the Estafan murder?"

Molly shook her head. "Sheriff Cox said he'd handle it, just like Fletcher's."

"Why?"

"Folks in Park County don't like strangers snooping around. Never have."

I repeated my words of welcome to Molly and went downstairs to unpack. I decided to check in at the office, then report what I'd found to Charlotte Perry. After that I thought I'd go back to Park County and talk to Meadows about Estafan.

Maybe because I was defending a local, I wouldn't be considered a stranger, I thought.

I was wrong.

Chapter Twenty

The usual late morning Monday crowd filled the waiting room of the Legal Aid Society. Bond had been posted for the DUI's, aggravated assaults, various batteries, and breaking and enterings that occurred over the weekend. After being released from the city and county jails, the first stop for those who had been arrested and had limited funds was our office.

I weaved through the accused lawbreakers and wished Mrs. Thompson a good morning. She looked up from her book of morning devotions and smiled. I was astounded. Mrs. Thompson hated Monday mornings. She pushed her cat-eye glasses up her nose and skipped the preliminaries. "Things are moving along quite nicely, Miss Randall."

I smiled back. "That's wonderful." On the way to my office, I stuck my head into Bernard's office. He was sitting behind his desk, ramrod straight and arms crossed, smoking his pipe. He nodded at my greeting. I stood for a moment and he didn't move. "What are you doing?" I asked.

"Waiting," he said through teeth clenched around his pipe.

I pursed my lips and nodded. When Bernard didn't expound, I said, "Waiting for what?"

After puffing on his pipe, Bernard removed it and placed it on his pecan shell ashtray. "The nephew."

"Eddie?"

"Indeed."

This was to be Eddie Thompson's first full day. I looked at my watch. It was eleven twelve. "He hasn't shown yet?"

Bernard shook his head slowly. "I am afraid that is not the problem."

I felt a tug on my shoulder. A voice behind me said, "Excuse me," and a man squeezed between me and the door. The man was carrying a file folder.

"Yes, Eddie?" Bernard said, a note of resignation in his voice. Bernard is unerringly polite. That tone of voice was as nasty as he ever got, except for occasional moments during questioning in court. Then he could be incredibly nasty.

Eddie moved behind Bernard, opened the folder, and placed it on the desk. Eddie's hair was brown and curly, almost wiry. He looked to be a little more than six feet tall and thin, but not too thin. A hint of five o'clock shadow was already showing. There was something different about the face. Unique. It triggered a memory. In high school, a group of gypsies had come through Maytown. From Lithuania, I think. Eddie had the same look.

I was thinking that he didn't look a thing like Mrs. Thompson, until he pushed his glasses up his nose, exactly the way Mrs. Thompson does.

Eddie said, "Mr. Fuchs, I *really* think we ought to go all the way on this one. This guy is a sad case. Really sad case. Three of his brothers are in the hospital—two of 'em were in car wrecks and the other one had a horrible accident on a construction site involving a wrecking ball. All of them are paralyzed for life. On top of that, his aunt just had a child born with no hands or feet.

"The guy's distraught. He couldn't have broken into the liquor store. He was in his church praying for his relatives Saturday night."

"Who?" I asked Bernard.

Bernard had donned his reading glasses and was perusing the file. "Dennis," he said. He didn't have to provide a last name.

I laughed. Because this was Eddie's first day, maybe I shouldn't have, but I couldn't help myself.

Bernard closed the file. "Eddie, once again, I must remind you to take your client's explanations with a grain of salt. While we do not want to form judgments too soon, and while we must do all we can do to be certain our clients' rights are protected to the fullest extent of our abilities, we must be wary of coming to precipitous conclusions as to the best action to take on their behalf."

"What?" Eddie asked, clearly puzzled.

Bernard looked up at Eddie. "A few minutes ago, I walked across the hall to brew some tea. I noticed that Selena Brown was waiting her turn."

I chuckled again.

"She was here a month ago. Selena explained that she had attempted to shoplift three dresses and a rather elegant robe from Macy's in order to raise money for her mother's operation. It seemed that her mother had contracted breast cancer which required a mastectomy. The family has no health insurance, which is surely sad, and needed the money badly."

Eddie said, "That's exactly my point with Dennis. I would think the jury would take that into consideration."

"Selena's case did not go to a jury. At my suggestion, she pled guilty. Because the merchandise was recovered immediately, the judge sentenced her to community service. I was not displeased with the outcome."

Eddie said with some indignation, "You should have tried harder." I could hear Mrs. Thompson's tone of voice loud and clear. "The job here, I would think, is to help these poor people."

"Eddie, please listen to this . . . carefully. The mastectomy Selena's mother suffered through . . ."

"Horrible thing," Eddie said and shivered.

"By my count, it was her seventh."

"Three with me," I added.

Bernard said, "Given my limited but, for this case, adequate knowledge of human anatomy, her explanations for stealing have given me pause from time to time."

Eddie looked puzzled again. It appeared, from the movement of his lips, that he was adding seven plus three.

Bernard handed Eddie the file. "My suggestion is that Dennis should plead guilty. You are familiar with North Carolina v. Alford aren't you?"

"Of course."

Bernard obviously had his doubts about that because he went on to explain. "The case established that there are times when it is in the client's best interest for his or her attorney to suggest a guilty plea. Even if the client claims innocence. That is particularly true when the prosecution's case is quite strong. My suggestion regarding Dennis is that you focus on the sentencing phase." Eddie's disappointment was obvious. Bernard added, "Please know that you *will* have some cases that deserve a more rigorous defense. I only caution you again to be wary of our clients' stories. Failing to do so will result in certain embarrassment in court."

Eddie nodded and left. After he was gone, Bernard looked at me and said, "Productive trip?"

I shrugged. "More questions than answers."

"Yes. That is not unusual at the beginning of an investigation."

I nodded toward the waiting room. "Need some help?"

Bernard shook his head. "We will manage."

Bernard's ability to persevere never ceases to amaze me.

After taking care of a few things in the mail, I drove to Charlotte Perry's house. The trip to Los Angeles had brought up some questions I wanted to ask her.

As I spoke to Charlotte, she held Lawton's picture in her lap. I couldn't imagine that Fletcher had talked to her about possible drug involvement and, at this point anyway, I didn't want to ask her about that. I carefully questioned her on what she knew about Lawton's interest in religion.

"He never spoke of anything like that," Charlotte said in

response to my question. Her eyes narrowed and she looked at his picture again.

I asked her if she knew Florina Harvey without mentioning that she was a stripper. Charlotte had never heard of her.

We sat quietly, which was easy to do with Charlotte Perry. I broke the silence by thinking out loud. "I just can't imagine why he wanted to buy that town."

"Maybe it has something to do with the Mexicans."

My head snapped toward Charlotte. "Mexicans?"

She shrugged. "I don't really know. The last time we talked, before he was . . ." She shook herself and breathed deeply. "He said something about all the Mexicans who were up there. The migrant workers who pick apples during the season."

"What did he say about them? Exactly."

"I don't really remember." She became quiet again. I didn't know if she was thinking about the Mexicans, or had gone off in another direction, or was just sitting, not thinking at all.

"Ms. Perry?"

"I just don't remember." I started to speak but she raised her hand. "He talked about the migrant workers making it more important."

"Making what more important?"

"Buying the town."

"Why would migrant workers make that more important?"

Charlotte shrugged.

I slouched in the wing chair and sighed.

"You are upset with me," Charlotte said.

"No. I'm just . . . frustrated. None of this makes sense."

"You will keep working on the case?"

"Ms. Perry, I want you to understand this. Because Freddy Meadows is indigent, he's stuck with me if he wants an attorney. He could decide that he doesn't want one, and based on what I've seen in Park County, the judge may go along with that request if it's made. If I do end up representing Meadows, my focus has to be on his defense. Your interests and his interests may coincide; but if they don't, my first responsibility would be to my client. If I end up not having a client, then I'm basically done with the whole deal."

She nodded, but didn't look satisfied.

I asked her if any funeral arrangements had been made.

She nodded again, slowly, and stared straight ahead. "I have made arrangements with Shedd and Plunkett Funeral Home. When the police officials release his remains, they will cremate him. I have asked them to send . . . him . . . to Mr. Adamson, his agent. Lawton's life was in Hollywood, not here. Perhaps there will be a service out there." She looked at me. "The phone doesn't stop ringing. People from newspapers and television shows keep calling. I find that to be very difficult." After a pause she said, "His friends are all out there, and I think that's where he should be remembered."

It was my turn to nod.

Charlotte looked at me. "I know this is awful to say, but I'm glad Mother's not here. She'd feel an obligation to make the arrangements." She looked away again. "She never did approve of what Lawton did out there, or of his friends. It would have been hard on her." Her eyes moved back to mine. "Very hard."

We said our good-byes and I got in my Yugo, but didn't start it. Instead, I sat and thought. Molly Malone didn't think Estafan's strange murder was connected to Lawton Fletcher's, but I wasn't convinced. Fletcher's comments to Charlotte about Mexicans reinforced that.

I was tired and needed to rest, but tomorrow, I thought, it would be time to return to Park County.

Chapter Twenty-one

The hour-long drive gave me time to think and I could concentrate because there was virtually no traffic on the highway to Braxton. The teenaged voice that gave the noon news on the Patsboro radio station did not mention Lawton Fletcher. With a week passing since his murder and with no new developments, I supposed the story had been pegged. I was glad.

I switched to the oldies of WFOX and thought about what to do in Park County. I decided that I needed to talk to Freddy Meadows again.

What if he refused my services? Go back to Patsboro and rescue Bernard from Mrs. Thompson's nephew? Forget Lawton Fletcher?

I wasn't sure that I could do that. Quitting something I've started is difficult for me. But, like my mama says, "Facts is facts, sweetheart."

I also wanted to find out about Estafan's murder and look into any possible cult activity in Park County.

Who to ask?

I glanced at my watch. It was twelve thirty and my agenda was getting full. I pushed the protesting Yugo above the speed limit. After all, Chief Lee and his town of Warrendale were on the other side of the county.

★   ★   ★

"Sheriff Cox ain't here, ma'm." The deputy blew a large purple bubble out of his mouth, then sucked it back in again. He was short—maybe five feet six—and looked young. Real young.

"When do you expect him back?" I asked.

The deputy shifted the huge wad of gum. "I don't rightly know, to tell you the truth." He blew another bubble. This time it popped and the gum covered the lower half of his face. He peeled it off with his fingers and stuck it back in his mouth. I prayed the man wouldn't offer to shake hands.

"Okay. I'd like to see Freddy Meadows."

A wide grin appeared. "I heard about when you visited him before. Oh, I'm sure he'd *love* to see you again. Yes, ma'm, I surely expect that he'd be most anxious to do that, for sure."

"Why don't you ask him?"

Another bubble. This time much smaller. "Sure, why not?" He turned and headed toward the door leading to the cells.

"If he does, I'd like to meet him somewhere other than back there." This time I wanted to talk to him in private.

Without turning, the diminutive deputy said, "Yes, ma'm, whatever y'all want ma'm. I tell you, ain't no way I'm gonna fool with somebody who beat the stew out of Freddy Meadows."

Meadows did want to meet with me. In fact, his attitude had changed dramatically since our last meeting. A week had passed and he was still in jail. That seemed to bother him.

When we were in the sheriff's office, I stood between Meadows and the door. He sat in a chair in front of the desk. I wanted to be able to make a quick exit if I had to. "Do you want me to represent you?" I asked.

Meadows sat with his knees spread, elbows resting on them, his fingers interlaced. His head was bowed. "Yes, ma'm, if you don't mind."

"Why the change, Freddy?"

"Ma'm?"

"Before, you didn't want to have anything to do with me.

You figured you'd be out of here with no problem. What happened?"

Meadows shrugged.

Remembering my conversation with Carl White after the preliminary hearing, I asked, "Somebody wants you to stay in here, Freddy. Somebody wants this deal to be closed. Who?"

Meadows shrugged again.

"Who?" I asked forcefully.

His head was still bowed. "I don't *know*, ma'm."

"I'm going to ask you this again, just like before. Did you kill Lawton Fletcher?"

He looked at me without unbowing his head. "No, ma'm. I didn't kill the man."

I looked at the deer head that hung on Sheriff Cox's wall. During the past four years I'd interviewed hundreds, though it seemed like thousands, of accused lawbreakers. I'd become, I thought, adept at recognizing when somebody was lying to me. Meadows wasn't. But he also wasn't telling all.

We went over his story again. He'd stopped in downtown Warrendale to use the telephone. He'd found Fletcher's wallet in the parking lot and took it with him.

I asked, "Do you know what privileged communication is?"

He shook his head.

"It means that if I am representing you . . . which I am, right?" He nodded again. ". . . that anything you tell me can't be repeated. Even the courts can't force me to repeat it. That's so you and I can talk freely without you worrying about what you say." I paused for a moment. "I want you to know that I take that very seriously. Do you understand?"

Another nod. Not good enough.

"Quit nodding and talk. That's important."

"Yes, ma'm, I under*stand*."

"Good. Now, I want to ask you, have you been involved in anything having to do with drugs? Using or selling?"

Meadows sat straight now. "Ain't no way." He stood and I

flinched, but he turned toward the window behind him. "I ain't no pothead."

I believed him. "Have you ever been involved with anything in the occult?"

He turned. "What?"

"You know, like satanism."

"I ain't no metalhead neither."

Now it was my turn. "Metalhead?"

"I listen to country. WBBC out of Commerce during the day. WPLO in Atlanta at night."

I wasn't sure the connection was absolute, but it is true that I hadn't heard of a cult founded on country music. I believed him on that, too.

"Look, when can I get out of here?"

"The bail is clearly excessive. Now that you've agreed to allow me to represent you, I'll file a motion to get it lowered. We'll go up the ladder if we have to, but it'll take a while."

"Sheeeit," Meadows said under his breath.

"Yes," I said.

Meadows was returned to his cell and I asked the deputy who I should talk to regarding the Mexican migrant workers.

Instead of blowing a bubble, he took the enormous wad of gum from his mouth and threw it in a trash can. "That'd be Miss Dorothy Sanford . . . over to the Family and Children's Services. She knows all about the spics."

"Pardon me?"

I had to wait a moment for the response. The deputy was busy unwrapping gum. He put a piece in his mouth and started unwrapping another one. "Excuse me, ma'm. I meant to say she'd know all about our friends from south of the Rio Grandey." As I turned to leave he added, "Oh, by the way. Dorothy'll be easy to spot. She's the only African-American type there."

I looked back at him. His eyes widened as a bubble appeared from his mouth. I backed out the door and bumped into someone. "Sorry," I said as I turned around.

"No problem."

I looked up at him. For the first time in a year, I felt a twinge at the sight of a man. A good twinge, that is. A twinge of attraction, rather than revulsion.

Chapter Twenty-two

I'm Jeff Warren."

I extended my hand. "Tammi Randall."

"It's good to meet you. You've been one of the primary topics of conversation around Warrendale." He paused. "Particularly with Chief Lee. He's quite taken with you."

I didn't respond immediately because I was too busy looking at Jeff Warren. His curly blond hair sat above bright, blue eyes and a crisp face. He was six-two, lean, and younger than I had imagined, probably in his early thirties. His hand in mine was firm, but not threatening. I let go. "I find it hard to believe that Chief Lee would think much of me."

Jeff Warren laughed. "Actually, he called you the *b* word on more than one occasion, but I believe that's a cover. He's quite smitten."

"Mr. Warren, please believe this. If that's the case, the smiting is not reciprocated."

Warren laughed again. "Please know that your esteem in my eyes has risen immeasurably."

A large part of me didn't want to care about that. In order not to betray the part that did, I redirected the conversation. "I understand you were negotiating with Lawton Fletcher for the town."

He waved a hand equivocally. "By long distance. We were to meet for the first time the night he died."

"I'd like to talk to you about that."

"It would be my pleasure." He looked at his watch and said, "I'm afraid I can't talk now. I have an appointment with Commissioner Jones."

I made a noncommittal sound.

"How about later? At my place. Could you join me for dinner?"

I hesitated.

"You're probably busy, I guess."

"No," I said, too quickly. "I'd be happy to."

"Around six?"

"Fine." He gave me directions to his house. I went out the front door and sat on the bench I'd visited the week before. My watch said one fourteen. I looked down at the dowdy wool dress I was wearing. I wanted to talk to Dorothy Sanford at the Department of Family and Children's Services. If that took an hour, I could drive back to Patsboro, take a bath, and change clothes before returning to Warrendale for dinner. Should be plenty of time.

I looked at the hills overlooking Braxton and wondered why I cared about what I was wearing.

Dorothy Sanford was loud. The longer we talked, the louder she got.

"You know how many black folks we have in Park County?" the Family and Children's Services director asked.

I shook my head, eyes wide at her volume.

"Twenty-two, honey. Twenty-two. You know why I'm working here rather than somewhere else?"

I shook my head again.

"Because I was born and raised here. Only back then, there was only us. Momma, Daddy, and my brothers and sisters. Goodness gracious, we've already doubled our population since I left here twenty years ago. Ain't progress something?"

"Sure is," I said.

"Of course, Washington, DC, told Park County they had to increase their minority representation in the social services to remain on the dole. Seeing how they knew me already, they called and asked, and I accepted the position. Ain't no place like home, right?"

Not knowing what else to say about that, I got to the point. "I'm representing Freddy Meadows. He's been charged with Lawton Fletcher's murder."

Dorothy slouched in her desk chair. "Yeah, I know."

"You don't approve?"

She sat straight. "Hey, honey. It's not for me to approve or disapprove. All I know is that Freddy Meadows is a low-down, raping, son of a bitch."

"Raping?" Icy feelings cut through me at the word.

"Can't prove it, but I tell you, honey, I *know* so. One of my foster babies, living down there next to him in the Bluerock community, was one of his victims. She didn't say nothing for six months. When she finally told me about it, all we found was her torn-up panties in the woods, but I know he did it."

"Baby?"

"Figure of speech. Lisa was sixteen then, but she's telling the truth."

I tried to shake that off. I already had enough on my plate. "I want to ask you something. There's some indication that Fletcher was involved in drugs or the occult . . ."

"Wouldn't be surprised a bit. Go out there to California and you get involved in all kinds of weird shit."

"Don't you mean 'sheeeit'?"

Dorothy howled. "You got that right, honey!" She laughed again, this time chuckling, "Sheeeit."

I said, "I'm looking for some kind of motivation for Fletcher's murder. It seems to me that his wanting to buy Warrendale might have played a part." I told Dorothy about his trips to Mexico and the Caribbean, and his having the shakes during the filming of his last movie.

"Sounds right suspicious," Dorothy agreed.

I told her about the religious tracts and the books on the occult Mitch and I found in Fletcher's room.

"Like I said, I'd believe anything about anybody who lived out there."

"Before his death, Fletcher told his sister that the Mexicans up here made it more important for him to buy the town. Do you think some of them could be involved with drugs or some kind of cult?"

"Drugs? Devil worshipping or some such stuff? *Ain't* no way. I know these folks. They're up here every fall to pick apples. Every single one of them is Catholic to the core. Have mass in the orchards every week. Wouldn't miss it. I surely do wish my fellow Baptists had that kind of commitment—especially in deer season." She paused. "The main problem our Mexicans have is that they're dirt poor. Kids take turns going to school because they have to share shoes. That kind of thing."

I reminded her of Estafan's death.

"First, Robert Estafan wasn't a migrant, if that's what you're thinking."

"I heard he might've been the child of one."

Dorothy shrugged. "That's true. But he stayed with his mama. She was thirteen when she had him and he was born and raised in Park County. She's working on her fourth marriage."

"You seem to know a lot about Estafan."

She nodded. "He was on his own before he died, but when he was younger, he was on our caseload."

"Would he be one to be involved in some kind of satanic activity?"

"Why're you so stuck on this Satan stuff? We don't have that kind of thing around here."

"How do you explain the blood, then?"

"What blood?"

"Estafan was covered with blood. Some kind of animal blood. And he was frozen."

"Animal blood? Frozen? What are you talking about, girl?"

I told her what Molly Malone had said.

"Look, honey. I know Park County and believe me, ain't no folks into that kind of stuff." Dorothy scratched her head. "Except for maybe . . ."

"Who?"

"New kid, up from Teal County. Joe Coulter. The school already referred him and this is only October. You probably heard of him, or his family. His stepdaddy got murdered down there in Teal County."

I had heard of Joe Coulter, even before Molly had mentioned him the day I arrived home from California. Lucas Anderson, chief detective in Teal County, had told me about him. Lucas had interviewed the teenager while investigating his stepfather's killing and thought Joe Coulter was trouble.

Dorothy said, "Joe came up here to live with his uncle. The boy has all the signs. Weird tattoos and all. But he's only been here since the summer. That'd be pretty quick to get some followers. Park County kids steal, lay drag, get pregnant, and get beat up and abused on a regular basis, but they listen to country mostly and go to Wednesday night services. Devil stuff's just not part of the culture."

I pulled a notepad from my purse. "Still, I'd like to talk to Joe. Do you have his address?"

Dorothy rolled her eyes. "You'd have to ask that." She swiveled her chair to a table behind her that was covered with file folders. "It's somewhere in there." She stood and shifted through the records. "Ain't got no help, honey, and I don't have enough time to file this stuff like I should." She found the folder she was looking for and sat down. As she looked through it, she said, "When you get done with Fletcher's murder, how about investigating what happened to my computer system?"

"What about it?"

Dorothy looked up from her file. "Supposed to get a system to get away from all this paper. About a year ago, I thought. Haven't seen hide nor hair of it. Commissioner Jones won't even talk about it no more." She pulled a paper from the folder and gave me directions to Joe Coulter's house. "You got a four-wheeler?" she asked.

I laughed. "I got a Yugo with four wheels. At least, last time I checked. Things keep falling off of it."

"Well, you can go up to Joe's uncle's place if you want to, but I wouldn't advise it. I did once. It's up in the north part of the county in the mountains and hard as hell to get to. If I were you, I'd try to see him at school."

I asked where the high school was. Dorothy said it was five minutes away on the north side of town. She said school was dismissed at three thirty.

I looked at my watch. If talking to Coulter took until school was out, I could get home by four thirty but would have to head back up by five to be at Jeff Warren's by six. That'd leave a half hour to bathe and change clothes. It also left no time to talk to Josie Beam. The therapist had given me her home phone number, but I'd never used it. I was feeling the need now. Something was happening to me and I hated it. I'd met lots of men in my work during the past year and had felt nothing. A two-minute meeting with Jeff Warren had changed that.

Why?

I glanced at Dorothy, who had a questioning look on her face. "Trying to calculate time," I said.

Dorothy nodded. I liked this woman. She was open and easy to be with. I suspected she was good at her job. I imagined that kids talked to her easily. I needed to talk to Josie, but couldn't. Maybe . . .

I asked, "Do you know Jeff Warren?"

"Oh yeah, my momma was his mammy. Jeff and I played together for years."

I nodded. I wanted to hear more.

"At least through grade school. After that, his parents made it clear to Momma that they didn't want me around."

"Uh-huh," I said.

She held up her hand. "Whoa. That wasn't Jeff's idea. In fact, stuff like that is why he got away from here as soon as he could."

"I need to talk to him about his conversations with Fletcher. I ran into him at the courthouse a while ago. He couldn't talk then, but he invited me to dinner tonight." Without thinking, I glanced down at my dress.

Dorothy put her elbows on her desk and leaned on them. "Honey, go back to Patsboro. Put on your best stuff. Jeff Warren's worth it, believe me."

I was embarrassed. She had seen through me so easily. "I guess I could talk to Joe Coulter tomorrow."

"Listen, honey. Fletcher's as dead as he's gonna get and the wheels of justice turn slow. Plenty of time for that. If I know Jeff, and I do, he's out of here as soon as possible. Go on home. Get prissed up. Like I said, he's worth it."

I closed my eyes, my stomach churning with conflict. I said, "Sheeeit."

Dorothy laughed. A rich, hearty, and knowing laugh.

Chapter Twenty-three

I stood in my bra and panties and stared at my closet, wondering why I'd bothered to drive all the way back to Patsboro to change clothes. Almost all of my clothes are of the functional variety—either business or casual. I did have the black, satin cocktail dress that I'd worn to the president's reception after law school graduation. It was much too formal for a casual dinner at Jeff Warren's.

I pulled out a baby-doll dress that I'd worn in my undergraduate days, held it against me, and looked in the mirror. No way. It stopped at midthigh. Besides, it probably wouldn't fit. After junior high school, I'd lost a lot of weight, but in recent years I'd gained some back.

I put the dress back in the closet and looked in the mirror again. For one of the few times since Crowe's attack, I appraised my body. I could pinch an inch at the waist, but just barely.

Suddenly, I shook myself. "What are you doing, Tammi?" I said to my reflection.

"Hi!"

I jumped at the sound coming from behind me, spun around, and crouched automatically in a defensive position and saw Misty.

I straightened. "You startled me."

"I'm sorry. I didn't mean to."

I walked to the closet to retrieve my robe. "That's all right.

I'm just not used to having anybody here."

"I should have knocked."

"The door was open. Don't worry about it." I put on the robe. "Is your mom here?"

"No. She called and said she'd be in around eight." Misty walked to my nineteen-inch television in the corner and turned it on. "I came down to tell you the cable guys, like, came today."

I marveled as she changed the channels. Each had something on it and the picture was clear as a bell. "That's great."

"I don't know how you could, like, *stand* having only three channels."

"I've never known anything else. In Maytown, where I grew up, we could get a couple stations if the weather was right. In college, I was generally too busy studying or swimming to spend much time watching television."

"Mother wants me to go to college. But I don't like studying that much."

I chuckled. "Who does? What grade are you in?"

"Tenth."

"Well, you still have some time to think about it." I looked at my watch. "I'm sorry, I've got to get ready to go."

"Going out tonight?"

I stood and returned to my closet. "Really, it's just a business meeting over dinner." I chewed on a knuckle, "But . . ."

"What's the matter?"

"Oh, nothing. I kind of want to dress a little differently than usual, I guess. I mean, I'm meeting with somebody who may be helpful in the case of a client I'm defending."

"Like, the Lawton Fletcher murder? Do you like this man you're meeting?"

I shrugged. "I just met him this afternoon." Misty gave me a knowing look. Am I so transparent, even to a fifteen-year-old? "I guess I was kind of attracted to him."

Misty joined me at the closet. "Let's find something right." Misty slid my dresses along the pole. "Yuck."

I laughed.

"I didn't mean, like, real, real yuck. It's just that, for the occasion, you know . . ."

"Yes, I know. That's what I was struggling with when you came in."

Misty stood back and looked at me. "You're about my size."

It hadn't occurred to me, but she was close to my height. But there's more to size than height.

"Come on," she said. I followed her up the stairs to her room. She started pulling dresses from her closet. "You wouldn't believe the yard sales at McCarty's Creek."

"I know. I've been to them myself. Your mother told me y'all go too."

After laying four dresses on her bed, she stood contemplating them while tapping a toe. "This is, like, business, right?"

"Right."

"But not all business."

"Oh, probably all business. I don't know . . ."

She chose a wine-colored, crepe column dress with crepe roses enhancing the neckline and held it up. "Something, kind of, like, in between. When I was taking social-dance lessons, mother found this for the recital."

"I'd look too fat in that."

"No you wouldn't. Try it on." I did. There were no mirrors in the room, but I imagined bulges all over the place. Misty said, "You look great. It's perfect. Elegant—a little business, but not too much. A little sexy, but not too much. Not too formal, but not too casual."

I looked at this fifteen-year-old. "How'd you learn all that stuff?"

"Young and Modern."

"What?"

She picked up a magazine from her nightstand and handed it to me. "You want to read it?"

"Sure." The last magazine I'd read that included fashion tips was when I was in high school. I had to hide my *Seventeen*s from

Mama. The Congregational Holiness didn't approve of such things.

She went to her closet. "Do you have some dark panty hose?" I said I did. She brought out some black platform pumps. "See if these fit." They did. "Great. Now wear your hair down. The black will look good against the dress."

"Thanks. I really appreciate your help." I turned at the door. "Do you have a boyfriend, Misty?"

"No way. My mother, like, won't allow it."

Good luck, Molly Malone, I thought as I left the room.

There were clouds to the west as I drove through Warrendale. I had watched the news on my TV as I finished dressing, and the map had shown a cold front on the way to north Georgia. Rain was due sometime that night.

The Baptist church in Warrendale appeared to be locked tight tonight. I was surprised until I realized it was Tuesday, not Wednesday. The trip to California had messed up my sense of time. I rechecked Jeff Warren's directions, and turned to the right just past Chief Lee's beer store and pool hall. It wasn't locked tight. Even at five forty-five on a Tuesday afternoon, the parking lot was filled with jacked-up Ranger pickups and Broncos. Ford should do a commercial there.

I followed a bending road up and down a mountain that Jeff Warren had called Shaking Rock. When the land leveled, I entered a broad, flat valley. Pastures were on the right. On the left, a white wooden fence paralleled the road for more than a mile before I found what I was looking for—two bricked columns topped by statues of roaring lions. The words Warren Hall were etched under each lion. I drove down the quarter-mile-long driveway of chopped granite, which was covered by a canopy of water oaks. After passing the last set of trees, the drive curved into a circle that fronted a house built on a granite foundation topped with reddish brown bricks. Rounded wings jutted on either side. A set of steps rose to an arched entrance with adjacent porches that were half screened and half bricked. Striped awnings hung over the porches.

When I arrived at the double doors, I looked back at my car. My Yugo looked pathetic against the backdrop of the immaculately kept premises. Before I could turn to knock, the door opened. I fully expected to be greeted by a servant, but Jeff Warren was standing there instead. He was dressed in a herringbone sports coat and navy pleated dress trousers. He wore a mauve knit shirt under the coat. The effect was businesslike, but not too much. It was also sexy, but not too much. Misty knew what she was talking about.

After greetings, he led me through a marbled entrance hall and under an arched opening into a large living room that featured a fireplace in the center of a wall of gray granite. Groups of chairs and sofas were scattered throughout, giving the room the feel of a club rather than a home. Lamps at each setting emitted weak light, contributing to the effect. I was led to a magenta sofa of crushed velvet that was in front of the fireplace. Warren sat in a chair of the same material. A substantial, square oak coffee table stood in front of the sofa.

"This is lovely, Mr. Warren," I said. Actually I thought the effect was cold and austere, but I was raised to be polite.

"Please, call me Jeff."

I nodded. "Tammi," I said.

He looked around the room. "I appreciate your sentiments, but I find this place to be cold and austere."

I laughed despite myself.

"Would you care for a drink?"

"A Coke or something like that would be fine."

He stood and moved to a portable bar and opened a cabinet underneath. "Are you sure you wouldn't like something else? Every liquor known to man is in here."

"No thank you. I don't drink alcohol."

Jeff closed the cabinet. "Same here." He patted the top of the bar. "This was my brother's." He turned and said, "Be right back."

Being left to myself, I noticed an uneasy feeling filling my gut. This was too familiar. After a short exchange, I was already finding Jeff Warren to be sensitive, open, and sure of himself. All the things that I find attractive in a man. Those were the same things that attracted me to Michael Hutcheson a year ago. He turned out to be a murderer and an untreated manic-depressive.

Jeff returned with a pitcher and two ice-filled glasses on a tray. "Is lemonade okay?"

"Perfect." We sat quietly for a moment and sipped. I wanted to ask him about his dealings with Lawton Fletcher, but it seemed inappropriate to get right down to business. Instead I asked, "Why do you live so far from Warrendale? I mean, it is your town."

"Actually, I don't live here at all. I'm just visiting."

I remembered then what Dorothy Sanford had said about his leaving home. I said, "But, this is your family's home, isn't it?"

"My family . . ." He paused, then said, "Well, I guess that's me now. . . . Anyway, the family never really owned the town. I do own the buildings, but there are public utilities, a government, and a lot of other stuff that I don't own. 'Selling a town' is a misnomer." He sipped his lemonade. "My great-great-grandfather built the mill. That brought in people who needed to buy things, so he built a general store. As time went by, he established a bank and other stores. But the family never did live there."

"The mill doesn't operate anymore," I said. "It looked like it has been a while since it did."

"The invention of polyester killed it. By the time cotton came in vogue again, it was too late. My grandfather had diversified. Got big into granite." He waved his hand toward the wall with the fireplace. "But the town persevered. By then, there was enough stuff going on around it to keep it going . . . in its own way."

I remembered the young woman holding the baby in Warrendale the night we found Fletcher. I remembered her saying she hoped Fletcher would make it better. "The area seems rather . . . depressed now."

Jeff rubbed his forehead with a finger. "Years of total dependence does that." He stood and freshened his lemonade. "It wasn't until after World War One that the mill workers were paid in US currency. Till then, they received Warren dollars, literally. Good only in Warrendale stores." He looked around the room. "All of this came from Warren bucks." He sat again. "Incest causes certain . . . abnormalities."

"And you didn't approve, so you left." He looked at me with questioning eyes. I set my empty glass on a coaster on the coffee table and said, "I spoke with Dorothy Sanford today."

Jeff chuckled. "Ol' Dot." A pause was followed by, "Yeah, I left. Went to the University of Miami, then stayed there."

Miami.

Florina Harvey had come from Miami. Florina Harvey was also connected to Lawton Fletcher in some unknown way.

Miami's a big place, I told myself. The odds of Jeff Warren knowing Florina Harvey had to be humongous. But sometimes what the head knows and what the belly feels are two different things. Suddenly I felt very uncomfortable in Misty's wine column dress that was a little business, but not too much, a little sexy, but not too much.

Chapter Twenty-four

Miami?" I asked. "Why Miami?"

"The university offered a scholarship. I was ready to get away from here." Jeff leaned forward to refill his glass with lemonade. "And I thought it was important to make it on my own. The scholarship allowed that."

"Athletic scholarship?" I asked.

Jeff chuckled. "Hardly. It was academic. I managed to do relatively well on my SATs."

"Was Miami the only school to offer?" I remembered my own scholarship package, a mixture of academic awards and athletic grants for the swimming team. I had a choice of several schools.

"No, but Miami seemed kind of exotic for a boy who'd grown up in Park County. I could have gone to Catledge in Patsboro, but that was too close to home. So was the University of Georgia. Like I said, I wanted to get away from here." A buzzer sounded from far away. Jeff rose from the sofa saying, "Sounds like dinner's about ready." He held his hand out. I took it and stood. Jeff said, "There're just a few things left to do. Why don't you come with me to the kitchen?"

I followed him through a huge dining room that held a massive table surrounded by chairs, along with a buffet along the wall. All were covered by sheets of clear plastic. We went through a swinging door to an expansive kitchen. He went to the stove, turned off the buzzer, and lifted the top off a Dutch oven. After stirring its contents, he turned off the flame under a smaller covered pot. "I hope you don't mind dining in here," he said while nodding to a small, round oak table at the far end. It was set for two.

"Fine with me." I was beginning to realize we were alone in this house. There were no servants. "Did you cook dinner?"

"Uh-huh." He opened a cabinet door, retrieved a container, and sprinkled red stuff into the Dutch oven. "I hope you like seafood."

"Love it," I said. "It smells wonderful. What is it?"

"Shrimp creole." He nodded toward the table again. "Why don't you have a seat?"

I moved to the table and sat. "Is that something popular in Miami?" I knew where creole cooking *was* popular. I was hoping Miami had adopted the dish. The city is, after all, on the ocean.

Jeff shook his head as he dipped rice from the smaller pot into a pair of flat bowls that sat on plates. "A woman from New Orleans gave me the recipe." With a ladle he poured a thickened red sauce filled with shrimp over the rice.

Another stab. I thought about odds again. Then I realized Theresa of Bourbon Street had said Florina had come *from* Miami, so she was in New Orleans *after* Miami. Then it occurred to me—I could just *ask* Jeff if he knew Florina Harvey. I had brought my purse with me into the kitchen and was still holding it. I started to open it to retrieve the publicity photos Mitch and I had obtained of Florina Harvey at Chealsea's on Bourbon Street, but something stopped me. If Jeff was connected to her, I didn't want him to know I knew she had been connected to Fletcher. I could learn more if he didn't know.

More important, I was alone with him in this house.

He opened the oven door and retrieved a loaf of French bread, which he placed on the table. The shrimp creole followed shortly.

When I told him how good the food was, he seemed pleased.

"Not too spicy?" he asked. I assured him it was perfect. We ate quietly for a moment, then I asked, "Why did you decide to sell the town?"

I'd caught him with his mouth full. He held up a hand and worked on swallowing. After a sip of water, he said, "When my brothers died, I was the only one left. My life is in Miami, not here."

"What do you do there?"

"Like everybody else in Miami, I'm in real estate."

I was surprised. "You sell houses?" He must be a broker at least, I thought.

"No. I own property. Started with some repossessions and things grew from there. Mostly apartment and office buildings. Mostly what I do is buy and sell."

"So you're a landlord," I said.

"So to speak."

"How did you connect with Lawton Fletcher?" Would he say Florina Harvey had been involved in the connection?

"He found me. Called one day from out of the blue. I was surprised until I learned he was from Patsboro. There'd been some stories in the Atlanta papers about Warrendale being for sale. I suppose it's unusual for a town to be offered. I assume he'd seen the articles."

"Did he say why he wanted to buy it?"

"No. And I didn't ask. I was too pleased that somebody with the wherewithal had come forward to wonder why he wanted it." I was happy to see him wipe his now empty bowl with a piece of French bread. That gave me permission to do the same. He added, "And he gave me some assurances. Want some more creole?"

I did, but I said I didn't. Despite the questions the conversation had generated about him, I was still concerned that Misty's tube dress might start to bulge.

He stood. "Do you mind if I have seconds?" I said I didn't and when he turned from the pot I was right behind him. "Change your mind?" he asked.

"Yeah. It's just too good to pass up." He took my bowl and refilled it. We sat and ate quietly for a minute. I said, "What kind of assurances?"

"What?"

"You said Fletcher gave you some assurances."

He put his spoon on the plate that held his bowl. "There are people who have worked in our stores all of their lives. Their parents and grandparents too. As I'm sure you know, employment opportunities in Park County are limited. I wanted to be sure they'd be taken care of."

"What'd he say?"

"He said that wouldn't be a problem. Their jobs might be different in some ways, but if they wanted to stay on, they could."

"Different?"

Jeff shrugged. "He didn't elaborate." He apparently saw my dissatisfied look. "It was a short conversation. He said he was interested and that was about it. We set a date for him to come look at the town and I agreed to be here. My attorney talked to his attorney. I assume his attorney contacted you."

"And you came up here from Miami to meet him."

"And he ended up dead. End of story."

"Who from here knew Fletcher was coming?"

Jeff shrugged. "As far as I know Harry Jones and I were the only ones who knew. My attorney said Fletcher wanted to avoid publicity at all costs."

"Who's Harry Jones?"

"County commissioner. The sale involved some dealing with the county about utilities. He needed to know."

"Maybe he told other people?"

Jeff shook his head. "I told him not to. I don't think he would. He's been commissioner for as long as I can remember and has always counted on my family to get him votes." Jeff drew a deep breath and let it go. "I don't think he'd want to irritate me."

While wiping my bowl with another piece of bread, I tried to think. Jeff Warren's answers came easily, but he didn't have many. I was confident of my ability to detect lies. I'd had a lot of practice with my clients. But he didn't fit the mold of the people I dealt with at the Legal Aid Society. I didn't trust my instincts that he was telling the whole truth.

"Want some more?"

This time my negative response was resolute. I was stuffed.

Why do I do that?

He said, "Let's go sit out front." I followed him through the dark dining room, through the living room, and out to the screened porch. He sat on a porch swing that faced the drive, oaks, and pasture that fronted the house. I sat on the other end of the swing and he began to push it slowly. The predicted precipitation had arrived in the form of a gentle mist.

I wanted to tell Jeff about my suspicions regarding Fletcher, but I couldn't. I didn't know enough about him, and the "woman from New Orleans" still bothered me. Instead I asked, "Have you had any thoughts on why Fletcher was murdered?"

He breathed deeply. "Only one. It passed through my mind, anyway."

"What?"

"Billy Ray Cunningham."

"Who?"

Jeff dragged his toe on the porch floor and stopped the swing. He looked at me. "Billy Ray Cunningham. Lives between here and Braxton. If the Dixie Mafia really exists, which I don't believe, he'd be the godfather. He's never been arrested, but he and his family were the major moonshiners around here years ago. 'Shine's pretty much passé anymore, even around here. But old habits die hard. I know for a fact he still runs the cockfights and I heard he's branched into dogfights." He paused. "He's probably into other stuff too."

"Drugs, maybe?"

A grimace crossed his face. "I don't know. Not much of a market here for that to be a major moneymaker. I'd think he's more into stuff like car parts, that sort of thing. But *that* is pure speculation."

"But you know about the cockfights."

"Yeah." He started the swing again. "I went to one a couple of weeks ago."

"A cockfight?" I'd never been to one, but I'd heard about them. Two roosters are put into a ring and they fight to the death. The matches are bloody and cruel. Lots of money is exchanged on the bets. Jeff's possible relationship with Florina Harvey was a long shot. An extreme long shot. His going to a cockfight was a sure thing. He just told me that. I was thinking I'd better be getting out of there.

"Right after I arrived here, Joey Peters came by. We went to school together all our lives. We rode around and ended up at the fight."

I remained silent.

He turned toward me again. "Look. Cockfights are a part of growing up male in Park County. It's like Little League and Cub Scouts. When Joey said where we were going, my first thought was to decline. But I knew it would be like a high school reunion and it was." He stretched his legs and rested his head on the back of the swing. "There were a lot of things I hated about this place, and cockfighting was one of them. That's why I wanted out of here. But, still, home is home. There are good people here. Hard-working people who love their children and take care of their families. A lot of them go to cockfights too. Who am I to judge them?"

I knew that. Maytown was no different. His last question was a good one. Who am I to judge? Confusion about Jeff reigned, and I abhor confusion, so I sublimated it by asking, "How would Cunningham be connected to Fletcher?"

He shrugged again. "I don't know. It's just that when you think of crime in Park County, it's hard not to think of Billy Ray Cunningham." We became silent and swung. He broke it by saying, "So, enough about Fletcher. Tell me about yourself."

I did and that led to our exchanging stories of our histories. Before I knew it, the sun was gone and it was approaching nine o'clock. The conversation had been easy, but I didn't want to overstay my welcome. As we said good-bye, I realized that the concern I'd felt earlier about Jeff Warren's possible involvement in Fletcher's murder had dissipated during the conversation. That concern returned, though, as I moved past the roaring lions at the end of his driveway. I'd had similar doubts about Michael Hutcheson a year ago, but had talked myself out of them. I shouldn't have.

As I drove through the mist over Shaking Rock's winding road in the pitch black of the cloudy night, an incredible sense of loneliness enveloped me. I became aware of Misty's dress clinging to me. Not too businesslike, but a little bit. Not too sexy, but a little bit.

I sighed deeply.

I drove slowly by Chief Lee's place. The sounds of country music poured from its open door as I passed by.

The stores of Warrendale and the church across the street were dark. I remembered Mitch's words the night we found Fletcher: "I don't like it here."

Suddenly, I was blinded by headlights in my rearview mirror. I reached up and flipped it to the night position, but the light continued to shine in the side mirror on the Yugo's door. The headlights sat well above my trunk. A tractor trailer? I wondered. No, the lights were too close together. And they weren't a foot from my bumper. I pressed on the accelerator, but the lights stayed with me.

The road straightened and I slowed down to allow the jerk plenty of opportunity to pass. He didn't. He stayed right behind me. Through the next curve, I sped up again. Nothing changed. It was as though I was towing him. A tingling began in my stomach.

I yelped when the Yugo lurched as the truck rammed me from behind.

Chapter Twenty-five

The Yugo slid on the wet road, but I stopped it. The truck's lights were still behind me, gaining again. I started to speed up, but thought better of it. I was going fifty-five and the car's engine was whining loudly. There was no way I could outrun the truck, and if it hit me again, I needed to be going slower, not faster. I eased off the accelerator and had just slowed to forty when the truck did ram into me again.

This time my car jumped forward slightly, but didn't swerve. The slower speed helped. The air was cool, but I was sweating as I gripped the steering wheel. After another bump, we entered a series of curves on the narrow road. The truck backed away as we went through them. I thought of my dad's Smith & Wesson Model 58. It was in Patsboro sitting in a drawer under the jeans I wore when doing yard work. The ammunition was locked in a file cabinet.

As the road straightened again, the thick woods that bordered the highway gave way to pastures on both sides. Road construction signs appeared and the road turned to loose gravel. Rocks were flying off the wheels and hitting under the car. I glanced back to see the truck gaining again. I searched ahead, looking for a house where I could seek shelter. No lights showed in the darkness. The truck's lights once again filled the mirror and I braced for another hit, but it didn't come. Instead, the truck swerved to my left and accelerated until it was next to me. I glanced over and saw a jacked-up pickup. I thought I saw red, but couldn't be sure.

As I was looking straight ahead, I sensed the truck's movement toward me. I swerved to the right and slammed on my brakes. The back end let loose and fishtailed as I swung the steering wheel back and forth. On the third swing, the tires on the right side of the Yugo went off the road and into the soft dirt, jerking me against my shoulder harness as the wheels dug into the mud. I sat for a moment, stunned, before my eyes focused ahead. The truck was coming back at me in reverse. When it was about a hundred feet ahead, it swerved and did a 180. The truck's headlights were once again bearing down on me; this time from straight ahead.

I pressed on the accelerator, but nothing happened. The right rear wheel was spinning in the mound of mud that the roadwork had caused. When the truck stopped forty feet ahead, its headlights glaring at me, I put the transmission in reverse and tried again. Nothing. A figure emerged from the truck, then reached back inside. It was difficult to see beyond the glare of the headlights, but I could see enough to tell he had retrieved a gun of some sort—a rifle or a shotgun. All I could think to do was run, hide in the darkness.

I grabbed for the door handle and pulled—too hard. Things had begun falling off the Yugo within a month of its purchase, and the door handle had come apart often. I moved across the passenger seat and crawled out the door headfirst. I'd taken three steps through the mud toward the pasture when the gun blasted.

I made a noise and stopped, breathing hard, and turned toward the truck. The man hadn't moved. He was still silhouetted behind the headlights. I stood, paralyzed. He yelled, "Lady you don't need to be comin' back to Park. You hear? Go on back where you come from and don't come back here no more!" Another crack from the gun and mud splattered next to me. He had shot from the hip.

His door slammed and he spun the truck around. As his taillights receded, I leaned on the top of my car with my head cradled in my crossed arms and breathed hard. I whispered, "Jesus," pulled my head up, and squeezed my neck, trying to relieve the tension. When I opened my eyes, they blinked against the rain that was falling harder now. Awareness began to return. I felt Misty's soaked dress clinging to me and I felt the mud surrounding my ankles.

I tried to pull my right foot up, but it didn't want to come. Another tug, harder this time, and my foot popped free without the shoe. The force of the pull pushed me over, and with my left foot still stuck, I fell, landing in the mud. I grabbed my left leg and pulled. The other foot popped free, again without a shoe. I hugged my knees against my chest and cried.

Damn it to hell, I cried.

"You *fucking* redneck!" I screamed.

The sound of the obscenity calmed me again. "C'mon. Tammi. Handle it," I whispered, then thought of Misty's shoes. I got on my knees and felt for the holes where my feet had been. After some groping, I found the shoes and pulled them free from the Georgia red clay.

I had to find a telephone. Call somebody. I knew there was nothing behind me for miles, so I began walking ahead, carrying the mud-filled shoes by two fingers. Surely, even in Park County, there'd be some kind of dwelling somewhere on this road.

There was. By the time I found it, my feet were raw from the gravel on the road, but when I headed toward the lights of the trailer and reentered mud, I longed for the gravel.

The rain had let up again and was now a swirling fine mist. The trailer had no lights on the outside, but enough light came through its windows to allow me to negotiate the slippery wooden stairs leading to a tiny deck and a door. From the inside, I could hear a television playing loudly. I knocked. No response. I knocked harder and yelled, "Hello!"

Some school friends had lived in trailers, but that was a long time ago and I had forgotten. Some trailer doors swing out, not in. When the door came toward me, hard, I stepped back, slipped on the wet wood, and tumbled down the stairs, landing on my elbows. I looked up at a tall, rail-thin man with a scraggly beard and mustache. "What you want?" he said in a voice that was surprisingly deep, considering his build.

I blinked the mist out of my eyes. "I need help," I said in a weak voice.

"What?"

Another figure appeared behind the man and pushed him aside. It was a woman, and she looked down on me for a moment before moving down the stairs. "Darlin', what's happened to you?" she asked while reaching out a hand. She was hefty, but not obese, and couldn't have been much more than five feet tall. I took her hand and she pulled me up easily. Clearly, muscle resided under the fat. "Oh my, you're a mess. Come on in the house."

Normally, I would have said something about not wanting to mess up her place. I didn't worry about that now. I was shivering and needed to get out of the rain. Once inside though, I became aware of my condition again. I was covered with mud and was dripping on the vinyl floor. The woman took my arm, saying, "Come on, honey." As I allowed myself to be pulled along, I glanced back at my muddy tracks. Apparently aware of my concern, she said, "Now don't you worry none 'bout that, darlin'. Henry does a whole lot worse than that every day when he gets through loggin'. Ain't no problem at all to clean that up." She laughed, "Believe me, I'm used to doin' that, I tell you."

She led me to a narrow hall, then into a small bathroom.

"I need to call the sheriff," I said.

After looking over her shoulder toward Henry, she cocked her head and said, "Honey, you ain't been . . . you know, have you?"

I shook my head quickly. "No. Got run off the road."

She said, "The first thing is to get shed of them wet clothes. We ain't got a phone nohow. I'll tell Henry to drive down to my maw maw's and call."

"Tell him I want the sheriff, not a deputy."

"I'll tell him." She stepped back and looked me up and down. "I tell you, I think you're about the size of my cousin Kendra. She left some stuff here last time. You just get out of them wet things and get a bath, and let me find them clothes and send Henry on his way." With that, she backed away and shut the door.

I stood, dazed. While desperately wanting to clean up, I didn't like the looks of Henry. When I took a step toward the door, it opened again. "Here, honey. I plumb forgot that I did the washin' today and there ain't a towel in here." She threw a towel on top of the toilet and said, "Now, do what I say and get out of them filthy clothes."

There was too much of my mother in that voice to ignore. After the door closed again, I stripped, started the water, turned the knob so the shower started, and stepped in. A bottle of shampoo sat on the ledge and I used it, thinking again how much easier it would be if I'd cut my hair. I thought about that every time I washed my hair, but my long hair was a part of the Congregational Holiness that I clung to for some reason beyond my fathoming.

I stayed there until the hot water began to fade. Just as I was about to turn the water off, I heard, "Now here's some clothes. I'm goin' to take your stuff and wash it out before it's ruint. Let this red clay stay on it, and you'll never get it out, I'll tell you that for sure."

The woman's cousin may have been about my size, but not exactly. As I squeezed into her jeans, I guessed she must be a size smaller than me. I let the tail of the white linen blouse hang out in order to cover as much of my bottom half as it would. It didn't cover much.

I walked barefooted into the small living room. Henry was sitting with a can of Budweiser beer on the arm of his chair. The woman was standing at the sink, cleaning my shoes. Misty's dress was hanging from a cupboard knob, dripping on the floor. Most of the mud was gone from it.

When I came between Henry and the television, he didn't

move or blink, just stared straight ahead. The woman turned as I entered the kitchen area. "Now, honey, I did the best I could on the dress. That red mud's a bitch, I tell you." She turned again, grabbed a paper towel from a wooden rack that stood on the counter, and began working on the second shoe. "What's your name, honey?"

I told her.

"I'm Wanda. Course, you already know Henry there. He's my brother."

"When's he going to call the sheriff?"

"Done done it."

"Your mother's house must be close by."

"It's my grandma's. We call her Maw maw. Just up the road." She handed me the shoes.

I put them on and they squeaked when I walked. Better than being filled with mud anyway. I thanked Wanda.

"Hush, darlin'. Now come on in here and watch some TV till the sheriff gets here."

The picture on the large TV was perfect. A rerun of *Mary Tyler Moore* was on. "You have cable out here?" I asked.

"Nuh-uh. Got a satellite."

I looked around the trailer. Wanda kept it neat, but there wasn't much here. I suppose if you don't have much, spending the money on a satellite dish makes sense. Gives you something to do.

Another rerun, this time *The Bob Newhart Show,* followed *Mary Tyler Moore*. While we watched, Henry sat silent, occasionally sipping his beer. Wanda laughed loudly throughout. I sat and tried to breathe in the tight pants. *Bob Newhart* was half over when there was a knock at the door.

When Wanda jumped up to answer the knock, I stood too. Henry sat and stared at the television. A man entered, wearing an unzipped rain slicker. He removed his plastic-covered hat, revealing a flattop underneath. His face was full, but firm. He nodded and said, "Henry."

Henry nodded back.

He looked at Wanda, then at me. "What's the problem?"

"Sheriff Cox?" I asked.

"Yes ma'm."

"I'm Tammi Randall, an attorney from Patsboro."

Cox held his cap with two hands and nodded. "Yes, ma'm, I've heard about you. You're defending Freddy Meadows."

Wanda said to me, "You're a lawyer?" I told her I was. Henry's eyes moved away from the television and looked at me for a moment, but not for long.

"So, how can I help you?" Cox asked.

I looked at Henry. I didn't want to say much in here. "I had a problem tonight. My car's stuck up on the road."

"That your car? Saw it on the way up here." He scratched his head. "Well, ma'm, generally when somebody gets stuck, they call Larry for his wrecker. Not the sheriff's office."

"Can you drive me back to my car?"

A look of irritation crossed the sheriff's face, but he said, "Yes, ma'm." He turned and walked out the door.

I took Wanda's hand, thanked her, and assured her that I would return her cousin's clothes. She gave me the dress and a plastic bag that held my underthings. As I walked out the door, she said, "Come see us."

In the sheriff's car, I said, "I've been trying to see you."

"Yeah, I know."

"My car didn't just get stuck. I was run off the road and shot at."

We were at the end of Wanda's driveway. Cox stopped the car and looked at me. "Say what?"

I told him the story. When I told him it was a jacked-up pickup he said, "Well, that's wonderful. Ought to narrow the suspect vehicles in Park County down to about five thousand." I told him I thought it was red. He pursed his lips. "Good. Very good. Now we're down to about thirty-five hundred." He pulled onto the highway and we were silent until we reached my car. He maneuvered his car so that it sat parallel to mine, its headlights shining toward where the pickup had been sitting when the man shot at me. "Stay here," he said, picked up a flashlight that was sitting on the seat, and got out.

The rain and mist had stopped completely. I watched as he searched with the flashlight. He kneeled down, picked something up, and returned to the car. After turning on the interior light, he held a shell casing between his thumb and forefinger and stared at its end. "Thirty-thirty. Not more than ten, maybe twelve thousand of those suckers in Park." He threw the casing in the ashtray. "Think I'll go right on out and make an arrest."

I could feel the anger welling in my belly. "Don't you think you should handle evidence of an attempted murder more carefully? You've ruined any chance for fingerprints."

Cox grunted. "First, it wasn't attempted murder. I'd bet the farm that if the guy wanted to drop you, he would have. Boys up here learn to shoot about a week after they learn to walk. Second, the guy's prints would have to be in some kind of database for that to do any good, and I doubt that's the case. My predecessors took care of the boys. Third, if we send prints off to the GBI lab on this deal, we might hear back in a year if we're lucky. They're way backed up on major stuff like dead movie stars. Fourth, if you're some kind of big-shot lawyer who defends criminals, why don't you know that already?"

I wanted to scream at him, but didn't. Instead, I pushed away my anger. I said, "You weren't shot at. I was." I immediately regretted saying that. It sounded petulant.

He looked at me and nodded. "True. Look, I'm sorry this happened to you. I'll ask around. See if I can find anything. I'm just warning you that I'll probably discover zip."

I reached under the blouse and released the top button of the jeans. I was tired of not breathing. Cox looked away when I did that. It was still hard to breathe, even with the button loosened. I said, "Since we're here, I want to ask you. Do you think Freddy Meadows killed Fletcher?"

Cox shrugged his shoulders. "Best suspect we got."

"He's not just a suspect. You arrested him."

"I didn't arrest him, Lee did. We're just holding him."

"But you can supersede Lee."

"Meadows had Fletcher's wallet and was seen in the area before the murder occurred. And I know Meadows. He's a mean son of a bitch."

"You have doubts, though."

"Hell, yeah, I have doubts. I've talked to the GBI crime lab people and asked around. Zip."

I retrieved the shell casing from the ashtray. "If it'd take a year to find out about this, how'd you find out about Fletcher's case so quickly?"

"You ain't a movie star and you ain't dead."

"True." I replaced the casing into the ashtray. "What about Billy Ray Cunningham?"

Cox's head snapped toward me. "What about him?"

"I heard he's into a lot of stuff. Criminal stuff. Have you thought about him?"

Cox slumped slightly. "Oh yeah. I've thought about Billy Ray Cunningham. I've thought about him a lot."

"And?"

"And, I'd rather not get blowed up."

"What?"

"Look. I've been sheriff for six months. It's going to take a while to go after Cunningham. The last sheriff who tried was ol' Arnold Ingle about twenty years ago. Just so happens that ol' Arnold's car decided to blow itself up one morning. Ol' Arnold was in it."

"Oh."

"Like I said, I'm trying to be careful about going after Cunningham. But I will. I guarantee you, I will." We were silent for a moment. "But that don't keep me from asking around. Haven't found anything connecting Cunningham to Fletcher."

"Drugs?" I suggested.

"Nah. Cunningham's not involved in that stuff. 'Shine, cars, cockfights. Not drugs though."

"You sure?"

"Of course I'm not sure. Just don't think so."

Silence entered the car again. Sheriff Cox didn't have to say that stuff about Cunningham. In fact, from what he said, he probably shouldn't have. He was being honest, and I felt relieved. It was good to know that Donald Lee and the bubble-blowing deputy from earlier today didn't represent all of law enforcement in Park County. Of course, what he told me hadn't helped with who killed Lawton Fletcher. That led to another thought. "Be right back," I said.

I jumped out of the sheriff's car, ran to mine, and got my purse. After getting in the patrol car again, I fished through the purse and found one of the pictures of Florina Harvey that Mitch and I had gotten on Bourbon Street. "Ever seen her?"

Cox looked at the picture and squinted his eyes. "Hmm," he said.

"What?"

"Yeah. But she sure wasn't dressed like this." He chuckled. "Or undressed like this."

My stomach leapt. "When did you see her?"

"This afternoon."

"This afternoon?"

"Yeah. I was going to the scene of an accident and a car pulled out in front of me from a driveway. Liked to had an accident of my own. I stopped and let her know that she needed to be watching where she was going." He gave the picture back to me. "Who is she?"

"A stripper from New Orleans."

"Hmm," he said again. "How about that. Makes you wonder, don't it?"

"Makes you wonder what?"

"Makes you wonder what a stripper's doing coming out of Jeff Warren's driveway."

Chapter Twenty-six

Jeff Warren *knew* Florina Harvey. I thought back to when I asked him about Lawton Fletcher's buying the town. Jeff had said, "He found me." Was he lying? I stared out the sheriff's car window. The mist had begun falling again.

I squeezed my eyes shut. Maybe Jeff *didn't* know her. Florina Harvey was one of Fletcher's two beneficiaries. Maybe she went to Jeff's to talk about the sale of the town. Maybe he met her this afternoon for the first time. Why hadn't he mentioned her this evening? Maybe he didn't see the relevance.

Maybe, maybe, maybe . . .

The thought hit me. The timing. The letters from Florina we found in Fletcher's apartment had been sent from New Orleans. The dates made it clear that she was in New Orleans *before* Fletcher expressed an interest in buying the town. So if Florina and Jeff knew each other in Miami . . . The sheriff's voice broke into my consciousness. "What?" I asked.

"What's this stripper have to do with anything?" He was still holding the picture.

Despite what he had said about intending to get Billy Ray Cunningham, I didn't know if I could trust this sheriff from Park County. In fact, I didn't know if I could trust *anybody* in this godforsaken place.

When I didn't respond, he turned in his seat and raised a forefinger. "Listen, lady, I'm still investigating this case and if you know something I should know, and I find out you didn't tell me, you're going to end up in jail on an obstruction charge. You understand me?"

My anger welled as I raised my own forefinger. "Sheriff, so far in Park County I've seen the work of Donald Lee, Carl White, and a judge who changes the bail of the accused from a thousand dollars to a million in less than a minute. I've been run off the road and shot at, and then I find out that a man everybody knows is a criminal, including the high sheriff, continues to run around loose. If I tell you what I know and that information is misused, I'll raise hell from here to Atlanta and beyond. Do you understand *me?*"

As soon as I asked the question, my anger diminished and fear replaced it. I was sitting in the middle of nowhere alone with a man I was threatening. The only witnesses to my whereabouts were weird Henry and his sister Wanda.

Lord help me, tears were in my eyes.

Cox turned and put both hands on the steering wheel. "You got a point." He took his hat off and ran a hand over his flattop. "And, I don't blame you for not trusting me. If I was in your position, I wouldn't either." He stared straight ahead. "My mother had me when she was fourteen. My granddaddy and grandma raised me. They died when I was in high school."

I wanted to say something, but didn't know what to say. Why was he telling me that?

"They got trapped in the basement when it caught on fire. The sheriff, the one who replaced Arnold Ingle, said it started from the gas heater down there."

I said, "I'm sorry."

"Yeah, well, the thing is . . . the thing is the sheriff failed to notice the chains that were wrapped around them and a pole. Nobody else did either. Except me."

"Chains?"

"Yeah. And I also noticed that earlier that day Billy Ray Cunningham had visited Granddaddy and Grandma. He was mad about something when he left."

"Jesus."

"I got a loan from the government and went to the Police Academy in Athens. I worked in Clarke County for ten years and eventually made chief deputy. Came back here and played the game and got elected sheriff." He turned to me again and said softly, "I'm going to get that son of a bitch, but you got to go along to get along. Now, will you tell me about this stripper?"

I did, along with everything Mitch and I had learned in Los Angeles and New Orleans.

The sheriff wasn't impressed by my theories of Fletcher's being involved with religious cults or drug deals. He said, "My guess is that Meadows probably figured he had money on him . . . big movie star and all."

It was my turn to disagree. "The only people who knew he was coming were Jeff Warren, his sister in Patsboro, the county commissioner, and me."

"I," the sheriff said.

"You knew he was coming?" When Fletcher's attorney called me, he said that nobody else knew, but it appeared that everybody in the county was aware of Fletcher's plans.

"No, I mean you should have said 'I,' not 'me.' 'Was' is a verb of being and is followed by a predicate nominative. You should have said 'I.' " Responding to my stare, he said, "My boy's in the ninth grade. I help him with his homework. First time I ever understood that stuff. I've decided you shouldn't go to high school until you're past forty. You say Harry knew?"

I was lost. "Who's Harry?"

"Harry Jones . . . the county commissioner."

"All I know is that a county commissioner knew. I don't know which one."

"There's only one."

"Ah." Park County had the single commissioner form of government. A form of government not uncommon in small counties in Georgia, but, to me, strange just the same. The power he (it was always a he) wielded was incredible. "You have a problem with the commissioner knowing about Fletcher's coming?"

Cox looked at me. I had the feeling he was trying to decide how much to say about Commissioner Jones.

I said, "You can trust me. I need to know."

"When I became sheriff, the first thing I did was go through the files. I found paperwork involving a grant application dated from the year before. It was for new equipment, and God knows we need it." He pounded on his radio. "Jones had signed it, so I asked him about it. His answer was less than satisfactory."

"What'd he say?"

"Said to leave the county's business to him and that I should stick to enforcing the law. I told him that'd be a whole lot easier if we had radios that functioned on a regular basis."

Something clicked in the recesses of my mind when he said that. "So?"

He shrugged again. "So, I'm left to wonder. Been eighteen months since the application was filed."

"Maybe it was turned down."

"Could be. But that would've been easy enough to admit."

"Be easy enough to check on, too, I would think. A simple phone call to whoever the application went to would do it."

" 'Whomever'," the sheriff said. "Objects of prepositions require the objective case."

I laughed. "Okay. Whomever. Why don't you just call and find out the grant's status?"

"The file just listed equipment needs and a mention that it was for a grant. Nothing was in there about who was doing the funding." Cox exhaled. "Anyway, that's my problem to figure out. If Fletcher was going to buy the town, I suppose it'd be natural that he'd meet with Jones." He looked at his watch and opened his door. "Let's get your car out. The wife'll be worried if I don't get home soon."

Cox retrieved a chain from his trunk and hooked it to something under the Yugo and to his cruiser. I went to my car and the Yugo was soon on the highway again. After returning the chain to his trunk, Sheriff Cox came to my car.

I rolled down my window. "Thanks."

He tipped his cap. "I think I'd like to follow you out of the county."

"That's not necessary. You need to get back to your family."

"Considering the circumstances, you might want to reconsider defending Meadows."

"I've seriously thought about that."

"And?"

"And earlier tonight, in the trailer, I thought I might try to get out of it."

He put his hands on his hips. "Good. Maybe Carl White can get it again. With him defending Meadows, my burden's eased considerable."

"—ly. The adverb modifies the verb."

Cox laughed. "Yeah. Answers the question How.

"But," I said, "you've changed my mind."

"I changed your mind?"

"I've finally met a man in Park County I think I can trust. And he happens to be the sheriff. Maybe there's hope."

Cox remained expressionless.

"I'll be back tomorrow morning. I plan to talk to a kid at the high school about your other murder."

"Estafan."

I nodded. "Seems odd. Two murders in this county within days of each other. Fletcher may have had an interest in the occult. A dead body covered by animal blood makes me wonder."

Cox narrowed his eyes. "Who do you plan to talk to?"

"Kid named Joe Coulter. Dorothy Sanford over at Family and Children's Services told me about him. There's a GBI agent who heard about him too. They think Coulter might be a candidate for Satan."

"Satan?"

"Yeah."

"I don't think so. Like I said, never had anything like that up here."

"Have you found anything on Estafan's murder?"

"Nothing yet."

"Do you know when he was last seen? Alive, that is."

"A week ago Sunday."

I thought for a moment. "That was the day Fletcher was killed."

"Yep. A couple of kids say they saw him heading for Warrendale just after lunch. Estafan lived alone and did odd jobs, so it's hard to pin anything down."

"Still . . ."

"Yeah, I know. But we only have two towns in this county that amount to anything. If you're heading anywhere, you're heading for either Warrendale or Braxton." The mist had turned to rain again and Cox bent his head to keep it off his face. "It's hard to imagine any connection. Satan stuff, especially." He looked at me. "Let me know if *you* find anything, okay?"

"I will, Sheriff." He turned, but stopped when I called his name. "You'll tell me, too? If anything turns up that I should know about."

"Yeah. I'll do that. Be careful now."

The sign announcing Teal County was a welcome sight. As soon as I passed it, I reached down and unzipped Cousin Kendra's jeans. Finally, I could breathe easily again, in more ways than one.

The Doors were singing "Riders on the Storm" on WFOX. Appropriate, I thought, as my wipers slapped in front of me.

The sense of safety I felt from being out of Park County released my mind to think about the day. Cox was right. The drug thing didn't make sense.

And Jeff Warren . . . What was his connection with Florina Harvey? And why hadn't he mentioned her? According to Cox, she had been to Jeff's house, and I knew she was connected to Lawton Fletcher. Why hadn't Jeff said something about her?

Just ask him, I thought. But not when I'm alone with him in his house.

And I'd see Joe Coulter. Beyond that I didn't know what I'd do.

That decided, I settled back and listened to Deon sing "Runaround Sue."

Out of the blue it hit me. What Dorothy Sanford had said about her computers. What did she say exactly? It took a moment, but her words returned. "When you get done with Fletcher's murder, how about investigating what happened to my computer system?"

Commissioner Jones, again.

Chapter Twenty-seven

The alarm clock didn't awaken me the next morning. I wanted to get some extra sleep, so the night before I hadn't set it. The pain from my scratched-up feet wouldn't allow me the luxury though. While growing up in Maytown, my shoes went off as soon as school was out. But that was a long time ago, and the leatherlike toughness of the soles of my feet was long gone. The gravel on that Park County road had done some damage.

When I lifted my head in an attempt to get out of bed, I lay back quickly in response to more pain that shot from my neck to the small of my back. The sudden stop in the mud last night must have strained something. I rolled to my right and stood gingerly.

In the kitchen, I found some English muffins and ate two of them covered with orange marmalade. One of the nice things about having housemates was that my food choices had increased dramatically. They kept the kitchen well stocked. The bad part was that if I kept this up, I'd become well stocked again myself.

After my regular Wednesday morning session at Jackson's Indoor Shooting Range, I took a long swim in the university's pool to loosen up my stiff muscles. Before, during, and after the shooting and swimming sessions, I called the Legal Aid Society asking for Bernard. The first two calls were from a pay phone, the last was from my house, where I went to return the Smith &

Wesson to my jeans drawer. Each time I called, Mrs. Thompson attempted to put me on hold, and three times she disconnected me. I gave up, deciding to try later. Bernard must have not been there anyway. If he had been, he surely would have beaten Mrs. Thompson to the phone on at least one of the three calls. Beating Mrs. Thompson to the phone was a necessary skill to work at the society. Failing to do so would mean a tremendously reduced client load, hence tremendously reduced funding.

The clock next to my bed indicated that it was almost ten o'clock. I wanted to talk to Joe Coulter. Given Dorothy's warning about needing a four-wheel drive to get to his home, I wanted to see him at school. The Yugo barely managed the hills of Patsboro.

But I also wanted to think this thing through with somebody first. I'd long ago learned the value of a second opinion. Talking to Dan had helped, but doing it long distance was difficult.

Maybe Mitch.

No luck. He was in Augusta visiting his store there. I hung up the phone hard, frustrated. I thought of Bernard again. I hated to do that. He was already handling a double load at the society, or triple, with Eddie Thompson there.

I moved out to the veranda. The morning had begun windy and cold, but the wind had died down and the temperature had warmed from the bright sun. I sat on the swing and pushed myself with a toe. You're on your own, Tammi, I thought. Florina Harvey flashed in my mind. She'd been at Jeff Warren's house. She knew Lawton Fletcher . . . somehow.

The thought of Jeff created a strange feeling. I had enjoyed my evening with him more than I wanted to admit, and later I learned he's connected to this whole thing in some way through Florina Harvey. In what way? I needed to find out how.

Back inside, I found Jeff's number in my little black book and called him. He said he'd be glad to see me. "How about an early lunch?" he asked, and suggested a café near Warrendale. I agreed.

I picked up my purse and stood. I winced as my tender feet

made themselves known once again. A reminder. From my drawer that held my jeans, I retrieved my daddy's Smith & Wesson Model 58. I loaded it with .41 magnum bullets and put the box holding the remaining ammunition in my purse. The pistol was next.

After that, I headed back to Park County.

Red paint peeled off the wooden siding of the Crooked Creek Grocery and Café and the awning above its front door was leaning heavily toward the road. The parking lot of cracked and broken asphalt was empty, except for an old black pickup truck that was streaked with red clay. I assumed Jeff Warren hadn't arrived yet, and I didn't want to go in by myself, so I sat on the hood of my Yugo and waited.

I hate waiting. To pass the time, I got a copy of the *Park County News* from an open basket in front of the café. A metal cylinder on its side asked you to insert a quarter. Park County may have murders, auto theft, and cockfights, but newspaper thievery evidently wasn't among its problems.

Just like in the Maytown paper, there wasn't a lot to read about, but one of the letters to the editor caught my eye. A man was complaining that his road had not yet been regraveled, despite assurances from Commissioner Jones that the state would pay for it.

I thought about that one for a moment.

After refolding the paper carefully, I replaced it in the basket. I had no further need of it and didn't want to add to the clutter in the Yugo. I have to admit that I considered retrieving my quarter, which would have been easy to do, but being raised right also meant being honest. I remember my father driving all the way back to a hardware store in Valdosta to return a box of nails that had accidentally been put in his bag.

My watch told me I'd spent twelve minutes waiting. Maybe Jeff had called and left a message. I decided to brave the Crooked Creek Grocery and Café by myself.

As I entered the store, I was hit by the heat from an open gas furnace that sat in front of the door and the luscious odors of open candy bins and lunch cooking. I moved across the scruffy wooden floor to the checkout counter that held hoop cheese under glass. A man behind the counter was reading a cockfighting magazine. I asked him if Jeff Warren might have called and left a message.

"No, ma'm. He ain't called."

I pursed my lips. "Mmmm."

" 'Course, no reason for that since he's right back there." He nodded toward the back of the store.

I looked around the shelves and saw Jeff leaning on a counter in the back, talking to a woman who looked a lot like my mother. She had short, black hair, a heavily lined face, and appeared to be in her sixties. "Thanks," I said before heading to the back.

I heard the woman talking first. "Land sakes, Jeff Warren, your mama would sure enough be proud of you."

Jeff looked away, as though he was embarrassed, and saw me. "Tammi. I was afraid you weren't going to make it."

"Been waiting outside. I didn't think you were here. Where's your car?"

"My truck's out front." He looked concerned. "You didn't see it?"

"Your truck?" I remembered the beat-up black pickup. "That's your truck?"

Jeff laughed. "You scared me for a minute. Stealing vehicles has always been a major pastime in Park County."

"If it's an old black truck covered with red mud, it's still there."

"That's it. Got it when I was sixteen. God, I love that truck. Sorry you were waiting. I got to talking to Miss Nell." He nodded his head toward the woman behind the counter. Miss Nell had her back to us now, stirring a pot on a large stove that sat behind the long counter. "Miss Nell, I'd like you to meet Tammi Randall. She's a lawyer from Patsboro."

Nell kept stirring, but looked back at me. "Pleased to meet you."

"Miss Nell cooked for us. Long time ago."

"Not so long ago," she said.

"Yeah, I suppose you're right, Miss Nell." He pointed to a blackboard that hung on the wall and said to me, "A meat and three vegetables. What would you like?"

Fried chicken, country steak and gravy, and liver and onions were the choices of meat. Beneath that were two columns of vegetables. Any of the choices would provide several thousand calories. I started to ask Miss Nell if she'd make a tuna plate or something, but my extensive swim had created a gnawing hunger. The heck with it, I thought, and ordered the country steak and cream gravy, along with macaroni and cheese, squash casserole, and green beans that I knew would be laced with fatback. After Jeff described Miss Nell's homemade sorghum, I chose biscuits over corn bread. I wouldn't eat supper, I promised myself.

The place was empty now, but Jeff said it'd be full shortly after noon, so he suggested an isolated table at the far end of the room. We sat on benches on either side of the table and waited for Miss Nell to fix our plates.

We sat quietly. I had called and asked for this meeting, so it was my responsibility to start. I didn't know how.

Jeff leaned forward, resting his elbows on the table. "I enjoyed our visit last night."

"So did I," I responded automatically. "The trip home was interesting too."

"What happened?"

I hesitated. How much did I want to tell him? Everything, I decided. I wanted to see his reaction. I related the previous night's events in detail. Jeff's eyes never left mine as I told the story. Except for occasional raised eyebrows, he showed no reaction as I was speaking. Miss Nell brought our heaping plates and they sat untouched until I was finished. Then, Jeff said, "You need to quit. It's not worth it."

I looked into his eyes. To quit would mean that the man who attacked me a year ago would have won. I'd be forever afraid. That had been the focus of my sessions with Dr. Josie Beam. I said, "No, I won't quit."

Jeff pursed his lips.

I waited.

Jeff leaned forward. "When I was in high school, we had a minister named Walton Peabody. My family was Methodist, and he was a student at Emory University who served the circuit of small churches around here. He was in his thirties, and had decided to give up his career as a teacher to be a preacher. He and I became good friends. He was, is, a brilliant man. But, more than that, he understood people better than anybody I'd met before or have met since.

"We spent a lot of time together. I remember one night right before I left for college. We were at the Waffle House in Braxton. It was after midnight. We talked about relationships between men and women. One of the things I remember most about that conversation is his talking about magic. He said compatibility was important, but a lasting relationship required some magic—a feeling that was inexplicable, but was there and could be felt." Jeff pointed an index finger to his temple. "I remember this clearly. Walton said, 'You'll know the magic when you feel it.' " Jeff paused. "God, this is so hard for me." Another pause. "Last night, for the first time in my life, I thought I might be feeling the magic that he was talking about." He put his hand on mine again. "I don't want you to be hurt."

Magic. Maybe that was it. I *was* attracted to him. That was a fact I couldn't deny to myself. And I was afraid, and couldn't deny that either. "You're going way too fast for me. I require a lot of space."

"I know. I'm moving too fast for me too." Jeff closed his eyes briefly, then looked at me. "Okay. Let's slow down. You were telling me about last night, but I suspect that's not why you called."

I started at the sound of a voice from behind me. "Something wrong with your dinner?" I turned to find Miss Nell.

Jeff said, "No. I'm sure it's fine. We got kind of distracted."

She picked up the plates. "Well, it's done gotten cold now. I'll get you some more." Before I could protest, she was gone. As I watched her go, I saw that half the tables were occupied. Most of the diners were men dressed in work clothes and wearing baseball caps that advertised Red Man chewing tobacco and John Deere tractors. I hadn't noticed them coming in. I turned toward Jeff.

"So why did you call?" he asked.

It took me a moment to remember. "I wanted to ask you about Florina Harvey."

In a puzzled voice, he said, "Florina Harvey?"

Don't deny knowing her, I thought. Please don't deny it.

"How do you know Florina and what does she have to do with anything?" His surprise sounded genuine.

"So you do know her?"

"Yeah. Or at least I did. In Miami. I haven't seen or heard from her in over a year. What about her?"

He's lying, I thought. God help me, he's lying. My stomach tightened again. I looked straight in his eyes. "She was at your house yesterday."

"At my house?" Surprise again. "What are you talking about?"

"Sheriff Cox told me he saw her coming out of your driveway yesterday afternoon. She pulled out in front of him and he stopped her and gave her a warning." My purse was sitting on the floor. I reached around the Smith & Wesson, retrieved her picture, and handed it to Jeff. "He identified her positively from that picture."

Jeff unfolded the publicity photo, looked at it, then looked at me. "Listen, Tammi. I swear to you I didn't see her yesterday and I haven't seen her for over a year." He handed the picture back to me. "I wasn't home yesterday afternoon, or yesterday morning either. I was in Atlanta at nine to complete negotiations on a piece of property in Miami. The guy was flying through

Atlanta, and we decided to go ahead and meet. I left there around eleven and was in Braxton around one. I have a very reliable witness to establish that. You want to know who?"

"Who?"

"You."

I winced. Of course. That was when he asked me to dinner. I felt stupid. "I forgot."

"After that I met with Commissioner Jones for about thirty minutes. By two I was at the high school."

"Park County High School?"

"Yes. Another old friend is the principal there. Jim Webster. He'd asked me to speak to their Marketing Education class. After that, we sat and talked over old times till four. You were coming at six, so I stopped on the way home and bought some shrimp, got home at five, and barely had enough time to get dinner ready."

I nodded again. Unless Jeff Warren was stupid, and he wasn't, his whereabouts yesterday afternoon could be confirmed by numerous witnesses, including me. "It's clear you didn't see her, but what was she doing coming out of your driveway?"

He shook his head. "I haven't the slightest idea. I also don't have the slightest idea of how you would know her, or what she has to do with Lawton Fletcher's murder."

I sat and thought for a moment. "What was your meeting with the commissioner about?"

"No big deal. He asked if anybody else had shown an interest in the town. We talked about the process . . . the surveying and the appraisals. He asked if the bank audit had been completed. Like I said, no big deal. It's part of his job to stay informed."

Miss Nell was back with fresh plates. My appetite had returned and there was a pause in the conversation while we began eating. Jeff was right. The sorghum on the biscuit was dreamy.

Jeff was dipping a piece of liver in Heinz 57 sauce. "Now, tell me, what's the deal with Florina?"

I told her about her letters to Fletcher. I also told him about Mitch and my trip to New Orleans.

Jeff said, "I was hoping she'd gotten out of the business. I gave her the opportunity."

"How'd you know her?"

"I own an apartment building that she lived in." He paused. "You have to understand that I own a lot of property. There's no way I can keep up with it all personally. Florina tracked me down and complained that the manager of the building was doing a lousy job. I showed up one day, and discovered she was right. I fired him and offered the job to her. She didn't want to do it. After that, we'd talk occasionally. I found her to be interesting." He was mixing butter in his sorghum, and looked up at me quickly. "I mean, she'd had a difficult life. Despite all that, and despite her job, she was . . . well, not what I would expect of a stripper. I always figured they'd be hard. She wasn't." He lathered the sorghum and butter mixture on a biscuit. "It's hard to explain." He chewed thoughtfully. "That must have been how Fletcher found out about Warrendale being for sale. I told her about the town." He used a napkin to wipe his lips. "I still can't figure how she was involved with a movie star."

I pushed my plate away. The belt of my pants felt awfully tight, and these were not borrowed. "Was she involved with drugs?"

He waved his hand equivocally. "Not that I saw, but you never know."

I shook my head. "The more I learn about this deal, the less sense it makes."

"What doesn't make sense? Maybe it would help if you'd tell me about it. You can leave out anything that you don't trust me to know."

Trust. Sometimes you have to jump into the fire and see what happens. I told him everything.

By the time I'd finished, the café's crowd was beginning to thin. Jeff said, "You're right. You need to find Florina."

"Like I said, Mitch is checking out the strip joints in Atlanta. He'll let me know if he finds her."

Miss Nell had removed our plates. Jeff sipped the last of his iced tea, then said, "I can help with Joe Coulter."

"When you said you were friends with the school's principal, I hoped you'd offer. Sometimes schools don't want to let you talk to kids."

"I can't promise, but Jim and I go back a long way. Maybe that'll help."

The parking lot was half filled when we walked out of the café. There were three jacked-up red pickup trucks among the vehicles. Jeff looked around and said, "Why don't I follow you?"

A mile down the road, we came to a stop sign. I glanced back and noticed that the rifle that had been in the gun rack of Jeff's truck was now in his passenger seat, leaning against the back window.

I turned on the radio. WFOX was playing, "You've Lost That Lovin' Feeling." I turned right and cut off the radio.

I didn't want to hear it.

Chapter Twenty-eight

The spasms began in Joe Coulter's hands. When they shook, he balled them into fists and his hands calmed down, but the trembling moved through his forearms to his shoulders. He squeezed his elbows against his body as he seemed to try to tighten all of his muscles. It ended as quickly as it began.

"Are you okay?" I asked.

He nodded twice quickly. "Yeah."

From behind his desk, Mr. Webster, the principal, said, "Joe, Miss Randall's a lawyer from Patsboro. She wants to ask you some questions."

Joe looked at me and remained silent.

I turned to the principal. "May I talk to him alone?"

Webster pursed his lips. "We really should let his uncle know about this."

"He don't care," Joe said.

The principal tapped the eraser end of a pencil on the wooden arm of his chair. "Okay." He moved to the reception area where Jeff was waiting and closed the door behind him.

I shifted my chair so that I was facing the teenager directly. He was pasty white and had fine bushy hair that fell to his shoulders. Homemade tattoos of hypodermic needles and pentagrams had been etched onto his arms. The sleeves were cut off his jean jacket. As I looked at him, the shaking began again.

Before the boy had been called in, Jeff and I had talked to

Webster. I told the principal that I was defending Freddy Meadows. Webster knew him.

"Meadows was one of the best running backs we've ever had," he said. "Quit school right after football season his senior year. A shame is what it was. He could've gone somewhere. Had the brains, but not the grades or SAT score for major colleges. He could've gone to a junior college, though, and transferred later." Webster shook his head. "That's the frustrating part of this job. We're fighting a hundred years of family tradition."

Jeff said, "It's hard to figure. You'd think a kid like that could be made to see what a difference some education could make in his life."

Webster leaned back in his chair. "Seems like that on the surface." He stroked his bearded chin. "Let me ask you something. Without thinking about it, just off the top of your head, what percentage of waking hours do you think kids spend in school from kindergarten through twelfth grade?"

Jeff and I remained silent.

"Just off the top of your head. What seems right?"

"About, oh, sixty percent," I guessed.

"More like seventy," Jeff said.

Webster shook his head. "Fourteen point seven percent. It's simple mathematics. Figuring six hours a day of class time and eight hours of sleep at night."

"That's all?" Jeff said in surprise.

"Yep. And that's something to think about. We've got them for less than fifteen percent of their conscious hours. The other eighty-five percent's spent out there with their families and in the community."

I thought of my seventh-grade English teacher who'd inspired me to learn standard English. Somehow, that had led to a whole new world for me. "Sometimes one teacher can make a big difference."

Webster rocked in his chair. "No doubt. That's what keeps us going. But those successes, up here anyway, are pretty rare. There's way too much competition out there in the world."

Now, alone with Joe Coulter, I thought of Webster's words. The teenager already looked wasted. I remembered what Joe'd said about his uncle: "He don't care." What chance did he have? His tremor started again. "Are you sure you're all right?"

He closed his eyes, then opened them halfway. A sheen of sweat appeared on his face. "Yeah." His voice was soft and weak.

My first thought was that the kid was on some kind of drug and coming down. I'd seen it often during the past four years. A good many of my clients had gotten high, done something stupid, and by the time I was dealing with them, they were falling off the cliff. But, somehow, this seemed different. Something was tugging at my unconscious, but I couldn't grab hold of it.

"Look," I said, "I need to ask you some questions, but I want you to know you're not in any trouble. I'm not the police. Like Mr. Webster said, I'm an attorney. A man named Freddy Meadows has been accused of murdering Lawton Fletcher. He was a movie star, you know?"

Joe shrugged. "Never heard of him."

I felt at a loss. I'd semi-lied because my purpose for being here was to discover something this kid had done that would implicate him rather than my client. I should have thought this through. What do I ask?

Joe's shuddering began again. I felt another inward tug.

The truth shall set you free.

The thought brought the clear memory of Preacher Smith at the Congregational Holiness back home in Maytown railing from the pulpit as my ten-year-old child's consciousness quivered. "Joe, there was another murder around here recently. A student from this school named Estafan."

The boy breathed deeply and his lips trembled. "He was half-Mex."

"You knew him?"

Joe's whole body nodded. "He was crazy about women. That was all he talked about. I told him to stay away from her."

The truth . . .

I said, "When he was found, his body was covered by blood. Some kind of animal blood." I waited for a reaction, but none came. "The fact is, Joe, that some people think you're involved in devil worship."

A smirk appeared on Joe's face. "Yeah. I know." He shivered again.

. . . shall set you free.

"Are you?" I asked.

When the spasm was over, he looked up at me, his eyes, again, only half open. "You're all right. You're not fucking with me."

I shook my head. "No. I'm not."

"I'm not fucking with you either. That devil stuff, I mean. It's fun to make 'em think I'm involved in it, but I'm not."

Something about his manner made me believe him. The fact was, I felt sorry for him. Feigning satanism is a desperate way to find self-esteem. "I believe you." Another spasm, this one worse than before. "But look, Joe, you need help. Now. What kind of drug are you on?"

He leaned forward, holding his arms around his waist. "Don't do drugs. Not anymore."

Stay up front, I told myself. I leaned forward and ran my finger across the hypodermic tattoo on his arm. "What's this for?"

He glanced to his left arm, then stared straight ahead. His stupor was intensifying.

This kid needs help.

Now!

I stood.

"That needle ain't for drugs," he said.

My memory banks flooded open. A fellow cheerleader in ninth grade who had a problem. We all knew the drill. I reached the door and swung it open. "Mr. Webster, I need a Coke. Now! Not a diet one. A real one."

The principal looked at Jeff questioningly, then back at me. He half laughed and said, "Pardon me?"

"A Coke, damn it! *Get it now!*"

"*Oh*kaay. You need a co-cola. I'll . . . go get you a co-cola."

I looked at Jeff. "Go with him, Jeff. Make him hurry."

Less than a minute later Jeff came into the office holding a red-and-white can. I opened it and held it up to Joe's lips. "Drink this," I said. He took a sip. "Good. Take a little more now."

"What's going on?" Jeff asked, clearly puzzled.

"He's a diabetic about two shakes away from going into shock. We need to get half of this Coke into him. About six ounces is right."

Five minutes passed. Jeff sat in the principal's chair and the principal leaned against the door jamb. Joe Coulter's color began to return and his sweating slowed. I put the can down. "What have you eaten today?"

Joe shook his head. "Nothing. Uncle Budge got mad when I forgot to split the firewood last night. He said something about no work, no eat."

"Does he know you're a diabetic?"

Joe nodded his head.

I turned to the principal. "You need to call DFACS."

He turned and said, "I'll call them now."

I set the Coke down, leaned forward, and took Joe's frail hands. "You mustn't let that happen, Joe. If it does, you tell Mr. Webster. He'll be sure you get what you need to eat."

"Yeah," he said.

"I guarantee it." I gave his hands a squeeze and sat back in my chair. We sat quietly again until the principal arrived with the school nurse. After taking his vital signs, she started to lead Joe toward the door. He stopped. "Can I talk to her alone again?" He nodded toward me.

The principal looked at the nurse. "He's okay now," she said, and left the room, followed by Webster and Jeff.

Joe remained standing. "Thanks for helping me."

I shrugged. I've never been good at accepting thanks. Preacher Smith had kept me humble.

"I want to tell you something." He put his hands in the pockets of his jeans. "Ain't nobody around here devil worshiping. I ain't, and if anybody else was, I'd know."

I nodded my head. A thought struck me. "Joe, who did you tell Estafan to stay away from?"

He looked at me, started to say something, but stopped.

"What?"

"You won't tell anybody I told you."

"You can count on it."

"At school. Estafan was messing around with Freddy Meadows's girlfriend."

Wonderful, I thought.

"Listen," Joe said, "as long as I eat right, I'll survive. If Freddy Meadows finds out I told you, I might not." He turned and left the room.

Chapter Twenty-nine

J eff was bent over the top of my Yugo, laughing. Hard.

"What?" I asked.

He looked up and wiped the tears from his eyes, took a deep breath, then laughed again and stroked the back of his head. "I've got to tell you . . ." He couldn't quit laughing.

I laughed too. I don't know why. I had no idea what was so funny. "What?" I said again, with emphasis.

Jeff calmed himself. "Jim and I are sitting there, you know, talking about old times. Some of the things we did . . . and then that door flies open. There you are, eyes wilder than grits. I think, God, the kid's attacked her. I start to jump up. Protect you from the punk, you know? And you scream"—he started laughing again—"and you scream, 'I need a Coke!' I sit back down. I mean, I'm thinking, she needs a Coke? I'm also thinking you've lost your mind."

I leaned against my car and crossed my arms, picturing the scene. The longer I pictured it, from his perspective, the more I understood his laughter. Soon we were both doubled over.

Finally, we stopped. He breathed heavily through his nose and looked up at the vivid blue sky. "So, is the kid a devil worshiper?"

I shook my head. "No, I don't think so. In fact, he convinced me that nothing like that's going on around here." I looked across the school parking lot to the back of the jail that held

Freddy Meadows. "I know small Georgia counties. I grew up in one. If there was any, even semiorganized, strange cult around here, Joe Coulter would have known about it."

"So what now?"

"You got me." Actually, I planned to talk to Freddy Meadows about his girlfriend and Estafan, but I wanted to think it through first, and I couldn't talk to Jeff about that. Meadows was my client.

Jeff looked at his watch. "It's just past two. Do you have to get back to Patsboro right away?"

I considered the question. At this point, I didn't *have* to get anywhere, except out of Park County before dark. A stab of guilt swept through me as I thought about poor Bernard, who was stuck in the office with Eddie Thompson.

"If you can stay a while, I've got something I want to show you."

My well-formed conscience told me I needed to rescue Bernard, but I didn't say that. Instead, I said, "What?"

"You have time?"

I buried my guilt. "I guess."

"Okay. How about following me? That'll keep you from backtracking to get your car."

My better judgement told me to say no. For reasons I still don't understand, I said yes.

I followed Jeff as he traveled south toward Warrendale. Shortly after passing a sign announcing that the town was two miles ahead, Jeff turned off the road onto an overgrown, graveled parking area that fronted a hollow, two-story red brick building sitting next to the Olkmolknee River.

As I stood by Jeff's truck, he pointed to the structure. "Another mill victimized by polyester. After it closed, somebody from Athens tried to make a go of it as a restaurant, but I supposed it was too far from anything."

I made noises of understanding, but wondered why he had wanted to show me this.

"Come on," he said.

I followed him around the mill and down a path that paralleled the river. The forest to the right was dense and I began to feel chilled again as we walked under the thick canopy that denied us the sun's warmth.

The farther we walked, the more uneasy I became. Where was he taking me? The suspicions that had been alleviated during our talk at the café began to emerge again. I thought of my purse with Daddy's pistol locked in the Yugo, and turned my head toward it.

Jeff said, "Whoa" just before I bumped into him. "Be careful here." He pointed to a small stream of muddy water that crossed the path. "I don't want you to mess up your shoes." He hopped across, turned, and reached his hand toward me. I hesitated.

Jeff wiggled his outstretched fingers. "Come on, we're almost there." I took his hand and hopped as he pulled me through the air.

A minute later, the path took a sharp turn and ended on a large outcropping of rock that overlooked the river. Jeff moved across the stone and sat on a ledge that was five feet above the flowing water. He removed his denim jacket and laid it next to him, turned toward me, and patted the coat.

In the open now, and with no wind, the air was comfortable again. I sat on his coat and dangled my legs over the side of the boulder. There was a rapids in front of us that caused the water to shimmer from the reflected light of the sun. Heavy woods lined the other side as far as I could see.

Except for the gentle sound of the river, there was absolute silence. Jeff broke it by saying, "I started coming down here when I was in high school." He picked up a stick and threw it in the river. I watched it bang against the rocks of the rapids and wondered if it would make it all the way to the Atlantic. "I told you before that I was basically a shy person. That was even more true in high school. Especially with girls." I felt my muscles tensing again. He said, "I'd come down here, always by myself, and . . ."

"What?"

"It's kind of embarrassing. I'd sit here and sing. Well, sort of anyway."

"Sort of sing?"

"The fact is, I can't sing worth a lick and can never remember the words. What I'd really do is . . . make noise, I guess."

I nodded, not really understanding.

"You know, just let it out. There was never anybody around. I'd just release. Let out all that stuff that was stuck inside. I always felt better afterwards." He looked at me. "Want to try it?"

I was staring straight ahead, but I heard him take a deep breath and hold it. A moment passed and he let it go.

"This is hard," he said. "I've never done it with anybody else here." He inhaled again and started. It was like he was attempting to sing a scale. Soon, he abandoned the scale and sang his own creations. He leaned forward and stretched his arms to the heavens. He stopped and looked at me. "You think I'm totally crazy, don't you?"

I nodded my head slightly. "A little, I guess."

"Why don't you try it?" He started again. As he sang, he looked at me and waved his hand. "Come on" was the message. Despite my misgivings, I couldn't help but chuckle. He raised his eyebrows and waved his hand harder.

What the heck, I thought. I started softly, but Jeff kept waving harder, so I moved it up a notch. Soon I was wailing away, oblivious to Jeff, watching the sparkling water flow by. The louder I sang, or hollered, or whatever you want to call it, the more relaxed I became. I leaned back on two hands, stared at the bright, blue sky and created nonsensical sounds. I lay back, closed my eyes, and let go. Really let go. It was glorious.

When I stopped, the silence was profound. It took me a moment to regain my senses, and upon opening my eyes, I saw Jeff lying next to me.

He smiled. "What do you think?"

"I think I needed that."

"I thought so too. I'm glad you let yourself do it."

We sat and talked about our histories, politics, all sorts of things. I learned that he was thinking about not returning to Miami.

"When I came back up here to meet Fletcher, I dreaded it. Miami is my life. This life was what I wanted to get away from." He paused for a moment. "But after being back here for a while now, I'm beginning to realize that a lot of those hard feelings were just growing-up feelings. Adolescent feelings. I'm beginning to realize that I left this place to prove something, that I could make it on my own." He squeezed his forehead with his fingers. "That part, I know now, I've done. I made it on my own, if making it means financial success." He looked at me, "The thing is, there ain't no place in Miami where I can go and caterwaul."

"So you might come back? For good?"

"I don't know. I'm thinking about it."

"If you did, would you still sell Warrendale if somebody else comes along who wants to buy it?"

"I don't know that either." He picked up a rock and threw it in the river. He looked at me. "I remember a time—when I was twelve, I think. Something like that. It was summertime and I was helping out in the general store. My granddad's office was there. Coach Revere came in and told Eldridge Johnson that his son was hurt. Coach volunteered for Little League during the summer, and said Joey'd cut himself on something at practice and it'd probably need stitches. Mr. Johnson took off his apron and went outside. So did Granddad Warren. By the time I got outside, Mr. Johnson was getting in Coach Revere's car and Granddad was hollering, 'This'll come out of your pay!' "

"That's awful," I said.

"Yeah. Maybe I left because of that kind of stuff too."

"You could make it different."

Jeff made a clucking sound. "Maybe. I'm the last of the Warrens. That's one thing I've been thinking about." He sat up. "Anyway, Fletcher was the only interested buyer. And even if somebody else showed up today, the bank audit still has to be done before a sale would be finalized. That'd provide time to think." He looked at his watch, and I looked at mine. I couldn't believe how the time had flown. He stood and said, "We better be going. I don't want you driving home in the dark."

We walked back to the old mill, this time hand in hand. After getting in our respective vehicles, his truck led the way again. As we approached Warrendale, he turned right and I turned left toward the south. Passing by Warrendale and the Fire-Baptist church, I watched cars and trucks parking for the Wednesday evening service.

I pulled the car to the side of the road and stopped. I wanted to get out of Park County and be back home, but something was tugging at me. I climbed out of the Yugo and leaned against it. My job was to defend Freddy Meadows, and other than a vague theory about Lawton Fletcher's being involved in some kind of religious cult and an even more hazy guess about drug dealing, I'd learned nothing to help him. Nothing to help Charlotte Perry either.

I heard the organ playing the prelude. Early memories invaded my mind. I pushed myself away from the car, moved toward the Fire-Baptist, and sat on a brick retaining wall that stood next to the church. The front doors were closed, but I could hear the music anyway. The preacher made a muffled entreaty, then the music began again.

I sat and listened to the service. I quit attending the Congregational Holiness when I was twelve, but I hadn't lost my faith . . . in God and Jesus anyway. What I lost was my faith in man's ability to pass along the message through churches. Still, my early years revolved around Sunday services and Wednesday prayer meetings and I found some comfort from sitting outside and listening to the ritual.

When the preacher started screaming, my attention wandered. I thought about Jeff and the afternoon I'd spent with him. A glimmer of warmth began to spread through me, but I pushed it away. I would not be hurt again.

My thoughts were interrupted by intensified sounds from the church. I turned around and watched as Deacon Bell stepped outside and lit a cigarette.

The organ started playing again. I recognized the hymn before the singing started and knew the words that would follow.

> There is pow'r, pow'r,
> Wonder-working pow'r in the blood of the lamb.

Estafan was seen heading toward Warrendale that Sunday. He was found dead, covered by the blood of an animal.

He'd been messing around with Freddy Meadows's girlfriend.

Meadows had been hunting that Sunday. He stopped at Warrendale to make a phone call.

What was Freddy Meadows hunting?

> There is pow'r, pow'r,
> Wonder-working pow'r
> In the precious blood of the lamb.

Blood.
Animal blood.
Memories of my daddy emerged in my consciousness.
What was Freddy hunting?
The thought seemed outlandish, but . . . I jumped off the ledge and ran to catch the deacon before he finished his smoke.

Chapter Thirty

T he deacon was standing to the side of the door. He saw me coming and said, "Evenin', missy. Where'd you come from?" This time he didn't hide his cigarette from me.

"I need to talk to you."

He looked beyond me. "Where's your colored friend? Sure would like to hear him talk again. Ain't never heard nothin' like it before, that's for sure."

"He's not here. Listen, I want to ask you something. You know that night when we found Fletcher?"

"Sure do."

"You told the GBI that Meadows had been hunting. How did you know that?"

The deacon scratched his head. "Well, I tell you. I was here early to get the church ready for the Sunday evenin' service. It's plumb amazin' what a mess good Christians can make during the mornin' service. Since I'm head deacon, I got to make sure—"

I interrupted him and repeated my question. "How did you know he'd been hunting?"

He flicked an ash. "Well, first off, I could tell he was huntin' by the way he was dressed. He had on a camouflage suit and boots."

Rural Southerners take forever to tell a story. Normally, I enjoy the richness of the details. Tonight, I didn't have time. The vision from a moment ago had reentered my mind. I'd seen my daddy going off to hunt a hundred times. "There was another way you could tell, wasn't there?"

"Hell, yeah. A body'd have to be real stupid to miss it. I remember thinkin' how he'd done gotten a big 'un. The ol' boy had a buck strapped to the hood of his Bronco. Biggest goddamn deer I ever seen. Had to be a goddamn twelve-pointer." He crushed his cigarette on the sidewalk with his shoe, making a mess.

"Where do people around here take their deer to be dressed?"

"Only one place to go." He pointed up Highway 28. " 'Bout five miles up there. C and C meat processors."

I thanked the deacon, hurried to the Yugo, and U-turned.

My watch read six eleven. About an hour of sunlight left—still time to see Chief Lee and be out of Park before dark. A minute later I was entering his beer store and pool hall.

From behind the counter that sat next to the beer coolers, a man hollered, "Yo, Donald, your girlfriend's back." The chief came from a door that apparently led to an office. Instead of his uniform, he was wearing jeans and a plaid shirt.

"I need to talk to you," I said.

"So talk."

"Privately," I said.

Donald Lee didn't move. The man behind the counter said, "Go on, Donald. She wants you all alone."

The chief looked past me. "Shut up, Budge." Joe Coulter's uncle. I wasn't surprised. Lee turned and moved toward the door in the back. "Come on."

The office was small, containing a desk covered with papers and two chairs. Donald Lee sat behind the desk, pulled open a drawer, and propped a boot on it. He waved his hand toward a chair in the corner. After sitting, I said, "I want to ask you about Estafan."

"Who?"

"The kid who was found dead last week."

"That's county business. Don't know nothing about him."

"All I need to know is where he was found."

"Yeah, well, I do know that. About five miles up Twenty-eight."

"North?"

"Hell, yeah. You ever heard anybody say, 'Up south'? Sheeeit."

"I'm just trying to be accurate, Chief. I've got another question. The night Lawton Fletcher was killed, you went and got Freddy Meadows."

"Sure did. Turned out I was right, too."

"Where'd you go? To his house?"

"Went to his trailer."

"Where is it?"

Lee took out a cigarette. He smoked Marlboros. Again, I wasn't surprised. "About two miles out on Stone Mill Run."

"Where's that?"

He blew a long stream of smoke. Ashes fell on Lee's shirt where it strained against his protruding stomach, and he flicked them away. "Why you asking all this?"

"Meadows is my client."

"Sheeeit."

"I have to admit, Chief, that your repartee is quite pedestrian."

Lee smiled and nodded. "Thanks."

"Could you tell me where Stone Mill Run is?"

"Go about a mile down Twenty-eight—that means south in case you forgot already—and turn left at Pirkle's store. Stone Mill's about a half mile from there."

"When you picked him up, did you see a deer he'd shot?"

Lee shook his head. "Nope. 'Course, I was kind of busy arresting him at the time." He lit another cigarette from the first one.

"Where's C and C meat processors?"

"What is this? Some kind of goddamned geography lesson?"

I didn't respond.

He shifted in his chair. "You go up—"

"North."

"That's the time. You go up Highway Twenty-eight, maybe six or seven miles. There's a sign. Got to go down this dirt driveway a ways before you get there though."

"You told me you stopped Meadows for speeding after you let him go that night. That's when you found Fletcher's wallet in his Bronco. What time was that?"

Lee leaned back. "Hell, I don't know. Let me think."

I remembered Mitch's reaction when the actress said those words in California. Lord, help me, I thought.

"Probably about two, I guess. It'd be on the ticket."

"Where'd you stop him?"

"Up on Twenty-eight."

"North."

"Goddamn, girl . . ."

I raised my hand. "I wasn't asking. I was thinking out loud. Was he coming or going? From or to town, I mean."

"He was coming this way."

"Unless you knew he'd gone out that way, you couldn't have been setting Meadows up."

"Look. Citizens been complaining about speeders on that side of town. I said I'd put a stop to it and I did." Lee's voice became louder as he spoke. "Meadows happened to come along and he happened to be speeding, and he happened to have Fletcher's wallet in his car, so I happened to arrest the son of a bitch for murder."

I stood. "Appreciate your help, Chief."

I turned to leave, but stopped when he said, "You ain't thinking about going out there, are you?"

"Out where?"

"C and C's."

"I wasn't planning on it, but why shouldn't I?"

Lee stood, placed both hands on his desk, and leaned on them. "C and C means Cunningham and Cunningham. Jimmy runs the place, but his brother Billy Ray owns it. I hear tell somebody doesn't want you messing around in the county, and generally that kind of thing doesn't happen without Billy Ray's say so."

"Who'd you 'hear tell' from?"

"Things just get around."

"Once again, I appreciate your help."

"What's all this stuff about the deer anyways?"

I was at the door. "I'll talk to Sheriff Cox about it. Like you said, it's the county's business. Not yours."

"Sheriff Cox? Better be careful with that."

"What?"

"Look, I know you don't like me much, but whatever you think, I'm an honest lawman."

"And the sheriff isn't?"

Lee reverted to form. "The man's sucked up on Billy Ray's tit, I guarantee it. How you think he got elected?" He stubbed the Marlboro in the ashtray on his desk. "I want to ask you something. How do you sleep at night knowing you're helping a plain-out killer?"

"My job is to be sure my client's rights are protected. It's the jury's job to determine guilt and innocence."

He tapped his fingers on his belly. "Looks to me like you ain't no better than Billy Ray Cunningham."

I didn't respond. I couldn't imagine what he was talking about.

"In fact, seems to me Billy Ray's doing a better job of it, seeing's how he got Meadows out of jail already."

"What are you talking about?"

"You hadn't heard?"

"Heard what?"

"Ol' Judge Gee had a change of heart. He released Meadows on his own recogtenance."

"Recognizance," I said automatically. "When?"

"This afternoon. And I'd bet dollars to doughnuts that Billy Ray was behind it."

★ ★ ★

By the time I was on the twisting road back to Patsboro, the sun was low on the horizon. I was busy thinking about deer hunting and about Billy Ray Cunningham and didn't see the truck until it was within inches of my back bumper. The pickup was red and jacked up. I was assuring myself that there were lots of them in Park County when the truck rushed forward and tapped my car's rear bumper.

Night or not, he was back.

I speeded up, hit my brakes hard, then immediately released them. I glanced back and the truck was well behind me. I jammed my brakes again, swerved left, turned the steering wheel to the right, and came to a stop at a forty-five degree angle across the road. I looked to my right and saw the truck come to a stop fifty feet away.

I pulled the Model 58 out of my purse, got out of the Yugo, and stood so that its trunk was between me and the truck.

A man climbed out of the truck carrying a rifle. As before, he stopped just behind the headlights, only now they weren't burning. The last turn of the road must have put us in an easterly direction because the sun was directly behind him. All that I could see was a silhouette. "Lady, I told you last night to stay out of Park. Tried to be nice and all. You done done it now." He started to raise his rifle.

A thousand reps at Jackson's Indoor Shooting Range came to bear on the moment. In one movement I squared myself, raised the forty-one-magnum Smith & Wesson, and braced my right arm with my left hand.

The noise that shattered the quiet afternoon was incredible.

Chapter Thirty-one

The headlight next to the man exploded. His rifle went flying as he screamed, "God*damn!*" I cocked the pistol, moved it up and to the right, and centered the sight on what I hoped was the bridge of his nose. As I squinted my eyes against the sunlight, all I could see was the outline of his face.

"Nuts," I said. "I was aiming for the center of the headlight. Missed by an inch."

We stood and stared at each other. I'd killed before, twice, but was at a disadvantage both times. I knew I wouldn't kill this man. I hoped he didn't know that.

Suddenly, he lunged for the rifle. In one motion, I swung my arm down and to the right and fired again. The rifle flipped from the impact of the forty-one-magnum round. The man, who had fallen in his attempt to get the rifle, remained still on the tar-graveled road.

I thought about what to do. I didn't want to try to drive somewhere with this guy while I was alone. And what if Chief Lee was right about Cox? I wasn't sure who I could trust around here, if anybody. Obviously, this guy had been following me. All day? Or did somebody see me and call him?

I moved slowly to my right until his face became visible. He had a neatly trimmed beard and mustache. His hair was black and combed straight back. The portion of his face that I could see was weathered. At least I'd know who to watch out for. I moved around him and around the truck. The license plate wasn't there. After sidestepping to the door of the truck, I felt in the glove compartment. It was empty. Taking quick glances into the interior yielded nothing that would identify him. After moving around him again so that my car was behind me, I said, "Throw me your wallet."

He stood and turned, patting his buttocks. "Ain't got one."

"Who sent you after me?"

The man headed toward his truck. I fired the gun again, this time shattering the windshield. He glanced at it. "Lady, I tell you that and you might as well shoot me now. I'd be dead either way."

I said, "Get in your truck and go home." He climbed in the pickup, turned it around, and headed toward Warrendale.

I retrieved the rifle and threw it in the backseat. Inside my car, I emptied the spent shells, reloaded my pistol, and held it in front of me. A year ago, I'd used it to kill two men. They deserved to die. The man tonight didn't. He was trying to scare me. I put the gun back into my purse and thought about what he had said: "I'd be dead either way."

The fact is, he did scare me.

When I passed the sign announcing Teal County, I relaxed a little. The road to Patsboro had been free of traffic, and now I allowed my unconscious mind to steer the Yugo while I went back in time.

Every fall my father spent a week at deer camp with his buddies. I knew the procedure. When a deer was killed, it would be field-dressed—slit from neck to tail underneath and gutted. Time was of the essence. If the animal wasn't refrigerated quickly, the meat would spoil and make the hunt useless. On their successful days, the men would make the thirty-mile trip from the camp to Kevin Farmer's place, which operated twenty-four hours a day during deer season. There, the deer would be hung in a refrigerator to age before being butchered. When

Daddy'd gotten a particularly nice buck, he'd bring it by the house before going to Farmer's so that he could show it off to Mother, my brother, when he was too young to go on the hunt himself, and me. I'd run out and count the points. Daddy would lean against his truck and say, "How about that un, girl?"

Part of me hated to see such a beautiful animal lying dead in the bed of his truck, but I'd always tell him how proud I was of him. A wide grin would appear on his face, and, smelling of cigarettes, Jim Beam whiskey, and several days of unwashed humanity, he'd hug me and kiss me on the cheek. Mama wouldn't let him hug her. She'd complain about how bad he smelled and tell him about how cleanliness was next to Godliness. He'd say, every time, "Got to get this big daddy buck to Farmer's 'fore it gets ruint." After climbing in his truck, he'd tell me how he loved me, take a swig from the bagged pint bottle of Jim Beam that lay on the seat next to him, and rumble into the night.

Freddy Meadows had told me he'd been hunting the day Lawton Fletcher was killed. Other than discovering that he'd been hunting alone, I hadn't thought about *what* he'd been hunting. That didn't seem important. The deacon said that one of the biggest bucks he'd ever seen was strapped to Meadows's Bronco. I imagined that the deacon had seen a lot of bucks, so it must have been huge. A buck that big could easily hold a relatively small body if the deer had been field-dressed. And I knew they were always field-dressed.

Estafan's body had been frozen and was thawing out when it was found a couple of miles from the place that the locals used to process their deer. Only hours after Meadows had been released by Chief Lee, he was stopped for speeding by Lee, but he wasn't coming from the direction of his trailer. He was coming from the direction of C&C meat processors.

Time is of the essence. Both for deer hunters and murderers.

And that thought bothered me. Lee'd said he'd arrested Meadows the first time at his trailer. Why would Meadows go there before going to C&C's?

Maybe he didn't. Maybe he went to C&C's first, then again

for some reason after Chief Lee let him go.

Or maybe Meadows had wanted to show off his buck to somebody first.

Whatever the sequence of events, a gruesome scenario involving my client was emerging in my mind. And that produced another problem.

On a first reading, the canon of ethics of the Georgia Bar Association is quite clear, filled with "shalls" and "shall nots." But, as is true in most human endeavors, real life provides multitudes of dilemmas. Back in law school, many hours were spent discussing hypotheticals posed by professors, and designed to help us when we would be faced with ethical decisions out in the world.

A basic tenet of the ethical code of my profession involves confidentiality. For the judicial system to work, a client must have full confidence that his secrets will be kept by his lawyer. There are clear-cut exceptions. If a client tells his lawyer he's planning to murder his cheating wife that night, the attorney has an obligation to reveal that. But when the lawyer in the course of defending a client discovers he might be guilty of another crime, what is her obligation?

In those classroom discussions, I'd insisted that once an attorney took on a client's case, all his past history must remain confidential. No matter what. Now, in real life, I wasn't so sure.

Suddenly, it seemed, I was parked in front of my house. The sun had set and as I moved between the magnolias that stood on either side of the walkway, I was comforted by the lights shining though the stained glass above the front door and the windows upstairs. At least I wouldn't be alone tonight when I dreamed about the man on the road, as I knew I would.

The door was locked. That didn't surprise me. Molly was undoubtedly careful. I held my keys toward the light from the stained glass above to find the right one.

The voice came from the dark side of the veranda to my right. "Tammi."

I dropped my keys and jumped away from the voice.

Chapter Thirty-two

I turned and backed against the locked door. The figure of a man was silhouetted by the streetlight. He spoke. "I'm sorry, Tammi. Didn't mean to scare you."

It was Dan. He moved forward and entered the colored light from the stained glass. I took a deep breath. "That's okay. When did you get back?"

"This morning, early."

"I thought you had another week to go up there."

"That was the schedule, but a bulldozer working on an addition to the school building hit a gas line that wasn't supposed to be there. That made everybody nervous so they called off school for a week until the digging gets finished."

We moved across the veranda and sat down.

"I suspect Meg and the kids don't mind."

Dan smiled. "We spent the day together. The kids played hookey." He glanced toward the front door. "You have house-mates now."

"Molly Malone and her daughter are living upstairs."

"Yeah. I recognized her from school. The daughter, I mean. She answered the door and told me she didn't know when you'd be back, so I decided to wait a while. Wanted to hear how the Lawton Fletcher thing was going."

"You sure? You've just come home."

Dan chuckled. "Yeah, and everything got back to normal in

a hurry. Samantha's at play practice. Meg's at a Girl Scout meeting with the other two."

"Okay," I said. It was comforting to be able to talk to him face to face. Once again I related the story, as I had done for Jeff earlier that day. There were some differences. I hadn't told Jeff about Mitch's incontinence in LA, but I knew Dan would enjoy it. He did, and laughed heartily.

When I got to the events of this evening, I told him about Meadows's being released and Donald Lee's suspicion that Billy Ray Cunningham had something to do with it. Then I said, "Dan, this next part has got to be confidential. I have some suspicions about my client, and I can't reveal them except in certain circumstances. The ethical canons are clear that revealing information about my client to those in my employ and have a need to know is allowed."

"I'm in your hire. My salary will be your paying for my breakfast Friday morning."

"You're going to join us again?"

"Absolutely."

So I told him. When I finished, Dan said, "Let me be sure I understand this. You think . . . what's your client's name again?"

"Meadows, Freddy Meadows."

"You think Meadows killed Estafan and hid the boy's body in the carcass of the deer, took it to the meat processors where it was frozen, then he dumped it in the woods."

"I don't know who dumped it, but I think he might have transported it."

"And all you've got to go on is what you've told me."

"So far."

"It's a reach, to say the least."

"I know. But it's all I've got. Two murders within a week. Meadows was definitely at the scene of one. Estafan was seen heading toward it. The deer thing's a guess. I just have this . . . feeling." I looked at him. "Don't you dare say it."

He raised both hands and spread his arms. "You know me. Wouldn't even think it."

"Now that I've said it out loud, though, it does sound outrageous."

"You going to check it out?"

"I'm not sure how." I nodded toward the house. "Molly's with the GBI and she's right in there. If Meadows wasn't my client, I'd ask her to help. I can't do that, though, without breaking the confidence."

"Maybe you could talk to her without really talking to her, if you know what I mean."

I shook my head. "She's too smart. I couldn't take that chance." I stopped the porch swing. "I think I might do this the easy way."

"What's that?"

"When I find him, I'll ask Meadows. Straight out. Act like I know more than I do. Maybe that would shake him up enough to say something."

"You did that before, with Radar Gilstrap. It worked."

"On the other hand, Meadows might die laughing."

"That'd tell you something too."

Dan and I both startled as the porch light came on. Molly was at the door. "Came downstairs for a snack and thought I heard voices out here. I'm sorry to intrude."

I stood. "You didn't. This is Dan Bushnell. I've told you about him."

Molly moved to Dan with her hand outstretched. "Misty's mentioned you too. It's good to meet you."

"Same here. Tammi's told me about you too. I was glad to hear about your moving in. I never have liked Tammi living here by herself."

Molly said, "That makes me feel better about being here without paying rent." She said to me, "I need to tell you that I've got to go to a conference. It's something on fiber evidence. I'll be leaving tomorrow morning and won't be back until late Sunday. Misty's staying with a friend."

"No problem," I said.

We all stood quietly in a bond of silence. I broke it. "Dan's helping me think through Meadows's defense."

Molly asked, "Anything new?" A split second later she held up her hand. "That's all right. I know you can't tell me." She looked at her watch. "Guess I'd better be heading to bed."

As she opened the screen door, a thought occurred to me. "Molly, do y'all at your place have anything new on the Estafan thing?"

She stood holding the screen door open with her back. "Not much. I did get a call from the lab today. They did the antigen test and found out the blood all over him was from a deer."

A jolt of electricity hit me. My outrageous theory might be right after all.

"But it gets weirder. They didn't just find deer blood on him, but bits of innards too. Small pieces of liver, intestines, that kind of stuff.

"Not really pieces," she went on. "Tiny specks of tissue, but enough to be identified. They can't understand it. It's as though somebody Cuisinarted it all together before putting it on him."

"Satanic?" Dan asked. I'd already told him I didn't think so, but he wanted Molly's opinion, I suppose.

Molly smiled. "I got a phone call late today from our guy who specializes in that sort of thing." She looked at me. "You remember. I told you about him."

I nodded.

"He said he talked to a kid who would be the prime suspect if that were the case. The kid I told you about. Joe . . . something. The kid said a woman lawyer had already talked to him."

I nodded again. "Coulter's his name."

"Right. The expert doesn't think Coulter's involved in anything. In fact, he's concluded nothing like that's going on at all in Park County."

"I don't think so either. So what do you do now?"

Molly shrugged. "Us? Nothing. We're out of it. Everybody's nervous about cults and stuff since Jonestown and Waco. Because there's no evidence of that sort of thing, it'll be up to the local authorities." She looked at me. "Just like with Fletcher."

She checked her watch. "Well, like I said . . . good night." She stopped again before going inside. "Oh. Your friend Mitch called. He wants you to call him back. He said it didn't matter what time." She paused for a moment. "You know, I read *Triple Threat.*"

"Uh-huh," I said warily. I was beginning to wonder why that book hadn't been a best seller.

"It's remarkable. He can do German amazingly well."

"Come on in," I said to Dan. "I want to call Mitch."

"All*ooo*" came over the wire when I called.

"It's me, Mitch."

"It is goot to hear your voice."

"Cute. What movie'd you rent tonight?"

"Kindergarten Cop."

Through a laugh, I said, "Forget it, Mitch. To do Arnold Schwarzenegger you'd have to work real hard on big."

"Just a telephone thing, you know."

"Maybe. So, did you find something?"

"Not some *thing,* some *body.*"

My stomach jumped a little. "You did?"

"Yep. Ms. Florina Harvey, aka Bambi."

"Where is she?"

"It was a rough assignment, Tammi. You know how many dollar bills I had to slip under garter belts the last three nights? And do you know how many strippers call themselves Bambi?"

"You didn't have to tip them."

"I'll claim it under contributions to the Legal Aid Society."

"You'll go to jail."

"I got receipts."

"That I don't doubt. So where is she?"

"You know Hightower County?"

"Yeah."

"There's a place called Thurman."

"I know it."

"In Thurman, there's a place called the Flashcube Lounge. The big city come to the country. She's dancing there."

"Did you see her?"

"Nope. I didn't want to do something that'd mess you up. During this arduous investigation, I found somebody who knew her. One of my salesmen who lives in Hightower checked for me. Quietly, you know. I didn't want to spook her."

"Good. I'll go up there tomorrow night. Want to come with me?"

"Sure. Can't hardly wait to see what the Flashcube's like."

I thought for a moment. "Are you busy tomorrow morning?"

"Nothing that I can't get out of. Why?"

"I've got some new information. I'm going to talk to Freddy Meadows about it tomorrow. It might be good to have some company."

"No problem. What's going on?"

"I'll tell you on the way up. Is eight okay?"

"Oh goody, I get to sleep late."

"I'll pick you up."

"Uh, Tammi. How about we go in my car? I want to be sensitive about this, but . . ."

"What's wrong with my Yugo?"

"Except for the part where things keep falling off it, nothing. Also, given the ethnic ratio in Park County, I'd rather not break down somewhere up there. I mean, I went up there once in the Yugo. That night, you know. To tell you the truth, the deacon and his congregation didn't inspire confidence."

"Mitch, I need to tell you something. Last night, and again today, a Park County resident suggested strongly that I shouldn't return there."

"I know how that feels," Mitch said.

"My Yugo became a target. It's got some bruises. You might not want to risk your Mercedes."

"The Mercedes is gone. Turned it in and got a Chevrolet." Mitch's business acumen had produced a wherewithal for him that he didn't flaunt, except in cars. Short-term leases and yearly exchanges were his style. In the last three years, he'd had a Jaguar, a Maserati, and the Mercedes.

A Chevrolet? I thought. "A Chevrolet?" I said.

"Yeah. A Caprice Wagon."

"What's that? Some kind of minivan?"

"Nuh-uh. Big old station wagon."

"A regular, old-fashioned station wagon? I didn't know they still made them."

"Sure do. I got to watching the Beaver's reruns and got nostalgic. All those white families on TV always had them. I'll be thirty soon, you know. Starting to reflect on the good old days in Newark, I think. I watched a lot of TV back then."

"And that's changed?"

"Tammi, one of the things that I find irritating about you is that you always try to change the subject. How about we go in my new Caprice?"

I surrendered. I decided it might be safer to be in a battle wagon if somebody else tried to run me off the road.

Mitch said, "Have you seen the latest edition of the *Star?*"

"Nope. That's one I keep forgetting to subscribe to."

"I read it at the grocery store tonight. You ought to get one. They've solved your problem."

"How's that?"

"It's on the cover. According to them, Lawton Fletcher'd had a long-time relationship with an alien from another solar system. When she found out he'd banged one of his costars, she directed her troops to the isolated town of Warrendale and confiscated his semen, killing him in the process. They say she plans to replicate him, but in a more faithful version."

"That's good to know, Mitch."

"Always try to be of help."

"By the way, Dan's back."

"Hey, great! He want to go? Make it harder to be outnumbered."

"I don't know. I'll ask him and let you know."

After I hung up, Dan said, "Sounds like Mitch found her. The stripper, I mean."

I sat back against the headboard of my bed and slipped off my flats. "Yes," I said. "Did you know there's a strip joint up in Thurman, in Hightower County?"

"No. Not particularly surprised though. Thurman's the only place in that county that sells liquor."

"Well, they got naked women now. We're going up there tomorrow night to see Florina Harvey." I looked at him. "Want to go?"

Dan thought a moment, then shook his head. "I better pass on that. They're doing a dress rehearsal of Samantha's play tomorrow evening. I told her I'd go." He paused. "But it sounded like Mitch is going with you tomorrow morning. To be with you when you talk to Meadows?"

I nodded. "Like I said, if we can find him. I'll try his trailer first. I'd like to see where he lives. If he's not there, I'll track him down."

"I'd like to go too. I'm not due back at work until next week."

"I'd like that." I didn't want to confront Meadows alone. I could use all the help I could get. "Mitch is picking me up at eight."

Dan stood. "I'll be here." At my bedroom door he stopped. "Molly's information supported your theory. Deer blood and bits of innards on the body. Like bits that would be left over after field-dressing a deer."

"Yes," I said.

A thoughtful look crossed Dan's face. "That's a fascinating notion."

"I guess," I said.

"You know, I haven't been . . . real happy lately."

I nodded. "Even you can't cover that up."

"Going up to Indiana clarified some things for me. It was very cathartic."

"Good."

He smiled. "Yes. Fascinating."

"What's going on, Dan?"

"You know that I was in the army?"

"I knew that you were in Vietnam, but you've never said much about it."

Dan remained silent for a moment. "Well, I'm still working some things out. Rather not say anything until . . ."

"That's okay."

What was that all about? I thought after Dan left. At least he seems more at peace now than before he went to Indiana.

I slid down on the bed and closed my eyes. As soon as I did, I pictured the river and the rapids and Jeff Warren.

It was a pleasant vision.

Chapter Thirty-three

I looked at the hand-drawn map that Chief Donald Lee had given me when we'd stopped in Warrendale on the way to see Freddy Meadows. "That must be it down there," I said, pointing down the narrow, rutted dirt driveway that seemed to drop straight down. Pine trees lined the narrow lane. A trailer sat perpendicular to it at the bottom of the ravine.

Mitch held both hands on top of the steering wheel of his station wagon and peered over its massive hood. "I sort of figured that might be it."

"Why'd you stop?"

"I was just contemplating how they got that trailer down there. I was also contemplating how in hell I'm going to get this station wagon down there."

From the backseat, Dan said, "Come on. You can make it. Put it in low."

"Easy for you to say," Mitch said as he did what he was told. He yelped a little every time a pine branch scraped his wagon, but soon we were at the bottom and stopped in front of Meadows's trailer. It was a white fourteen-footer that sat on concrete blocks and had rust streaks down its sides.

Mitch started to get out, but hesitated when Dan said, "Wait." Dan opened his door and left it open as he stepped out. A yellow blur making a ferocious noise leaped from the side of the trailer. Dan quickly retreated to the car.

"I was afraid of that," Dan said. As we watched, a large yellow dog with long yellow teeth threw himself at Dan's window. Soon, the dog backed up and snarled, his tail tucked under him. "Oh well," Mitch said, with phony resignation. "It doesn't look like anybody's home anyway."

I said, "Even if no one's here, I'd like to look around."

"Mmmm."

"No problem," Dan said. I looked back. Dan was digging into the pocket of the denim jacket. He held up a Ziploc baggie. "Lesson learned from a lot of home visits. Wieners are essential." He broke a piece off, rolled his window down a couple of inches, and threw the meat toward the dog. "Come on," he said, and climbed out of the car.

I opened my door and stepped out. The dog growled, but ran for another piece of the wiener, which Dan threw well away from us. As soon as the dog inhaled the meat and turned, Dan tossed another piece. After chomping that one, the animal still had his tail tucked under, but he had quit growling.

From the car, Mitch asked, "Is that all you got?"

Dan held up the last piece and tossed it directly in front of the dog this time. It was gone in an instant.

Mitch said, "If that's all you got, I ain't getting out."

Dan made a clucking noise, held out his hand, and approached the dog. "Come on, fellow," Dan said and carefully reached around the dog's head and scratched behind its ears. Its tail relaxed and began wagging slightly. Dan dropped to a knee, grabbed the sides of the dog's head, and rubbed vigorously. The animal responded by nuzzling up to Dan's body, the tail now wagging with vigor.

I walked to Dan and stroked the dog's head. "I think you can get out now, Mitch," I said.

We approached the steps to the trailer and I knocked. No reply. I knocked harder. Still no answer. "Let's look around, anyway," I said and started to back off the steps.

The door opened. I turned to see a woman, or really a girl, standing there. I would have been surprised if she was sixteen.

Her mussed black hair fell across her shoulders and she was wearing a T-shirt that stopped midthigh above her bare legs and feet. Her face was pretty but, right now, puffy. "What y'all want?" she asked.

"Is this Freddy Meadows's place?" I asked.

Her eyes squinched against the weak sunlight that filtered through the pine trees. "Yeah. But he ain't here."

"Shucks," Mitch said. "Guess we got to go, then."

I said, "I'm Freddy's attorney. My name's Tammi. I need to talk to him. Are you his wife?" I knew she wasn't. I knew Meadows wasn't married.

"I'm gonna be," she said defensively.

"That's good," I lied. "What's your name?"

"Anna."

"When's the date?"

"Pretty soon," she said.

I nodded. "Shouldn't you be in school?"

"I didn't feel good today."

My guess was she didn't feel well enough to go to school fairly often. "Listen, you know that I am defending Freddy against a charge of murder, don't you?"

She nodded. "He told me about you. A little bit, anyways."

"It would help Freddy if I could talk to you. Okay?"

Anna looked at Dan and Mitch. "I don't know if he'd like that."

"He will," I said, and walked up the wood steps to the door. I took her arm and moved her inside. "Really, it's for his own good."

The trailer was identical to Wanda's, the woman who took care of me the night I was run off the road. A kitchen was to the right, a hall leading to bedrooms was on the left, and we were standing in a living room. The furniture was the same—I knew from friends in Maytown that the furniture comes with the trailer. Anna sat on the miniature sofa and I sat next to her.

When Anna sat, her T-shirt rose up her legs, making it clear that she had nothing on underneath. I nudged her arm and nodded toward her legs. She got the message and tugged the shirt down as far as she could. I looked at Mitch and Dan. They were assiduously examining the bare walls of the trailer and absolutely avoiding examining the bareness of this child.

"How long have you been with Freddy?" I asked.

"A long time. We're havin' our third anniversary next week."

"Third anniversary?"

"You met in July?" Dan asked.

"July twenty-eighth," Anna said.

Three-month anniversary, I thought. I looked at Dan. He shrugged. He'd worked with teenagers for a long time. He knew the deal. I'd forgotten. Actually, I was never involved in that part of it, even as a teenager.

I said, "So you were here when Chief Lee arrested him a couple of weeks ago."

"Donald Lee's a fuckin' bastard. I know his sister, and she thinks so too."

It was hard for me not to agree. "But you were here then."

"Yeah, I was here. It wasn't fair. Donald just come up with that big ol' gun of his and took Freddy. He'd of beat the shit out of Donald if it wasn't for the gun."

"You remember that night pretty good?" I asked.

"I remember it. It was the worst time in my life." Her eyes filled with tears.

I've learned from experience that girls like Anna often go from glistening eyes to hysterics in a hurry, so I moved on quickly. "What happened before Donald Lee came? If you want to help Freddy, you have to remember that." I felt a stab of guilt. I didn't know if that'd help Freddy or hurt him.

Anna wiped her nose with her hand and wiped that on her shirt. "Freddy was real excited. He'd gotten a big ol' buck and said we'd be eatin' good from it. When I got on the steps, I could already tell it was a good one. I wanted to go count the points but he wouldn't let me."

Excitement hit me. It looked like my wild hunch was being

confirmed. "Why wouldn't he let you? Count the points, I mean."

She shrugged. "I don't know. Said he had to get it to C and C's. I thought it was funny. Always before, he wanted me to count 'em."

"How many times before?" Dan asked.

"Well, only once, I guess."

I looked at Dan. He shrugged. "They tend to exaggerate," he said quietly.

Freddy Meadows didn't want Anna to count the points. He didn't want her to get near the buck.

A body falling out of it would have spoiled the effect. Even with Anna. More than ever, I was sure I was right.

"Anna, I want to ask you about something that happened at scho—"

Suddenly, Dan stepped back from the door. It flew open and Freddy Meadows entered the trailer. He looked at Mitch, then stared at Anna momentarily. Her T-shirt had eased up her legs again. Meadows's gaze returned to Mitch. A moment later, Meadows was on top of him.

Chapter Thirty-four

It was incredible.

I knew Mitch was quick-witted the first time I met him five years ago. Now I knew he was just plain quick. One moment Freddy Meadows was grabbing for Mitch; the next moment Meadows was hugging thin air and Mitch was standing behind him.

Dan was quick too. Before I could move, he had Meadows's right arm behind his back. "Calm down, son," Dan said quietly. Meadows tried to jerk his arm free. Dan pushed Meadows's arm up a notch, grabbed his left wrist, and jammed him against the back of the recliner that Mitch had vacated moments before. In an instant, Dan released Meadows's wrist and pressed a thumb against his neck. It was one of the pressure points Chico had taught me to use. Dan said, again in a quiet voice, "I said, calm down, boy." Dan's thumb moved again, pressing harder.

Meadows gave a cry of pain and Dan eased his thumb back. "Now," Dan said, "I'm going to let you go, but you better, by God, turn around and sit down. Do you understand that?"

Meadows nodded. Dan released his grip slowly, but kept his hands on my client until he was turned around and sitting quietly. Dan backed up and looked at me. "You just don't know," he said, "how often I've wanted to do that at school. Another cathartic experience." He looked at Meadows. "If you move again, maybe I'll get to have yet another one."

Freddy wasn't paying attention, which was undoubtedly one of his major problems. He rubbed his neck and looked at Anna, then at Mitch, Dan, and me. "What the hell are you doing here?" he asked us petulantly.

I said, "I came to talk to you about some important stuff relating to your case." I waved a hand toward Mitch and Dan. "These are my . . . co-workers." Each of them smiled graciously and nodded.

Meadows responded in the Park County fashion to which I'd become accustomed. He said, "Sheeeit."

It was time, I thought, to start bluffing. "I hope you can come up with a more coherent response in court when the time comes. You're going to need it," I said.

"What the fuck does that mean?"

"That means you need to tell me about a guy named Estafan."

If Meadows played poker, he must have been lousy at it. He flinched at the mention of the name. "I ain't saying nothing with him around," he said, looking at Dan. He shifted his gaze to Mitch. "Or him either."

Mitch said, sounding exactly like Clint Eastwood, "That's too bad, scum sucker."

I grabbed Mitch and Dan by their arms and pulled them back a step. I said quietly, "Com'on y'all, I need to talk to him."

Dan asked, "You going to be all right with him alone?"

I looked at Freddy Meadows. "Am I going to be all right with you alone?"

He didn't respond.

I said, "You remember that day when you were in jail?"

He sat motionless.

"I think he remembers. I'll be okay. How about y'all taking Anna outside and entertaining her while I talk to my client?" Anna squirmed on the sofa. "But first, Anna, go back and put some pants on."

Soon, I was alone with Freddy. "We have a problem," I said.

He hadn't moved from the recliner. "What?"

"Do you know what confidentiality means?"

"Yeah. You already asked me that. It means you can't tell stuff. You said a guy's lawyer can't tell stuff he tells him."

"Her," I said. "I'm a her."

"Fu . . ." He stopped, midword.

I moved to the sofa and sat. "I need to tell you this. I know you killed Estafan."

He looked at me, hard.

I skipped over the details of the killing, which was good because on that part I didn't have a clue, and went with what I thought I knew. "After you killed him, you put his body in that big buck you shot that Sunday and took him to C and C's. A few days later you took him out in the woods and dumped the body."

"I don't know what you're talking about."

"Yes, you do," I said firmly. "The time has come, Freddy, to tell me the truth. You're charged with killing Lawton Fletcher. He was a major movie star. We're not talking about typical Park County stuff here." I didn't mention that Fletcher's fame was fading fast and that nobody but the people around here cared much about him anymore. I figured Freddy didn't know that, so I lied some more. "This is a whole new ball game. People from all over will be digging into this. It's only just begun. And the fact that somebody pulled some strings with the judge to get you out of jail is purely temporary. There is no doubt about that."

"I didn't kill Fletcher."

"I believe that. The question is, will anybody else believe that? You'd better start talking to me."

He didn't.

"Listen. Defense attorneys don't just sit around waiting for the trial to begin so their clients can burn in the electric chair. We go out and investigate. It didn't take me long to figure out that you killed Estafan, and I'm just one step ahead of the law." Was my nose growing? I had no doubt that the law, if any existed in Park County, knew nothing of any of this. "I also believe you know something about Fletcher's murder. I don't think you did it, but I think you know something you're not telling me." Another shot in the dark.

I continued, "Nobody around here cares a whit about a poor part-Mexican kid. I know that and you know that. The best-case scenario is we do some kind of plea bargaining and trade the Fletcher murder charge for a manslaughter charge on Estafan. You agree to tell them what you know about Fletcher and spend a little time in jail.

"On the other hand, you go down on the Lawton Fletcher thing, and you're looking at life without parole at best, and Ol' Sparky down in Jackson is a real possibility. I'm suggesting to you that you better start getting real."

Meadows's hand was bouncing off the arm of the recliner. "I didn't kill Fletcher."

I leaned forward. "So tell me about it. I'm trying to help you."

Meadows leaned back and stared at the ceiling and nodded. "Okay."

"You went hunting that day," I prodded.

"Yeah. Nothing happened all day. Not a deer in sight. Finally I got tired of sitting there and decided to go home."

"What time was that?"

"Five, or thereabouts. I climb out of the stand, turn around, and there's the biggest goddamn buck I ever seen in my life. Just standing there, about sixty yards away, looking at me. It was easy." He raised his arms and shot an imaginary arrow into the ceiling of the trailer.

"And . . ."

"I field-dress him, just like my daddy taught me, and tie him to the hood of my Bronco."

"And you head home."

"Yeah."

"But you stop along the way?"

He didn't respond.

"Come on, Freddy," I said. "Your choice is six months in the county farm or sizzle."

Where'd that come from?

He looked toward the trailer's kitchen. "I saw him."

"Estafan?" I guessed.

"Yeah." The word was backed by anger.

"What was your problem with him?"

"He was messing with Anna. At school. She told the assistant principal but the spic mongrel kept doing it. That Friday, before . . . it happened, she came home and said he'd grabbed her breast."

I thought of Joe Coulter and what he'd said about Estafan.

"I was going to see Estafan after school on Monday. But when I stopped in Warrendale to call Anna, there he was, walking across the parking lot. He sees me and runs. He knew what he done and he's a chickenshit. Won't face up to me." Freddy's eyes moved to mine. "I remember what Coach Martin always said. 'Ain't nothin' worse than a quitter. Quitters ain't nothin' but chickenshits.' "

"So . . ." I prodded.

"He ran in that old mill. I chased after him and caught him. He said some stuff that pissed me off. We started fighting and all of a sudden I had my hunting knife out."

"And?"

"And blood started spurting . . ."

"And?"

"And he was dead, goddamnit. Are you stupid, or what?"

I repressed my instinct to put into practice what I'd learned at Chico's and said, "I need to know this stuff if I'm going to help you. What happened after that?"

"I didn't mean to kill him; I just couldn't stand the thought of him having his hands all over Anna. I figured I'd better get out of there, so I went for the door that was closest to my Bronco and there was this other guy there."

"Other guy?" I asked the question despite my certainty of who it was.

"Yeah. This other guy's laying on the floor deader'n hell,

blood coming out the back of his head. I started thinking straight again. I knew I was in trouble."

I remembered what Principal Webster had said. Freddy Meadows wasn't stupid. I wouldn't have thought that, but Webster knew him better than I did.

Meadows continued. "So I went back to Estafan and drug his body over to the other one. Figured they'd think Estafan's blood was the dead guy's. I took off my jacket and shirt, wrapped the Mex's neck up with my shirt, and put my jacket back on. I carried him out and put him in the deer and took off."

"Wait," I said. "You have to tell me everything if I'm going to help you."

"What?"

"The wallet."

"Yeah, well. The guy was dead so I got his wallet. If I'd of known the guy was some kind of movie star I wouldn't of got it."

"Then you came back here to show off your big buck to Anna."

He narrowed his eyes and looked to the door.

Anger flew through me. "You better listen to this. Anna told us you'd brought the deer here that night. That's all. I'm going to make it a habit to check on her. If I ever find out you've hurt her, I'll . . ." I'll kill you, I thought. I said, "You *will* wish you hadn't."

I couldn't believe it. Tears appeared in his eyes. He said, "I wouldn't hurt her. I love her."

God help the girl, I thought. That was a seriously true prayer. I'd dealt with too many women whose husbands and boyfriends would sit in my office declaring the same thing. That would be the morning after they'd beat the daylights out of their true loves. Almost always, the women went back to the men and a month later we'd be going through the whole thing again. Men are jerks and women are stupid. That's what I'd concluded.

I said, "So after you left here, you took the deer and Estafan's body to C and C's."

Freddy wiped his eyes. "I ain't talking about that."

I didn't blame him. C and C was owned by Billy Ray Cunningham. If I was in Freddy's position, I'd be a whole lot more afraid of Billy Ray Cunningham than of the judicial system. I was sure that Cunningham didn't have a parole board and his death sentences didn't harbor appeals.

"How'd Estafan's body end up in the woods off Highway Twenty-eight?"

Meadows shook his head. "I don't know."

I believed that too. "Do you work for Cunningham?"

"I ain't talking about that. I told you what I did to Estafan and that's all I'm saying."

Donald Lee was right. It had to be Cunningham who influenced the judge to let Freddy out.

From Mitch and my visit to California, I'd formulated two tenuous theories. One was that Fletcher had become caught up in some kind of religious thing. Knowing the origin of the animal blood that was found on Estafan had removed one of the factors that had strengthened that notion in my mind.

The other possibility was that Fletcher was involved with drugs. His behavior on the set was suspicious, as was his change in lifestyle. And there were those trips to Mexico and the Caribbean.

Nothing much to go on in either case.

But somebody in Park County was obviously disturbed about my investigating Fletcher's murder. Because of that, it seemed likely that there was some kind of connection between Fletcher and someone here.

I had to go with what I had, as little as that was.

"Okay. But I've got to ask you something else and you need to tell me the truth, whether you like it or not. Like I said, we can deal with the Estafan thing." At that moment, I hated my job more than anything I've hated in my life. "We *must* deal with the Fletcher murder, too. If we don't, you're dead whether it's Cunningham or the state of Georgia."

Freddy took a deep breath and let it go.

"Is Cunningham involved in drugs?"

He looked relieved. "No way. He hates 'em. He preaches about that all the time."

"He doesn't traffic?"

"No way. Billy Ray hates the motherfu . . . He hates pushers. Like I said. Ain't no drugs in Park County. Billy Ray makes damn sure of that."

Billy Ray Cunningham, moonshiner, gambler, auto thief, murderer, and only the Lord knows what else, hates drugs.

What to do now? I needed to find somebody for Freddy to confess to about murdering Estafan so I could negotiate a plea bargain. Donald Lee wasn't a candidate and he had said Sheriff Cox was tight with Cunningham. I couldn't chance that. The only other person with any semblance of jurisdiction who I *knew* I could trust was Molly, and she wouldn't be back until Sunday night.

The answer was clear. I'd have to wait for Molly's return. I said, "You don't plan on killing anybody else in the next couple of days, do you?"

Incredibly, Freddy looked hurt. "I didn't mean to kill him. If he hadn't been such an asshole and fought me, I wouldn't have."

"Okay. I want you to stay here, in the trailer, until Monday morning. Can you call in sick, or something, until then?"

"Yeah. I don't work any particular hours."

That wasn't surprising, if he worked for Billy Ray Cunningham. I stood. "I'm telling you, Freddy, you better stay here. It's for your own good. Believe me."

I went out the trailer and spoke to Anna. I gave her my card and told her to call me, day or night, if Freddy ever hurt her. She insisted he'd never do that, but I insisted she take the card anyway. She went in the trailer and I stood next to Dan while we watched Mitch try to get his station wagon turned around in the tight space in front of the trailer. Dan's suggestions during the process were less than helpful. Finally, we were on our way back to Patsboro.

Despite Dan's offer to be my employee in return for buying

breakfast, I couldn't bring myself to fudge further on my ethical constraints. What I'd said the night before was conjecture. What Freddy had told me today would remain private.

Seeing Florina Harvey had become more critical than ever. More than anything else, I needed some solid information about Lawton Fletcher.

Chapter Thirty-five

I'd like to talk to Florina Harvey," I said to the bearded man behind the bar of the Flashcube Lounge.

"Who?"

"Bambi," Mitch said.

The man looked at Mitch. "Why?"

I gave him my card. "I'm an attorney from Patsboro. I need to talk to her about a case I'm working on."

"Hell, she just got here a couple of weeks ago. If she's in some kind of trouble, I'll fire her ass."

"She's not in trouble. It just turns out she knew somebody important to the case. From a long time ago."

In heavy redneck, Mitch said, "Hey, you tol' me she was 'sposed to be heah tonight. After six, you said." Mitch looked at his watch. "Shore 'nuff it's done got after six." It was the voice he'd used that afternoon when he called from my house to find out if Bambi would be working tonight.

The man gave Mitch a hard look, followed by one of puzzlement. "You're the guy who called today?"

"Shore 'nuff," Mitch said, and grinned.

I leaned on the bar. "Look, Mr. . . . ?"

"Sheats. Tracy Sheats."

"I just need to ask her some questions, Tracy. About a guy she knew. No big deal. Is she here?" I felt dumb. Being coquettish wasn't my strong suit. It worked, though.

"Yeah. She's in the back. I'll go get her." He turned, then stopped. "You ever think about dancing?"

I half-smiled and shook my head. After Tracy left, Mitch said, "You seem to have that look. Maybe in your former life you were a stripper."

"Not in this life," I said. While we waited, I surveyed the Flashcube. There wasn't much to survey. On my right, the bar ran the length of the wood-frame building. To the left were two rows of tables with laminated tops. Only three were occupied. T-shirts covered by opened plaid flannel shirts were the prevailing fashion, except for one man, at a table by himself, who wore an Izod sweater and a tie. He was in the back corner, writing on a paper napkin.

The music was subdued compared to the place on Bourbon Street. Maybe Thurman had a noise ordinance. Or maybe this place didn't want to draw attention to itself because it was located smack-dab in the Bible Belt. A young girl with that hard country look was dancing on the bar at the far end of the room. She was down to a G-string, and a single dollar bill was hanging from her garter. It appeared Hightower County men were lousy tippers.

Tracy reappeared. Behind him was the woman whose picture I'd been carrying around for a week. Florina Harvey was wearing a bikini bathing suit covered by a sheer top and was obviously older than the dancer on the bar by a good ten years but, strangely enough, didn't look nearly as hard. In fact, she looked better than the picture.

She remained behind the bar. I said, "I'm Tammi Randall and this is Mitch Griffith. We'd like to talk to you."

"What about?"

Tracy had resumed slicing jalapeños, but was obviously interested in my answer.

I said, "You mind sitting at a table?" I turned toward the empty tables near the door.

"Tracy said you were a lawyer. What do you want?"

"I just need to talk." I nodded at the tables. "Come on." I walked to one and sat down.

Florina hesitated. Mitch followed me and sat.

"Come on," I said again.

She looked at Tracy, shrugged, rounded the bar, and sat next to me.

I said, "I won't keep you long."

She shrugged again. "Don't matter. Thursday nights suck around here anyway. Country boys don't seem to start partying till Friday." She twirled an ashtray that was sitting on the table. "So what's the deal?"

"Theresa told me you'd come to Atlanta."

She stopped twirling the ashtray. "Theresa? From New Orleans?"

"I met her last week." I nodded toward Mitch. "We went there looking for you."

"Why?"

"We'd been in Los Angeles. Investigating a murder. I work for the Legal Aid Society in Patsboro. I'm defending a guy named Freddy Meadows. He's been charged with murdering Lawton Fletcher."

She closed her eyes at the mention of Fletcher's name. "What makes you think I'd know anything about a movie star?"

"The main clue were some letters we found in his apartment. They were from you."

She opened her eyes. They were wet with tears. "I don't want to talk about that in here."

"Where can we go?"

"Tracy has an office."

Mitch and I followed Florina around the bar. She said to Tracy, "We need to use your office."

"No way," Tracy said. "As soon as I finish up here, I've got some work to do in there."

Mitch tapped Tracy on his shoulder. "Bambi heah's tryin' to

talk Tammi into dancin' for you." He raised his eyebrows twice.

Tracy laughed. "Yeah, right. She's going to give up lawyering to be a stripper." He looked at me. "Hey, who knows? Maybe Bambi can talk you into it. Worth a shot. Go ahead."

I punched Mitch in his ribs as we moved toward the office.

"Just trying to help," he said.

"Gee, thanks," I said.

There were two chairs in the office and Florina and I sat in them. Mitch squatted, avoiding the filthy tile floor, and leaned against the door.

"Tell me about Lawton Fletcher," I said.

Tears came to Florina's eyes again.

"How did you know each other?" I asked.

"We didn't. Not until a year ago, anyway. We never met in person." She wiped her nose with her hand. "At least that we could remember."

"That you could remember?"

"My maiden name was Fletcher. Florina Fletcher."

Sometimes I'm real slow. It took a moment, then I said, "You were Lawton Fletcher's . . ."

"Sister. Soon after he was born we were sent to foster homes. Different ones. Different counties. I sort of remember going to see a baby for a while, but nothing else. I ended up being sent to New Orleans because we had an aunt there. That didn't work out and I was in foster homes there."

"How'd you find each other?"

"He found me. Lawton said it wasn't hard. There was a trail of paper to work from Family and Children's Services. He called one night, out of the blue. We talked and wrote letters. We were supposed to meet last weekend." She sniffled, then buried her head in her hands and cried. Through her tears, she said, "All my life, I've been alone. Felt that way anyway. When he called, I felt . . . a connection. Finally, a connection with somebody. And now he's . . ." Her words turned to a wail.

I scooted my chair over, put my arm around her. "I'm so

sorry," I said. A minute passed and the crying stopped. I knew from personal experience that the body can take only so much of that.

She sat up and drew her hands down her face. Streaks of mascara ran down her cheeks. "I don't know how I can help you."

I said, "When Mitch and I were out in LA, we looked through his apartment. It wasn't much for someone with as much money as he had. That's where we found your letters."

"He'd decided *things* weren't important. He told me that. He didn't want to waste money on . . . material stuff."

"Florina, I know you want to believe that, but he was about to spend millions of dollars to buy a town. That's a lot of stuff."

"He wasn't going to buy it for himself. He had a plan."

"What was the plan? Why would he buy the town?"

She shrugged. "He never told me, except he was going to help people like us. I wrote and told him he was doing the right thing. I didn't know exactly what he was going to do, but I knew it would be something good."

I didn't want to disabuse her of the vision she had of her long-lost brother, but I also wanted to know everything she knew about Lawton Fletcher. I'd learned that even a tiny bit of information can help turn a case. As much as I hated to, I had to tell her about his shakes and memory lapses on the set, his trips to Mexico and the Caribbean.

I never got around to that.

She started crying again. "He was dying. He told me what it was. Some kind of 'syringe' something. A disease that ruins the muscles and nerves. He said there wasn't a cure. He found me to tell me that. He said the doctors said I might have inherited it too. He wanted me to know. In case I wanted to have children."

I sat straight, stunned.

"He told me it was horrible. He was getting to where he couldn't count on holding things. Even walking was getting hard to do at times. The last time we talked, he said he had to force himself to go to the set. He'd get so worried about moving, he'd forget his lines. He said it would be his last movie. He told me he'd gone to Mexico and some other places where people said they could cure him, but he was just getting worse, like the doctors told him he would." Tears fell again. "He said he knew he was going to die and he wanted to do something before it got so bad that he couldn't do anything and it had something to do with buying Warrendale."

I was still stunned. Lawton Fletcher was dying and he knew it. Of course, we're all dying and we all know it. It makes a difference, though, if we know when it's going to happen. I suppose that's why Preacher Smith kept harping about dying at the Congregational Holiness. Death can be a great motivator to take care of business.

I said, "So you had told him about the town being for sale. You learned that from Jeff Warren when you were in Miami."

At the sound of the name she looked at me. "How'd you know that?"

"Like I said, I'm defending the guy who's accused of murdering your brother. I'm investigating the death and he died in Warrendale. I talked to Jeff Warren."

She didn't react to the name the way I thought she might. "Jeff told me about his town. After I left Miami, Lawton found me down in New Orleans. The first time we talked, I told him I knew a guy who was trying to sell a whole town. I figured he'd found out what I do for a living and I was embarrassed. I was trying to impress him by telling him I knew somebody important enough to own a town. I guess I didn't want him to think I was just . . ."

I nodded, letting her know I understood.

"At the time, I didn't know that Lawton had grown up sixty miles from Jeff's town. He got real excited and said that that was exactly what he was looking for. I asked him what he meant, but he never told me. He said he had to figure out some stuff first. He said he didn't know if it would work."

I nodded again and we sat quietly. Florina Harvey had just blown my theories, tenuous as they were, all to hell. The only evidence I had about Lawton Fletcher's involvement in drugs was hearsay based on his behavior. Every bit of that behavior had been explained by Florina. She had no reason to lie about any of that, I thought. And why would anybody try to start some kind of cult thing when he knew he'd be dead soon after buying the town?

Then it hit me. Without thinking, I popped my forehead with the heel of my hand. Florina looked at me. She was a beneficiary. According to Fletcher's agent, who was also his lawyer, Florina and Charlotte Perry inherited. Who benefits? That's the first rule of crime investigation. Charlotte Perry's parents had left her in comfortable circumstances, and Lawton was sending her more. On the other hand, Florina had nothing but her aging body. In her profession, she was coming to the end of the line. The Flashcube Lounge was absolute testimony to that.

Was Florina grasping at straws? Diverting suspicion from herself by creating a story about Fletcher's terminal illness? She knew she'd been seen in the area recently. Sheriff Cox had stopped her as she was exiting Jeff's driveway.

Another thought hit me. She'd been at Jeff's. He claimed he didn't know she'd been there, and he had an airtight alibi for the time. He'd been with the county commissioner and the principal of the high school. But who could trust whom in Park County?

Then Mitch asked this question: "Why didn't he tell anybody about his illness? We talked to his lawyer and the leading lady on that last film. They didn't know anything. Nobody knew anything about his illness."

Florina said, "He told me he didn't want pity. That was real important to him. He said he grew up with people feeling sorry for him and he hated it. In fact, he said that's why his last foster parents had saved him. They didn't pity him. They just expected him to act right."

If she's lying, I thought, she's good at it. She should be an actress.

"Lawton told me his doctor's name. He's in San Diego.

Some kind of expert on what he had. I called him, hoping he'd tell me Lawton was wrong. He wasn't. The doctor told me Lawton would die within a few years."

"Do you know the doctor's name?"

"I got it at home. And his telephone number, if you want it."

She wasn't lying. I'd get the number and check it out, of course. But I was convinced that she wasn't lying.

"Did you know that you're inheriting half of Lawton's estate?"

She nodded. "He sent me a copy of the will. But it didn't matter. He started sending me money and said any time I needed some more he'd send more."

"He sent you enough to live on?"

"Ten thousand a month, each month for the past year."

I swept my palm at her outfit. "Then why . . . ?"

A smile of resignation crossed her face. "I quit for a while. Lawton wanted me to move up here to Georgia. He said he was going to move here as soon as he got the town. He said we could spend some time together. So I moved and planned to retire. After a month, I was going crazy just sitting around. I've worked all my life. Or at least since I was fifteen. That's when I started dancing. And I don't know how to do anything else. I mean, I can't type or do computers." She looked at me. "And the fact is, I like this work. I know somebody like you doesn't understand that, but I do. I'm putting the money into CDs for when I can't anymore."

She was right. I didn't understand it. I did understand that I was back to square one.

Charlotte Perry clearly didn't care about Lawton Fletcher's money. She still had the checks he'd sent her a year ago. She showed them to me the day after Fletcher was killed. Florina Harvey knew about the will and she knew he'd be dead soon. Why risk killing him?

Lawton Fletcher wasn't a druggie and he wasn't buying Warrendale to start a cult of some kind. He was dying and was planning to do something good with Warrendale.

And that meant that Freddy Meadows's revelation about Billy Ray Cunningham's attitude about drugs meant nothing.

Freddy Meadows had confessed to murdering Estafan. To me, anyway. I didn't think he'd murdered Lawton Fletcher, but he was still charged with that and I was charged with Freddy's defense.

As I watched Florina Harvey wipe away her tears, I realized that I was left with nothing but confusion and uncertainty.

Chapter Thirty-six

Mrs. Thompson peered over her book of morning devotions when I arrived at the Legal Aid Society the next morning. Her glasses slipped and she pushed them back up her nose. "My goodness, Miss Randall. Did we decide to come to work today?" She lowered her eyes back to her Bible study. "Of course, it is Friday so we can look forward to the weekend, can't we?"

I put my briefcase down and leaned on the counter that fronted her desk. "And good morning to you, Mrs. Thompson. What is the topic of today's devotional?"

"Love thy neighbor as you love yourself."

Knowing that Mrs. Thompson's capacity to detect irony was nil, I said nothing and went to my office. Surprisingly, there were some messages on my desk. Four, to be exact. Of course, I'd been away from here for four days and had undoubtedly received more calls than that, but considering Mrs. Thompson, to get even four messages was miraculous.

One was from Detective Macleod from California who reported that he'd found nothing new. I returned the other three. All were from women who told me what a wonderful job Eddie Thompson was doing for the society. They didn't sound like typical clients, and I suspected that Mrs. Thompson had set up some ringers for her nephew.

That business taken care of, I leaned back in my chair and

stared at the top of my desk. It was empty. I felt disoriented. Normally when I was in my office, there was never enough time to get done what needed to be done. Now, I had plenty of time. When Molly returned on Sunday, I'd tell her about Freddy Meadows and Estafan and make plans to turn him over to her. Until then, there wasn't anything else to do on that case, and I had no others.

Bernard's booming voice sounded from the reception room. "Good morning, Mrs. Thompson."

"You'll never guess who's here," Mrs. Thompson said.

"No, I probably would not. Perhaps you will simply tell me." I could hear him unlocking his office. "By doing it that way, you may return to your devotional quickly, and I will be able to avoid the suspense. I do hate feeling suspenseful."

Before Mrs. Thompson could reply, I was in the hall. Bernard looked up and said, "Oh, it is you, Tammi. Grand! I have missed you."

I couldn't see Mrs. Thompson, but I would bet she was pushing her glasses up as she made a harrumphing noise. After following Bernard into his office, I closed the door. "What's wrong with her?" I asked.

Bernard stood in front of his desk and waved his hand toward the chair on the opposite side. He would never sit before me, so I sat. He followed suit. "Sometime earlier in the week, Tuesday, I think, Mrs. Thompson asked to speak with me. She was concerned that you did not like her nephew and may be undermining his work here."

"What?"

Bernard looked thoughtful. "Yes, I believe that was the gist of her complaint."

"I haven't even been here. In fact, I've only seen him twice."

"Over the years, I have come to the conclusion that Mrs. Thompson does not require logic, nor facts, to form her opinions. She simply adopts them without rhyme or reason."

"I know that. But this one's really weird. I haven't even thought about Eddie Thompson, much less undermined him."

"I would not worry about it, if I were you. By next week she will have another agenda and will have forgotten about this one. I have no doubt."

"I'm not worried." I crossed my legs. "Not about her anyway."

"But you are concerned about something. Is it the Fletcher case?"

I nodded. "So far, I've determined that my client is guilty of murder."

"That always makes a case interesting."

"But not the one he's charged with. In fact, he's not even a suspect in the killing he committed."

"That, I would think, moves the case from interesting to fascinating."

"*Frustrating* is the word. I still have to defend the charge of murdering Lawton Fletcher and have gotten nowhere along those lines." I tapped the arms of the chair. "I thought that I was heading in the right direction, but I was wrong."

"Would you like to tell me about it?"

"Yes. That's really why I came in today. I was hoping you'd be able to listen to this."

"Shoot," he said.

I'd gone through this with Jeff and Dan, but had to leave things out with them. With Bernard, I could reveal everything. Freddy was a client of the society, so any attorney here represented him. Midway through my story, Bernard stopped me and retrieved a legal pad from his desk and took notes. When I was finished, he sat quietly and flipped through them. Finally, he packed his pipe and lit it. "At one point during your story, I was thinking of suicide. That certainly is not an unusual reaction for someone who knows he faces a painful death. I thought that perhaps your Freddy Meadows may have picked up the gun, along with the wallet, but did not want to tell you about that."

I nodded. "I woke up sometime last night with that thought. But it doesn't make sense. First, why wouldn't Freddy tell me he'd found a gun? That'd be in his best interest."

"He may not realize that. People do panic when faced with a murder charge. Or perhaps yet another person happened onto the scene and took the gun."

"That could be. Nobody saw anybody else around, though. All Mitch and I saw was an empty parking lot." Something clicked when I said that. Where did Estafan live? He'd been seen heading toward Warrendale. Freddy Meadows had killed Estafan and carried him away from the town tucked inside the deer. How had he gotten to Warrendale?

I shrugged inwardly. If Estafan had left a car somewhere in the vicinity, it would have been found by now. Besides, Meadows had already confessed to the murder.

"Tammi, are you there?"

"What?"

"We were discussing the possibility that Fletcher took his own life."

I shook my head. "There was nothing in what Florina Harvey or Charlotte Perry said about Fletcher to indicate he was thinking like that. In fact, it was just the opposite. He was trying to make the best of the time he had left. And why would he go to Warrendale to commit suicide?"

"As I said, the thought crossed my mind, but I believe you are right. Suicide does not make sense."

"What does?"

Bernard puffed on his pipe. "There is someone out there who benefited from Lawton Fletcher's death."

"That's what I've been trying to figure out. The logical ones are Charlotte Perry and Florina Harvey. They inherited. They also told me, independently, that Fletcher was already sharing his money with them."

"There are some people for whom sharing is not good enough."

"I know. But neither of these women even spent what they had. Charlotte Perry inherited a good bit from her parents, and Lawton was sending her money, yet she lives in a modest house in Forest Glen. Florina Harvey continues to be a stripper despite

Lawton giving her enough money that she doesn't have to be."

Bernard looked at his notes again. "Given his history as you have described it, the next logical candidate would be Billy Ray Cunningham. Perhaps he benefits by Fletcher's death in some way that does not involve the drug trade."

I shrugged. "Could be. I don't have a clue on that, though."

"It is not required that benefiting involve money. Perhaps Mr. Cunningham is more interested in protecting his power. He does appear to have quite a lot of that and, I suspect, he would not like to lose it. Perhaps he was afraid a Hollywood movie star would infringe upon his authority."

The hymn went through my mind. *Pow'r, pow'r, pow'r in the blood.* "Could be," I said.

"So what are your plans now?"

"I don't have any. Except to have Freddy Meadows turn himself into Molly Malone when she gets back. I'll work on having the Estafan charge be manslaughter. My hope is that Molly can have some influence in getting the charge of murdering Lawton Fletcher dropped. In other words, I'll work to minimize his sentence, even though I don't really want to."

"There are times when our lot is odious."

"Amen," I said.

There was a knock at the door. I reached over and opened it. Eddie Thompson came in, carrying a folder. "I need to check something out with you." Then he saw me. "Oh, hi."

I smiled.

He placed the folder in front of Bernard and opened it. "There's a guy named Joe Packer in my office. He got arrested last night for a B and E over at the university. After going through his file, I wouldn't be surprised if he did it, but the evidence is weak. I think it'd be worth going not-guilty on this one and seeing what happens. What do you think?"

"If you believe it would be in your client's best interest, I think that is what you should do," Bernard said. He noticed my raised eyebrows. "Eddie has turned out to be a quick learner."

The phone chirped. Bernard and I grabbed for it, but Eddie

beat us to it. "It's for you," he said, handing the phone to me. "Boy, I don't know how you guys can tolerate having a secretary who can't figure out how to transfer a call."

I held the phone and watched Eddie pick up his folder and leave. I looked at Bernard. He said, "I was speaking the truth, believe it or not."

Jeff Warren was on the phone. After preliminaries, he asked me if I wanted to go to a football game that evening.

"A football game?"

"I know it's not real exotic, but on fall Friday nights in Park County, it's the biggest show in town. If the Cougars win tonight, they'll clinch a playoff berth."

My feelings were mixed. A little tug pulled at me when I heard his voice. On the other hand, I was looking forward to staying out of Park County until Monday when Molly would be with me.

"I'll come pick you up. That way you won't have to drive up here alone."

"I'd like that," I said. "I haven't been to a high school game in years."

"Good. Would six be okay? The game starts at seven thirty."

I agreed and handed the phone to Bernard, who put it in its cradle. "Jeff Warren," I said.

Bernard sucked on his pipe and nodded. "From what you said earlier, he seems to be a nice fellow."

"Seems to be," I said trying to hide a blush, even though I knew hiding things from Bernard was useless. He never missed anything. I changed the subject. "So Eddie's working out?"

"I have been amazed. Perhaps I was guilty of passing the sins of the aunt to the nephew. I now believe he will be an asset."

"Amazing."

"Yes," Bernard said. "And now, I suggest that you take the rest of the day off. It is clear you have been working night and day for the society, no matter what Mrs. Thompson thinks. The grant we are hoping for is very important. I continue to believe we must show a need for our services in the outlying counties.

You have been doing good work. Go home and rest."

"Well, I really don't have a lot to do around here. And I need to get my hair done. It's driving me crazy."

Bernard laughed. "I would never have noticed."

I stood. "Thanks, Bernard. You are wonderful to work for."

Bernard held up his hand. "There is no need for that. Now, go get your hair done and have a good time tonight at the football game. Perhaps it will take your mind off the case."

That was one of the few times since I've known him that Bernard Fuchs turned out to be wrong.

Chapter Thirty-seven

Oh ho! Look who's here! I'll bet you came to relive the glory of your days on the gridiron here at the home of the Cougars." Principal Webster was standing beside the ticket booth. He had a full money bag in his hand.

Jeff did not hesitate to make it clear: "My glory days were spent on the bench unless we were ahead by fifty points. Jim here, on the other hand, was our star running back. He went on to play at that national powerhouse, Mars Hill College."

"Hey! We were second in the conference two years in a row."

"We'd better go on in," Jeff said, "so we can find a seat before they fill up."

Webster said, "Y'all hold on a minute. I got a place for you but I need to put this up." He held up the money bag. After putting it under the seat of his truck and locking the door, he waved for us to follow him. He led us behind the wooden bleachers to a steep set of stairs leading to the roof of the press box. We walked across the shingles of the roof to a where a man was standing behind a video camera. He was bent down, adjusting a black-and-white television that was attached to the camera. Webster said to the man, "Roland, this is Jeff Warren, a distinguished alumnus, and his friend Miss . . . uh . . ."

"Tammi Randall," I said.

"That's right. Tammi Randall."

Roland looked up. "Yeah, I know Jeff. Everybody in the county knows Jeff."

Webster slapped Roland on the back. "Good deal. They've got my permission to watch the game from up here. Let the coaches know, if they ask about 'em. Okay?"

"Sure." He looked at Jeff and me. "Just so you don't mind the real distinct possibility that this press box might fall down." To Webster, he said, "I thought we were going to fix up the facilities around here."

Webster said, "Ran into a problem." He pointed across the field. "You know that brand-new parking lot we got? The commissioner made some kind of deal with the state Department of Transportation for that, so we went ahead and did it. And then the money never came through. It cost a pretty penny. We'll have to wait on the stadium improvements." Webster stomped his feet on the roof underneath him. "But this old thing's all right." He looked at Jeff. "Got to get back to the ticket booth. It looks like we're going to have a big gate tonight, and I don't like leaving too much money sitting around. I'll be taking it to the bank, but I ought to be back by the second quarter. See you then."

Jeff and I propped our elbows on the railing that faced the field.

"I wouldn't lean too hard on that thing," Roland said. "It's a mite rickety."

Jeff shook it with his hands. It moved, but not much. "Just be careful," he said to me.

We watched the teams warming up. A boy wearing number ten was obviously the starting quarterback—I could tell from his swagger and the way he took his helmet off at every opportunity. The stands were already packed, and now and then he'd walk to the fence, which was lined three deep with people, and talk to somebody in the crowd.

I used to watch Paul Starling do that. He was the captain of the Maytown Hornets and had his picture in the weekly *Maytown News* every Tuesday during football season. He now reads water meters for the city.

I guess it's okay, I decided as I watched number ten preen in warm-ups. If it wasn't for football, most of these guys wouldn't have anything to make them proud. It'd just be better if they weren't such jerks about it.

"Want something to eat?" Jeff asked. "The booster club grills some great hot dogs and hamburgers, if things haven't changed."

"Sure," I said. "A hot dog sounds good."

"Do you want slaw on them?"

"One's enough and slaw would be good."

"Okay. Be back in a minute."

I watched him back down the steps off the roof and felt a strange sense of contentment. If most men had asked me to a football game, I'd have figured they were jerks, trying to relive their moments of glory. But Jeff had readily admitted he had no moments of gridiron glory. He also had enough money to take me to Atlanta and dine on high cuisine, but he seemed genuinely excited about the booster club's hot dogs.

That's what he was, I decided. Genuine.

The game was exciting for a quarter. Both teams scored on their opening drives. Two Park County coaches had joined us. Each wore headsets with microphones so they could relay information to the coaches on the field. One of them didn't need a microphone, though. In a booming voice, he hollered, screamed, and cursed. After a play in which the Shawton tailback ran for twenty yards, the coach yelled, "Goddamn! I told that retard of a linebacker to shoot the gap whenever they split both flankers. What in the hell is wrong with that son of a bitch?"

I looked down into the crowd. A few parents were looking up to the press box, smiling and laughing. Football is amazing. These are the same people who would be challenging a book if it talked about witches.

Principal Webster appeared as promised at the beginning of the second quarter. He pointed out several people in the crowd and told stories about them. One woman was having an affair; a man sitting directly below us, who was an officer of the elementary school PTO, had been arrested for DUI a month ago. He pointed toward the fence where a portly man in overalls was moving down the line of spectators shaking hands. "There's Commissioner Jones, politicking."

The crowd below us roared and we looked to the field in time to see number ten crossing the goal line. The announcer said it had been a ninety-three-yard run, but we had missed it.

The principal said, "Roland, how about backing that up so we can see it?"

"Let me get the extra point first." After Park County successfully went for two, going ahead by a point, Roland fiddled with the camera and replayed the touchdown run on the television screen.

Jeff said, "That's not bad, Jim. Instant replay here in Park County. Things *have* changed."

The principal left shortly before halftime, saying he had to supervise the concession area. I enjoyed the bands and thought about how those kids, unlike the football players, were learning something they could use throughout their lives. I still wished I'd been in the band instead of being a cheerleader. I mean, how many times in the past ten years have I had the opportunity to bounce up and down and scream, "Rip off their arm, and hit 'em with it, hit 'em with it!" I would love to be able to go home at night and play the clarinet.

Jeff went to get us some popcorn and Cokes. I leaned against the railing, feeling more confident because it hadn't succumbed to the blows of the coach throughout the first half. There was the commissioner again, just below me.

Every time I heard the commissioner mentioned, something clicked. What was it?

I thought back. The first time, it seemed, was when Dorothy at the Department of Family and Children's Services complained about her computers. She told me the commissioner had helped get a grant, but the money hadn't come through. The night I was run off the road, Sheriff Cox had complained about new radios for his department that had been promised but not delivered. Tonight, Principal Webster talked about the parking lot. Same thing. The commissioner had arranged for funding and it hadn't come through.

Click, click, click.

I paid no attention to the game in the second half. Instead, I watched the commissioner as he continued to mingle and shake hands. He turned and began to struggle up the hill that led to school. Suddenly, the coach shouted, "Oh, Jesus, God, mother of Mary!"

I looked down to the field and saw that the Shawton Patriots were on Park County's two-yard line. I looked to the scoreboard. Park County was ahead by seven points with thirty-seven seconds left in the game.

The coach hit his colleague on the shoulder. "How in the *fuck* could he let that happen?" He whispered the *f* word. Apparently the *f* word wasn't tolerated even in football in Park County. At least not on the front porch.

The coach said, "Hell! If the IRS did an audit on that kid's brain, he wouldn't owe no taxes. I guaran-goddamn-tee you that! How many times did I tell that jerk to watch for the post pattern on third and long?" He slapped the railing again. "Goddamn it!"

Audit. It hit me like a ton of bricks. The Warrendale Bank. When I first met Jeff, he was going to meet with the commissioner. At Miss Nell's café, Jeff told me the commissioner had asked him about the bank audit that day. Why would he ask about that?

I looked for the commissioner again. It took a moment, but I saw him between the two wings of the high school. He was standing under the flagpole, talking to another man. No, not talking. Arguing. Both of their arms were moving in a definite pattern of disagreement.

I pulled on Jeff's arm. "Who's the commissioner talking to?"
Jeff looked where I was pointing. "I can't tell. He's in the shadow."

The crowd on the other side of the field roared. The Shawton Patriots had scored. An extra point would tie the game. If they went for two, they could win or lose.

The coach was shouting into the microphone. "No way they're going for two. They'll go for the sure thing and take it into overtime. We got to go guts! *Guts!*"

I looked back at the commissioner, who was still gesticulating at the other man. I said to Jeff, "Guts?"

"That means everybody goes after the ball. Everybody. It's a risk. If they're faking the kick, two points would be a cinch."

"I want to know who that guy is."

"What guy?" Jeff asked.

"The one talking to the commissioner."

He looked in that direction again and shrugged. "Can't tell from here."

Roland pushed my arm down. "Excuse me, but I've got to get this." He peered again into the video camera's viewfinder and pressed the zoom button. I looked down at the television that was at the base of the videocamera's tripod. The players became bigger until only the kicker was on the screen. Roland backed the zoom up, so that both lines came into view. I watched the play on television. The kick was blocked and bedlam broke out in the stands below us. The game was over. The Cougars had won and would advance to the playoffs.

I grabbed Roland's shoulders and pulled him back. "Excuse me. Can I use this for a minute?" Roland was a big man and I had to stand on my tiptoes to see in the viewfinder. I turned the camera, found the commissioner, and zoomed in.

"Look, Jeff," I said, pointing to the television. The commissioner's face was clear, as was the face of the man who was pointing a finger at the commissioner's nose.

Jeff squatted on a knee and looked at the television. "It appears that the commissioner and Billy Ray Cunningham are in the midst of a disagreement."

I leaned toward the TV. "That's Billy Ray Cunningham?"

"Sure is."

"How about that?"

It was ten o'clock. Jeff wanted to go to the Cougar's Den for old-times sake. We sat in a booth, drank malts, and watched the kids hang out.

"Are you okay?" Jeff asked.

I was watching three girls who were sitting at a table across the room. They were studiously, and obviously, ignoring a group of boys who were sitting in a booth next to them. Some things never change.

I smiled at Jeff. "Yes. I'm fine. It's fun to remember. Particularly since I don't have to play the games anymore. Being a teenager is awful. Never again for me."

"Me neither," Jeff said. "And I won't. Sit and wonder like a teenager, that is. You seem distracted. Would you rather go someplace else? Or go home?"

"I'm sorry. I know I'm not being much fun."

"That's not it. I just would feel bad if you weren't happy being here. Or if you'd rather not be with me, that's all right." He paused. "Well, not really all right, but I'll survive."

I leaned toward him. "No. I've enjoyed being with you tonight. And at the river."

He smiled. "That's good to hear."

Being in this place did something to me. I opened a packet of sugar, poured it on a napkin, and ate it with a wet finger. Just as I used to do.

"Why the interest in the commissioner and Billy Ray?" Jeff asked.

"You guessed it."

"I guessed it?"

"What I'm thinking about. I can't help it. Something connected tonight."

"What?"

"How well do you know the commissioner?"

Jeff shrugged. "He's been the commissioner for as long as I can remember. Always been there, so I guess I don't think about him much."

"The day we met, here in Braxton, you told me you were on your way to meet with him. Remember that?"

"Certainly."

"Remind me of what you talked about."

"He asked me if anybody else had been interested in buying Warrendale, other than Fletcher."

"The other day you said he'd asked you about the bank audit."

"He just asked if that'd been done yet. I had the feeling he might've heard about somebody else who was interested in buying Warrendale and was playing it close to the vest. Really I didn't care, though. I'm not interested in Park County political intrigue."

"Tell me about the audit."

"What about it?"

"What does it entail?"

"It's not a big deal. If the bank was going to sell, the Fed would come in and be sure the regulations had been followed. I assume they have been. Chad Rabun, who runs the bank, is a good man. Quite fastidious, actually. His *t*s will be crossed, I'm sure."

"So they don't audit individual accounts?"

Jeff shook his head. "I don't think so. The only way that happens, usually, is when IRS gets interested, or something like that."

"Maybe Commissioner Jones didn't know that. Maybe he heard the word *audit* and panicked."

"What are you talking about?"

"I'd like to examine some accounts."

"Whose?"

"Does the commissioner have any accounts in your bank?"

"I don't know, but it wouldn't surprise me. It would be prudent to spread your business around if you were a politician."

"How about Park County accounts?"

"Same thing, I would think."

"Can we look?"

"I think that would take a court order. Customers are entitled to privacy."

"Yeah." I took another dip of sugar and thought of Dan's breaking and entering skills. Only he always objected to the breaking part. He was better than that. "How secure is your bank?"

"That's a weird question, Tammi."

"I'd like to take an unofficial look. If you don't want to be involved, it can be handled in other ways."

Jeff wet his finger and dipped sugar too. "I own the bank. I can get a key. That'd probably make it easier."

I thought of Dan's skills. "A little. Yes. Certainly less tense."

"When?"

"Is the bank open tomorrow?"

"Until noon."

"Tomorrow afternoon?"

"Okay."

"Somebody will be with me. At least one, maybe two. The first has an expertise in finance."

"I trust your judgment."

"Good."

"That stuff will kill you." I hadn't seen the boy approach the table. He adjusted his glasses and said, "You're old enough to know better."

"What?" Jeff asked, puzzled.

The boy pointed to the sugar. "That stuff."

I said, "Thanks for your concern. The truth is I haven't done this since I was a teenager. Sometimes I put it in coffee and I eat an occasional brownie, but other than that, I don't touch the stuff."

"That's sick," he said. "You must've been some kind of hippie or something."

I'd missed hippiedom by ten years. I looked at Jeff. He was containing laughter.

The boy said, "I'm president of Stop Drugs at the Source at Park County High School. I intend to report you to the authorities."

"Drugs?" I said stupidly.

Jeff dipped a finger in the sugar. "Suspicious-looking white substance." He licked his finger. The boy stalked away and out the door.

I said, "But, this doesn't look anything like—"

"We better get out of here before we get busted for snorting sugar."

I laughed. And Jeff laughed. And we held each other up as we laughed our way out of the Cougar's Den.

Chapter Thirty-eight

T his is a pleasant change," Mitch said.

"What is?" I asked.

"Breaking in someplace by using a key."

Jeff turned the key to the security system. The red light on the panel went out and the green light below it lit. "That should get it." He used another key to open the back door to the bank. We stood expectantly. When no bells rang, Mitch and I followed Jeff into a hallway that led to the bank's lobby.

Mitch stood in front of a computer workstation on a desk to the side of the lobby. "Where's the mainframe?" he asked.

Jeff said, "I don't know. I'll look around." He moved around, opening offices with his master key.

"Where's Dan?" Mitch asked. We'd come in separate cars today and hadn't had a chance to talk.

"He's in Athens. Somebody gave him some tickets to the Georgia–South Carolina game and he'd made plans to take the family. He felt bad about not being able to come until I told him Jeff could let us in. Like you said, that took the fun out of it for him."

Jeff appeared from the hallway through which we'd entered the bank. "I think I found it."

Mitch and I followed him to a small office that held a desk and a workstation. Mitch knelt next to a nondescript metal box, about two feet tall and a foot wide, which had a couple of switches and a keyhole. A key was in the keyhole. Mitch said, "I don't know why they bother to put keys on these things. Nobody ever takes them out."

"That's the mainframe?" I asked.

Mitch said, "It's an IBM System Thirty-six. It can hold a lot of records, but I would have thought they'd have a bigger system."

"It's a small bank," Jeff said.

Mitch sat behind the workstation and flipped a switch. "Good. It's up. That'll save time." He stood. To Jeff he said, "Go ahead and log on."

When I had talked to Mitch this morning, he told me that to get into the computer system, he'd have to know a log-on and a password. He said the bank would have hard copies of records, but that it would be much more efficient if he could get into the computer system. When I suggested that the Warrendale Bank may not have a computer system, he scoffed. He was right.

Jeff sat where Mitch had been. "After you called this morning, I came over here and asked Chad Rabun about my being able to get into the system. I was afraid he'd wonder why, but he didn't question it." Jeff typed in his name next to the word LOGON, and typed something next to the word PASSWORD. That part remained blank as he typed. The master menu appeared on the screen. Jeff stood and said, "I guess being the boss has some advantages."

"Definitely," Mitch said as he turned on a printer next to the desk. He sat in front of the station. "Let's go to D space U."

"Do what?" I asked.

Mitch hit some keys and pointed to the screen, then hit some more keys. "Great!" He pointed to a listing on the screen. I followed his finger across to the words "system operator."

"So what does that mean?" I asked.

"Jeff's log-on has access to the entire system. Of course, since Jeff has access, I do too. Let's do an F-five."

"F-five?"

"Yeah. I want to print out the buried menus." After perusing another menu, Mitch hit a couple of keys and the printer came to life. He turned toward Jeff and me. "How about you guys going out and entertaining yourselves. I've got to concentrate."

"You're suggesting that we're superfluous."

Mitch was at the printer. "Yes."

"I'm hurt."

Mitch ripped paper off the printer, then looked at me. Clark Gable said, "Frankly, my dear . . ."

"All right. We're gone."

Jeff and I sat in the lobby and talked idly. After forty-five minutes, I checked on Mitch. He was staring at the screen, hitting keys, and making notes on a legal pad that sat next to the workstation. "How's it going?"

He kept his eyes on the screen. "Nothing yet."

I went back to the lobby and sighed as I sat.

"Bored?" Jeff asked.

"Waiting's not my favorite thing."

"Want to take a walk?"

"Might as well," I said. On the way out the back hallway, I stuck my head into the office where Mitch was and told him we'd be out for a while. He continued to stare at the screen and flipped his hand. The message was clear.

Jeff and I walked down Highway 28 for a hundred yards and came to the stores of Warrendale. When we went into the general store, the manager came out to greet "Mr. Jeff." His genuflection obviously embarrassed Jeff. When we were back on the sidewalk, he said, "I hate that."

"It's good that you hate that," I said.

We approached the old men in overalls who were playing checkers in front of the appliance store. One of the men watching the games said, "Hidy, Mr. Jeff."

Jeff said, "How you doing, Gene?"

"Can't complain," Gene answered, then went on to complain about all of his various ills until one of the other men told him to hush up about all that.

After some more small talk, Jeff and I moved on. Soon we

were at the old mill where Fletcher and Estafan had been killed. We went inside.

Light from the painted window filtered into the mill. Jeff said, "I guess I need to get this cleaned up. I hadn't thought about that." We were standing next to a streak of blood on the floor.

I followed the streak to the far end of the mill. Molly had said the lab guys assumed this was Fletcher's blood. They figured he'd been shot up here, then dragged across the mill. Now I knew that it was Estafan who was killed at the far end. The GBI had no reason to examine all this blood. Fletcher's was the only body they had. Why type all of it? Of course, that won't be necessary now. Freddy admitted his guilt about Estafan's murder.

I stood and stared at the bloodstains. Two separate and unrelated murders had taken place at virtually the same time in a small country town. The odds of that happening had to be astronomical.

Those normal patterns, coupled with logic, dictated that there had to be some connection between the two events. What was it?

Jeff and I walked back toward the Warrendale square. "Looks like something's going on," Jeff said.

The checkers crowd, along with another twenty or so people, surrounded a car in the parking lot. As we approached, the crowd separated to reveal Chief Donald Lee and his patrol car.

Chief Lee said, "They said you were around here someplace, Mr. Jeff."

"What is it?" Jeff asked.

Donald Lee opened the back door to his car and pulled a handcuffed man from it. It was Mitch. The chief said to Jeff, "I was making my rounds and noticed the bank's security light was off. I checked it out and found this boy in the bank fooling around with the computer." Lee hitched up his pants. "He says you knew he was in there, but I didn't swallow that one bit."

Jeff pulled Donald Lee away from the crowd and spoke to

him quietly. Chief Lee nodded throughout the conversation. Jeff slapped him on the back, and Lee moved back to Mitch and unlocked the handcuffs. "Sorry about that," Lee said. He turned and said to the crowd, "Y'all can go on now." When nobody moved, he put his hand on his holstered gun and yelled, "Go on, I said!"

There was some mumbling, but the crowd dispersed and Chief Lee drove his car away.

"What'd you tell him?" I asked.

Jeff smiled and looked at Mitch. "I told him Mitch was conducting an audit for the Internal Revenue Service. He was impressed."

"Good thinking," I said.

"First, though, he was confused. He said he'd seen Mitch with you the night Fletcher was murdered."

"Uh-oh," Mitch said.

"But then I reminded him how all of y'all look alike. That seemed to satisfy him."

"Yassuh, Masser," Mitch said. "That shore is somethin' I done noticed. Yassuh, that shorely is amazin'."

I said, "Did you find anything?"

"Yep," Mitch said. "Something interesting. Mighty, mighty interesting."

Back in the bank, Mitch shut down the computer system and we sat in the lobby looking at a printout he provided. "It took me a while to find it. I looked under all of the obvious things. Found a couple of business accounts Commissioner Jones had. Not big ones. There were some Park County accounts, mostly having something to do with bonds."

I was looking at the printout. Jeff was behind me leaning over my chair. "Is this one of them?" I asked.

"Nuh-uh. It is a county account, though, sort of."

I looked at the top of the printout. The only identifying reference I could find read P.C.S.F.

Mitch said, "All of the accounts I could find where you would expect them to be looked okay. No problems. Nothing obvious, anyway. So I started looking around. Started looking for acronyms first and hit pay dirt."

Jeff asked, "What does P.C.S.F. mean?"

"It's cross-referenced as Park County Sunshine Fund."

I looked at Mitch. "Sunshine Fund?"

He nodded. "That's what it said. Usually that's some kind of fund that's collected from employees to buy flowers and gifts for each other for birthdays and funerals and stuff like that."

Mitch moved next to my chair. "Check this out." He moved his finger to the top of the printout. "Three months ago, the account held over two fifty."

I nodded. "So?"

"That's over two hundred fifty grand. That's in thousands of dollars. Two hundred fifty-three thousand one hundred fifty-nine dollars and nine cents to be exact."

"A sunshine fund with over a quarter of a million dollars?" Jeff mused.

"Not anymore. The account started to diminish in the last couple of months. It's down to a couple of thousand dollars now."

"Who are the signatories?" Jeff asked.

"That's -tory. Signatory. There's only one. Good ol' Commissioner Jones. And guess what else?"

I looked up from the printout. "What?"

"More than likely this account has never been examined by the state. The law requires that public accounts be audited. This wasn't listed that way. It was like a private account. For the record, anyway."

"Jeff, when did Fletcher first express an interest in buying Warrendale?" I asked.

"I'd just returned from Chicago when he called. That was around the first of August."

I said, "And you told Commissioner Jones."

"Yes. Like I said, he was the only one that I mentioned it to. But to get the ball rolling, I had to."

Mitch said, "So you get a call at the first of August, tell Jones about it, and by mid-August he starts taking money out of this account."

"He was nervous," I said.

"About an audit by the Fed," Jeff added.

Mitch said, "He couldn't just come in and get it all at once. That'd draw attention to the account."

Jeff sat in my chair. "So you're thinking that Commissioner Jones heard about the possible sale and got nervous about that account."

Mitch said, "He started taking money out slowly. Somewhere along the line he heard the bank was going to be audited if there was a sale."

Jeff said, "But he was still nervous. He asked about the audit a week ago."

I said, "Taking the money out wasn't good enough. The records would still be there. The only way to be sure he was in the clear was to stop the sale."

"Stop Fletcher," Mitch said.

"Kill him," I said.

"Jeez," Jeff said. "Like I told you, that audit wouldn't have even looked at that account."

"He didn't know that," I said.

Of course, this is all conjecture, I thought. When Molly gets back tomorrow evening, I'll hand Meadows over to her for Estafan's murder and lay down some heavy-duty hints about checking out a certain account at the Warrendale Bank.

I walked toward the back hallway. "Come on. Let's get out of here. I'm tired of thinking about this."

Outside, Mitch and I said good-bye to Jeff. Before I got in the Yugo, Mitch said, "I wonder where the money came from."

"I'm pretty sure I know the answer to that," I said.

"Where?"

"Radios, computers, roads, and parking lots. All funded but none paid for."

"What?"

"When one commissioner runs a county, Mitch, there's just too much power. Eventually, it gets in their blood and they can't help themselves so they help themselves."

Chapter Thirty-nine

As I hooked up my brand-new twenty-inch television, I felt the angst I always suffer when I spend money on things that aren't absolutely necessary. Mama had drummed economy into me.

What's done is done, I told myself.

On the way home from Warrendale, I'd stopped at Mitch's store. He had gone there rather than straight home. He wanted to give me the television, as I was afraid he would, but I insisted on paying for it. I finally agreed to buy it at cost.

I wanted the television for several reasons. First, Molly had installed cable at Professor Gatlin's house and had paid for an outlet to be put in my room. The cable company boasted thirty-six channels, but the television I'd inherited from Aunt Ouida needed a converter to get more than twelve. The mathematics favored buying a new television rather than renting a cable box.

I also told myself that I'd gone to college for seven years and I ought to be able to buy a new television, by God. While it was true that I didn't make much money at the society, I had some money in my savings account, lived rent-free, and had nobody else to spend it on.

The third reason was that I was tired of thinking about Lawton Fletcher, Freddy Meadows, and Warrendale. I needed a distraction and I figured that somewhere in thirty-six channels I'd find something to take my mind off all that.

I was wrong.

After stripping to my bra and panties and putting on my robe, I lay on my bed and used the remote control to flip through the channels. How could there be so many channels and yet nothing that I wanted to watch? Vanna White was selling a tooth whitener on one channel. It took me a while to realize that we'd never get back to the show. The commercial *was* the show. ESPN was broadcasting beach volleyball. No thanks. I watched wrestling on WTBS for a few minutes in honor of my new stepfather, Big Jack Pelham. He had retired from wrestling and I'd grown to care about him a great deal, but that sense of loyalty could not engender too much enthusiasm for the sport.

Finally, I settled on MTV, mostly to spite my mother. Once again, I remembered my days of listening to rock and roll on headphones attached to my portable radio and singing gospel whenever Mama passed by.

"Hee, hee, hee," I said aloud as I openly watched the decadence right there on television.

The phone rang. I almost didn't answer it. I *knew* it was Mama. She'd found out somehow.

But I had to answer it and it wasn't my mother.

An automated computer voice announced that I was receiving a collect call. A moment later, I heard a recorded voice say, "Anna."

It took a moment to remember who Anna was. As soon as I did, I answered "Yes" to the recorded request, accepting the call. The female automaton said, "Go ahead, please," and I said, "Hello?"

"Tammi?"

"Yes."

I could hear the sounds of traffic, but Anna said nothing.

"Anna? Are you all right?"

"You said I could call."

"Yes. What happened?"

"He did it. Freddy beat me up. You said I could call."

"Are you hurt?"

There was another hesitation that was undergirded by traffic noise. It was hard to hear. "He hit me. I need help."

Part of me wanted to jump up and go get her. Another part of me was ticked off. I'd just started to relax and forget about Park County. But, as much as I wanted to, I couldn't ignore the first part. "Where are you?" I asked.

"I'm at the Waffle House. Just out from Braxton. On the Athens Road."

Surely there was another way, I thought. "Anna, do you have anybody who you can stay with? Any family up there?"

Another loud silence followed. "I ain't got nobody. You said I could call."

I stared at the television. Steven Tyler of Aerosmith was grabbing his crotch. I hated to admit it, but maybe Mama was right about some things.

I looked at the clock radio on Aunt Ouida's nightstand. It was seven thirty-two. "Does Freddy know you're there?"

She sounded relieved. "No."

"It'll take forty-five minutes, at least. Stay there."

She said she would and we hung up. As I dressed, something kept knocking on my brain.

Something wasn't right.

How'd Anna get to Braxton? She lived with Freddy outside of Warrendale, which was twenty miles from there. And there was her tone of voice. She did sound distressed, but not panicked.

I didn't want to drive through Park County by myself again. Last time, I'd surprised the guy in the truck. Surprise seldom worked more than once. Even with stupid people.

I picked up the phone, held it, then slammed it down on its cradle. When are you going to grow up, Tammi? I thought. Handle it. Handle it. I got my purse, buoyed by the heftiness of the Model 58 in it, and headed to the front door. On the veranda, I stopped.

There's a difference between being independent and being

stupid. It wouldn't hurt to have somebody with me. If Molly was here, I'd ask her, but she wasn't.

I retreated to my room and called Mitch. When he answered, I heard female laughter in the background. I wanted to hang up without speaking, but when you're raised right, which is to say you're raised with southern grace, you don't do that, so I said, "Hi, Mitch. It sounds like you're busy. I'll call back later."

"Come on, Tammi, out with it."

I lie when I have to, but I'm not very good at it, especially with people who are important to me. I gave it a shot anyway. "I just wondered how you were doing."

"Oh, I'm doing fine. To tell you the truth, not a whole lot has happened since I saw you two hours ago. Now, what's going on?"

"Really. It's okay. I'll call you tomorrow."

He said, "Hold on." A moment later, he said, "They're in the kitchen. Eating pizza."

"They?"

"Uhh, yeah."

"Don't worry about it, Mitch. It's not important."

"You've got to help me," Mitch said.

"What?"

"Actually, something has happened since I saw you last. You know that research I was doing."

"Research?"

"You know. Looking for Florina Harvey."

"Uh-huh."

"One night, I sort of got . . . carried away, I guess. You know?"

"No."

"Apparently, I invited Kimberly over tonight. She brought a friend and some pizzas."

"You *apparently* invited her over?"

"Kimberly says I did."

"I've never known you to drink much, Mitch."

"Like I said, I got carried away. If you tell me you need me, that'll give me an excuse to send them away."

"Why don't you just tell them you made a mistake?"

"I hate to be rude."

"That's not being rude. It's being honest. There's a difference."

"You're right. Hold on." He put the phone down.

Over the phone I heard the Arnold Schwarzenegger voice again. "Oot. Oot. Both of you. I must travel to the past and capture the one who has escaped. Soon I will be vaporized into nothing but nuts and bolts. Take the pizza with you."

A woman said, loudly, "Man, you're crazy!"

Mitch said, "Hasta la vista, baby!" and I heard a door slam. A moment later, he was back on the phone and Arnold was gone.

I said, "I thought you were going to be honest."

"Somehow, Arnold was easier. Now, what's happening?"

I told him about the call from Anna.

Mitch said, "You *don't* need to go up there alone. We'll go with you."

"We?"

"Yeah. Dan and I."

"Dan's got other stuff going on."

"He told me all about it. He also said he needed to be involved in something. Hold on."

The phone clicked and sounded dead. A minute passed and Mitch was back. "You there, Tammi?"

"Yes."

"We're on three-way. Dan, you still on?"

"Yeah."

"Tammi, tell Dan what you told me."

I said, "Look, Dan, I don't want . . ."

"What's going on, Tammi?"

I repeated the story.

"I don't like it," Dan said. "Girls like Anna, who are in abusive relationships, don't just suddenly decide enough's enough. I've worked with a bunch of them. It's one of the most frustrating things I deal with. Sometimes their mamas will finally do something. But not the girls themselves. Anna could be an exception, but it'd be hard for me to believe."

"Yeah," I said. "I think that's why I called Mitch. I can't just ignore her, but I think I need some . . . backup."

"No problem," Mitch said. "We'll go up together."

"No," Dan said. A moment of silence passed. "How about Mitch and I following you?" Another pause. "Something's funny going on. If we're together, there's no cavalry. And if Anna really has decided she's had enough, there's no harm done if we're in two vehicles. I'll go by your place, Mitch, and pick you up. Freddy Meadows saw your battlewagon yesterday. If he's screwing around, it'd be good not to be obvious."

"It appears to me that you are casting aspersions about my taste in vehicles," Mitch said.

Dan laughed. "It's logistics, Mitch. How many brand-new, huge, old-fashioned station wagons do you think exist in northeast Georgia?"

Mitch said defensively, "The Beaver's family had one."

I broke into the argument. "Dan's right. If something funky's going on, there's no sense in taking chances."

Mitch surrendered. "Okay, we'll go in your Previa."

"My VW," Dan said.

"The bus?" Mitch said incredulously. "You've probably forgotten this, so I'll remind you. Hills exist between here and Braxton. It'd be good to get there before dawn."

Dan said, "It'll handle the hills. You just got to get some speed on the downhill parts. Besides, I know it can keep up with Tammi's Yugo. It's a moot point anyway. Meg's mother borrowed the Previa tonight. Her bridge group went to a tournament in Atlanta."

Mitch surrendered.

He shouldn't have.

★ ★ ★

A half hour later, as I passed the sign announcing Park County, I looked in my rearview mirror at the round lights of Dan's 1969 Volkswagen bus. As I negotiated the hills of the piedmont, I realized Dan had been wrong. It was hard to believe that there had ever been a vehicle built that would have to struggle to keep up with my Yugo. Dan's VW was struggling.

It was on one of those hills that I lost him. I saw the logging truck start to pull out from the woods. I tried to slow down so Dan could catch up, but before I could, the truck moved onto the road behind me. Soon my mirror was dark. I slowed and looked for a place to pull over and wait for them, but the forest that surrounded the road provided no respite. I slowed to thirty, waiting for the logging truck to catch up. Before it could, I saw the Waffle House sign.

I pulled into the parking lot, stopped near the road, and looked back down the highway. I saw nothing but darkness. Where are they, I thought?

I looked at the Waffle House. There was Anna, standing outside the door. If I made it this far without incident, maybe she had had a revelation, I thought. When I opened my door, I was staring into the barrel of a major-league pistol.

Chapter Forty

Keep both hands on the wheel. None of that judo stuff." The barrel of the pistol was against the back of my head. Freddy Meadows had quickly released the seat lock and climbed into the back of the Yugo, smashing me against the steering wheel as he did.

"What are you *doing?*" I asked in a stern voice. Stern wasn't what I felt inside. What I felt was icy fear. I didn't want him to know that.

"Somebody wants to see you. Pull on up to Anna. I got to tell her something."

I focused on the restaurant. Anna was still standing in front of the door.

"Who wants to see me?"

"You'll see." He pushed the barrel against my head harder. "Move it."

An involuntary shudder coursed through my body. I squeezed my hands tightly on the steering wheel, shut my eyes, and took a deep breath. All I could do was talk, I told myself. Stay calm. "And if I refuse?"

"Then I'll kill you. Maybe I spend a few years in jail. Big shit. I don't bring you in, and I'm dead for sure." I felt his breath against my ear. *"Move it."*

Freddy wasn't bluffing. I started the Yugo and drove toward Anna. Through the passenger-side window, Freddy said to her,

"Call that number I gave you and tell 'em we're on the way and take the Bronco back to the trailer."

"I don't have the keys," Anna said, fear in her voice.

"Oh, shit," Freddy said. I heard rustling in the backseat, then he leaned toward the window and threw the keys out the window. When he did that, the gun backed away from my head.

I turned and looked at Anna. She said, plaintively, "I'm sorry."

The gun was back against me. "Shut up," Freddy said to Anna. To me he said, "Get going."

"Where?"

"You'll see when we get there."

Strangely, my fear was replaced by irritation. "It would be real helpful if you'd tell me which direction to go."

"Oh, yeah." He moved the gun and pointed it toward the north. "That way."

As I pulled onto the highway, I looked in vain for Dan's bus. The highway was empty.

Clearly, the hot spot in Braxton on a Saturday night was the Waffle House. The rest of the town was dark and empty. Shortly after we left Braxton, Meadows told me to turn left. As I negotiated the curvy road, I said, "There are people who know where I was going. And why. You're just digging yourself in deeper."

"I'll take care of Anna. She won't say nothing." A moment later, Freddy said, "Slow down." His gun moved in front of me again. "There it is. Where the hay sign is."

I looked ahead and to my left and saw a mailbox with a sign hanging on it that said Hay For Sale. As I turned into the driveway, the Yugo's headlights illuminated a large house with barn red siding. A porch stretched across its front.

"Go on by the house," Freddy said.

We were on a narrow lane that went through a stand of trees. Beyond the woods were two chicken houses, illuminated by the full moon. Freddy's gun appeared in front of me and he pointed to the house on the right. "There he is."

I turned my car in that direction and the Yugo's lights fell on a man standing by the door of the chicken house. I recognized him. The last time I'd seen him was on a black-and-white television when Jeff and I were on top of the press box at Park County High School.

After I stopped the car, Freddy poked the gun against my head again. "Get out." He followed me and we approached Commissioner Jones.

The commissioner was dressed in overalls that covered a red-and-black plaid flannel shirt. He said, "I appreciate you coming up tonight." He looked beyond me to Freddy. "Goddamn, boy, what the hell you doing with that gun?"

"You said to get her up here, Uncle Harry."

"I didn't say to kidnap her, for Christ's sake. Put that thing away."

I looked around at Freddy. He put the pistol in the large pocket of his army fatigue jacket.

"Sheeeit," the commissioner said in disgust. "I apologize for my nephew, m'am. Sometimes I believe he's got oatmeal for brains."

The commissioner was Freddy's uncle? Did he get Freddy out of jail, rather than Cunningham? Why didn't I know he was the commissioner's nephew? A bunch of stuff would have made sense sooner if I'd known that.

" 'Course, he ain't blood kin. He belongs to my sister's second husband. Judging from him, oatmeal brains run in the family." Jones rubbed his arms. "It's getting nippy out here." He turned to the chicken house and opened the door slightly. To Freddy, he said, "You stay out here." He gestured for me to follow him.

I wasn't sure what to do. It appeared that the commissioner was unhappy about Freddy's forcing me to come here. Maybe I could just say, "No thanks" and leave. On the other hand, his irritation may have been an act—the country gentleman thing. I looked toward my Yugo and saw Freddy leaning on the driver's-side door. I looked back at the commissioner and decided I'd rather take my chances with him.

As soon as I walked in the door, I had to cover my nose with my hand, attempting to shield myself from the powerful smell that permeated the chicken house. The ammonia in chicken droppings gives the same jolt to the system as smelling salts.

The commissioner closed the door behind me. He said, "Give it a little time. You'll get used to it."

Over my hand, I looked around the building. It ran the length of a football field and was about forty-feet wide. The floor was completely covered by chickens. Everywhere. They backed away, climbing over one another in panic, clearing a space of about ten feet around me.

The commissioner said something, but I couldn't understand him over the panicked clucking of thousands of chickens. I felt his hand on my arm as he tugged me toward the wall on the right. We walked alongside a trough that was hanging by chains from the ceiling and was filled with feed. He led me to the wall where a two-by-ten plank formed a ledge about two feet off the ground around the house. Chicken droppings covered the plank. Jones pulled an empty burlap sack off the wall, put it on the ledge, and gestured for me to sit. He sat without worrying about covering the ledge.

Once we stopped moving, the chickens quieted down.

Jones said, "I apologize again for meeting out here. I wanted to talk to you, but I didn't want the missus to know. She don't need the worry."

Once again, anger replaced my fear. I moved my hand away from my face and said, "If you wanted to talk to me, all you had to do was make an appointment and come to my office."

He had both hands on his knees. "I needed to see you right away. I knew you was representing Freddy, and I asked him to see if you'd come up here to see me tonight. I don't know why in hell that boy didn't just ask you." He was silent for a moment. "Or maybe I do. He's done got hooked up with Billy Ray Cunningham and learned his ways, I guess."

I thought of the sunshine account we'd discovered earlier

that day. Getting hooked up with his uncle wasn't all that great for Freddy either, I thought. "So what do you want?" I asked.

The chickens, who had apparently become used to us, scattered again when Jones stood. He scratched his head and said, "You know, Miss Randall, this here's a big county landwise, but it ain't got a whole lot of people. Word spreads pretty fast when something unusual happens."

He knows we know, I thought. Fear edged back into my gut.

"I heard the IRS was up at the Warrendale Bank today."

Chief Donald Lee, I thought.

Jones leaned on a hand against the wall of the chicken house. "When I heard that, I called Chad Rabun at home and asked him if he knew what was going on at the bank. He hadn't heard anything about it, and that kind of surprised me since he's the president. He told me that the Warren boy'd been by the bank that morning to find out how to get into the computer." He sat on the ledge again, supporting himself with his elbows on his knees, and stared out toward the chickens. "Chad said there was a way he could tell on the computer what they'd looked at, so he went and checked. He told me they were looking at my accounts and the county's accounts.

"He said there was one account they was particularly interested in. He said they printed that one out." Jones looked at me. "I heard you was there too."

"What do you want from me, Commissioner?"

"I want your help."

"My help?"

"I'm going to need an attorney to help me when I confess come Monday morning."

Apparently, Jones didn't understand that I worked for Legal Aid. We represented only indigent clients, but I was too interested in the turn this conversation had taken to mention that. "Confess to what?"

"Miss Randall, I was raised by two of the finest people you ever seen and I been to the Sunday morning services at Calvary Baptist near about every week of my life. I done lived with this long enough." He looked to the chicken house's roof. "I know Mama's seen ever thing I done from up there in heaven, and I can't stand the shame no more."

His remorse seemed genuine, but I'd seen the same act a zillion times in my office. His saying he wanted to confess and wanting me to represent him was an interesting touch. What did he *really* want from me?

He sighed heavily. "The fact is I've been stealing money."

"That's what we guessed. You've been putting it into the county's sunshine fund."

He nodded slowly. "It started with the drought of '89. I overbought on cattle that year and lost a bunch of money. And the hay didn't grow, so I had to buy feed that winter. Everything I did after that to try to recover didn't work. In '91 eighteen cows got killed by lightning and I lost another load to shipping fever. 'Course I'd canceled my insurance after the '89 drought 'cause I couldn't afford it." He looked around the chicken house. "Now, this is all I got. The poultry company puts the chickens in here and pays for the feed. All I do is baby-sit."

I said, "So you started selling off county property and diverting money from state and federal grants."

"You know more than I thought. Guess that means the IRS does too." He stood again and put his hands in his back pockets. "Started off just to pay the property tax. Ain't no way I could still be commissioner and not pay the taxes. One day this check come in for some computers for the welfare. I sat there and held it and looked at it. It'd be easy to do. We had this sunshine fund that never got audited by nobody." He kicked at a chicken that was pecking at his boot. "Figured I'd pay it back soon as it came time to sell the cattle, but that year we had plenty of rain. The bottom dropped out of the prices. I didn't even get back what I'd put into 'em. No way I could pay back the welfare, and I had to pay the bills coming due for fertilizer. Two tractors broke too."

"So you stole some more and it got easier."

His eyes moved quickly to mine. "Didn't get no easier. I hated it."

"How much land do you have?" I asked.

"Couple of hundred acres."

"If you hated stealing so much, why didn't you sell some land?"

"First, it was kind of like gambling, I guess. I kept figuring I'd make it back next time." He looked toward the roof again. "This land's been in my family since before the War Between the States. I went and mortgaged it off before I started. . . ." He looked at me again. "But that money's all gone too."

The wood plank I was sitting on was digging into my legs. I stood and rubbed the sore spots. "So you killed Lawton Fletcher to keep him from buying Warrendale so there wouldn't be an audit?" I regretted the question as soon as I asked it. I'd gotten caught up in his story and had forgotten my predicament. His apparent sincerity had lulled me.

"What?" He sounded incredulous.

It was too late. I couldn't just say "Never mind." Besides, I felt fairly confident. It was just the commissioner, the chickens, and me in here. I wasn't sure about the chickens, but I knew that I could handle the commissioner. I was also ready to know the truth about Fletcher's murder. "I know you were worried about a bank audit if the bank sold. Kill Fletcher and the audit's off. That'd give you time to close the account and get rid of the evidence. What you obviously didn't know was that when a bank sells, the auditors don't look at individual accounts. They're just interested in the overall health of the bank. You killed Fletcher for nothing."

For the first time, anger entered Jones's voice. "Look, missy, I know I done wrong, but I ain't no murderer. I don't know nothing about that movie actor." His anger left as quickly as it came. He sat on the ledge again and bowed his head. He was staring at the floor. "Lord, ain't this ever gonna end?"

This wasn't an act. He was telling the truth. I knew it. And I also knew I was back at square one, again, on who killed Lawton Fletcher. Of course, at this point, part of me didn't care. There was no way I would continue to represent Freddy Meadows after tonight. Hell, I thought, the bastard probably did it.

There was another part of me, though. The part that forced me to finish college and law school. I'd come this far. I wanted to know. I sat down again next to the commissioner. "A while ago, when you were telling me why you didn't sell your land so you could quit stealing, you said something about gambling and the land being mortgaged, but there was something else, wasn't there?"

His head was in his hands. "Yes."

"What?"

"Billy Ray Cunningham."

Back to Cunningham, I thought. "What about him?"

Jones stood again. "He found out what I was doing. We had some surplus graders that I figured I could sell with nobody knowing. Turned out I was dealing with the same organization Cunningham sells his cars to. After that . . ."

"He blackmailed you and you had to keep diverting funds. He got a cut."

"That's about it, except it got to where I got a cut and he got the rest." He picked some feed from the trough and let it slide through his fingers. "So how about it? Like I said, the bank owns my land now and I ain't got no cash. At least that's not stolen. Can't afford no lawyer, so if you don't take my case, I'll be stuck with Carl White."

Before I could respond, chaos broke loose. The chickens began screaming and jumping on each other. I turned to see the door flying open.

Just as I had the commissioner, I recognized the man from Friday night's football game. Billy Ray Cunningham. He kicked at the chickens as he entered and was followed by Freddy Meadows, who had his pistol out again. Behind him were Dan and Mitch.

They were being held at gunpoint by Sheriff Cox.

276

Chapter Forty-one

Billy Ray Cunningham adjusted his round, wire-rim glasses and said, "How you doing, Harry?"

The commissioner didn't respond to Cunningham. Instead, he looked at his nephew. "What are you doing, Freddy?"

Freddy said, "You're a son of a bitch, *Uncle* Harry."

Cunningham leaned against a support post and kicked a chicken hard. It went flying across the house. Other chickens scattered when it fell among them. It was clearly dead. "He knows, Harry. I told him Wednesday that you set it up with the DA to get a bail set that'd keep him in jail."

"You son of a bitch," Freddy said again to his uncle.

Cunningham moved his hand from the pole and stroked his nose. "God, I hate these places. Smell like shit." He looked at Commissioner Jones. "When I got back from the deer camp and found out, I had a little talk with the judge and got that fixed and told Freddy about how his favorite uncle was keeping him in jail to save his own skin."

The sympathy I'd felt for the commissioner began to diminish. My guess was that he figured if Freddy's arrest for Lawton Fletcher's murder held up, the investigation would be limited. He was afraid that an investigation into the killing would result in somebody looking into all the business of Warrendale, including the bank. He was right, of course. That's exactly what happened. Despite Jones's apparent remorse about being a thief, he still tried to manipulate the system and keep himself out of trouble until he believed that the IRS had showed up. Then, he figured there was no way out.

Cunningham sighed deeply, clearly for effect. "You never have understood, Harry. Ain't nothing ever going to happen to anybody who works for me, for ever and ever, amen." He kicked at another chicken, but missed. "Unless you cross me, Harry. When Freddy told me you wanted to see her," he nodded at me, "I knew you were crossing me. That just won't do, Harry."

I looked across the sea of chickens to Mitch and Dan. How'd they end up here? I thought. I knew they didn't follow me. My eyes moved past them to Cox, who was leaning against the door, his pistol aimed between them and the commissioner and me.

Cunningham said, "Now, we got to do something about all this." He looked at the commissioner. " 'Course, you ain't no problem, Harry. You're local. A simple fire'll do." He waved his hand toward me, then at Dan and Mitch. "But, for these three, something special's got to happen. It's a pain in the butt." He walked through the chickens to Freddy and put his hand on Freddy's shoulder. "Looks to me like we need to have a tragic traffic accident." Cunningham looked at Cox. "Freddy and the sheriff'll take care of that."

I looked at Mitch and Dan. They were standing impassively. Dan twirled his fingers slightly. Talk, was the message. Delay them and see if something happens. I said, "Freddy, I need to know something. Did you kill Fletcher?"

At the sound of his name, Freddy raised his pistol toward me. "I already told you what happened. Fletcher was dead when I saw him."

Cunningham said, "The truth is, I'd like to know who killed that boy. I don't like things happening in my county without me knowing about it." He waved his hand around the room. "Look what it's caused. But I'll find out, and I'll take care of it." He looked at Sheriff Cox. "Ever since you got elected, you been sucking up to me. Well, now's your chance. Take care of this deal." He pointed to me.

Cox stood still.

I looked at Dan. His eyes locked on mine. He barely nodded, then moved his eyes from me to the sheriff. He closed his eyes for a moment before shifting them toward Freddy, who had dropped his arm again.

I understood Dan's message. Given the opportunity, I'd go after Cox, who was closer to me, and he'd get Freddy.

I turned toward Cox just as he started to move. To provide balance, I shifted my feet as nonchalantly as I could.

Strangely, I wasn't afraid. I was angry.

Cox moved toward me. I stared into his eyes. When he was five feet from me, it happened.

He winked.

It was subtle, but I knew I saw it. The wink was deliberate. I looked to Dan and shook my head slightly. I hoped he understood.

Cox passed by me and walked to Freddy and Cunningham. Before Freddy knew what was happening, the sheriff had the barrel of his gun under Freddy's chin and had grabbed his pistol. "Give it up," Cox said. When Freddy hesitated, Cox threw a knee in Freddy's groin and pulled the gun out of his hand. Freddy yelped and fell on the floor, rolling in the chicken droppings and holding himself between his legs.

The sheriff pointed his pistol at Cunningham, then looked at me and said, "Come here." I walked through the chickens and he gave me Freddy's pistol. "From what I hear, you know how to use this."

"From what you hear?" I asked.

Cox smiled slightly. "I stopped Ralph Brooks today for driving with a messed up windshield. He told me about what Billy Ray made him do and about what you'd done. I guess he figured that I was working with Billy Ray and that'd make it right. Ralph'll be in jail before the night's over."

"Good," I said.

"How about taking the commissioner and Freddy out front. My car's in the other direction. I don't want to handle them all in the dark. When I get to the car, I'll call for some backup and drive around."

I accepted Freddy's pistol and cocked it. Dan and Mitch grabbed Freddy underneath his armpits and pulled him up. Mitch said, "Ohhh, gross."

I looked at the commissioner. He looked at the gun and said, "You don't need that."

I nodded, and Jones and I followed Mitch and Dan toward the door. They were holding Freddy Meadows between them. As I was closing the door to the chicken house, I looked back at Sheriff Cox and Billy Ray Cunningham.

"You'll be sorry, Cox." Cunningham said. "You're a dead man, just like your grandpappy."

When I got outside, Freddy was spreadeagled on the ground, with the commissioner sitting next to him. Dan and Mitch were leaning against the hood of the Yugo, watching them. I got between Mitch and Dan, training the gun on Meadows. "So what happened?" I asked.

Dan made a clucking sound. "Got behind that logging truck and lost you. When we arrived at the Waffle House, you were gone, but Anna wasn't. She was inside eating a hamburger. It didn't take much persuading for her to tell us what was going on and where you and Freddy were going."

"She felt real bad about how she got you up here," Mitch said.

"Yeah," I said.

Dan continued. "So we get here. It takes a while because we had to find the address in a phone book and get directions. As soon as we get out of the van, the sheriff and that other guy are there and we're caught."

"Billy Ray Cunningham," I said.

Dan said, "There's a bunch here I don't understand."

I said, "You're not alone. After all this, I still don't have a clue as to who killed Lawton Fletcher."

"That isn't what I'm talking about. Why did Cox capture Mitch and me, then let us go?"

I recounted my conversation with the sheriff when we were in my car the night I was stuck, about his grandparents and Cunningham. He also had said something about how you have to go along to get along. Apparently, he was biding his time while he waited to find Cunningham in a situation where he could put him in jail.

"There won't be much jail time on this deal," Mitch said. "Some kind of charge on terroristic threats, or something like that. A few months, maybe."

"You don't know the whole story," I said. "Cunningham got in on the commissioner's sunshine fund deal. They were both stealing the county blind." I nodded toward Jones. "He's ready to tell all and that ought to mean more time than a few months." My arm was tiring, so let my arm and the pistol drop to my side. Freddy obviously wasn't going anywhere. "The only problem is that a Park County judge and jury will be trying Cunningham. It's hard for me to imagine getting a conviction, much less jail time, for him in this county."

"There's something else I don't understand," Dan said.

"What?" I asked.

He turned around and pointed toward the lane leading to Jones's house. "My van's up that way. After they got us, we walked by the house and through some woods to get here. I'd swear I saw a police car sitting in the woods." He turned around. "So why'd the sheriff say his car was in the other direction?"

"Umm," I said, and thought for a moment.

Suddenly, visions of sitting with Cox in his cruiser that rainy night flashed in my mind. Before I could move, three gunshots resounded through the silence of the night. The cacophony of thousands of chickens going berserk followed.

Dan sprang forward and landed a fist on the back of Freddy

Meadows's neck as Freddy was trying to stand. Freddy fell back to the ground, limp.

"What the hell?" Mitch exclaimed.

The door to the chicken house opened and Sheriff Cox walked to us. He looked down at Dan, whose knee was resting on Meadows's back. "Good," Cox said, "looks like you got things under control out here."

I looked at Cox, and he looked at me. The sheriff said quietly, "The son of a bitch resisted arrest and I had to defend myself." He put his pistol into his holster. "Guess I'd better go call an ambulance. Actually, I'd better call the coroner too."

He stood silently for a moment. "By the way, we got a break on the Fletcher case late this afternoon. A crew that was clearing pipelines found a motorcycle in a ravine behind the mill in Warrendale. It was well hidden."

It took a moment for what he said to register. I was still trying to absorb what had just happened.

Cox said, "We found a Colt DA thirty-eight in the cycle's saddlebag. I'll bet that the bullet that killed Fletcher will match that old Colt. There's just not that many turn-of-the-century guns around." The sheriff scratched his chin. "So I figure whoever was driving that motocycle killed Fletcher. The problem is, it appears the cycle was stolen. Showed up on a sheet out of Atlanta."

I remembered Molly's words when she told me what the lab had discovered. "We find that gun, and we've found the murderer." Sheriff Cox would know that too.

The night Fletcher died, the parking lot had been empty when Mitch and I'd arrived. That was also the night Freddy Meadows killed Robert Estafan. I looked at Freddy, who was still lying facedown on the ground. I knelt next to him and said, "Estafan had a motorcycle, didn't he? You got rid of it before you took the body to C and C's."

"Yeah."

I knew Freddy Meadows had killed Estafan, and why. But why would Estafan shoot Fletcher? Against all odds, what'd happened was the most unlikely of events: a stranger-on-stranger murder in Park County.

Then Cox said, "We found something else in the saddlebag. Ten thousand dollars in cash." He looked at me. "You reckon Fletcher'd be carrying that kind of money on him?"

No, I thought. He wouldn't. But ten thousand dollars was a familiar figure. That's the exact amount Lawton Fletcher had sent Florina Harvey and Charlotte Perry each month for the past year.

Charlotte hadn't cashed her checks. I saw them. Florina had cashed hers, but she'd put the money in CDs.

That's what she said, anyway.

I looked up at the multitude of stars that sparkled through the pitch black sky. I heard Sheriff Cox as he moved away toward his car, but I continued to stare silently at the heavens.

There was a rustling to my left as Mitch and Dan pulled Freddy up from the ground. Meadows said, "Hell, the boy was half Mex, you know. He ain't got no people of his own. Who's gonna care?"

A beat passed, then I snapped my head toward Freddy.

The money.

The antique gun.

What Dorothy Sanford had told me about Estafan.

Ask enough questions. Pay attention to what you see and hear, even if none of it seems to matter. Eventually, something will come together. That's what Dan had preached during the Jarvis thing and a year ago with Crowe.

There were still questions to ask and calls to make.

But—if I was right . . .

Why?

Chapter Forty-two

Charlotte Perry sat on her worn sofa, exactly where she'd sat the day that she asked me to search for her adopted brother's killer. She looked at Dan and Mitch, who were standing in front of the fireplace. "I'm so pleased you're here. I've read all about both of you, you know."

Molly Malone and I were sitting in matching wing armchairs across a coffee table from Charlotte. Molly said, "Ms. Perry, I'm afraid that I must place you under arrest for being an accessory to Lawton Fletcher's murder." Then she recited the Miranda rights. Charlotte said she understood them.

It was just after ten on Monday morning. Molly hadn't arrived home until late the night before, but I didn't mind waiting. I needed to make a couple of phone calls to confirm my hunches and they had to be made this morning, and I was certain Charlotte Perry wasn't going anywhere.

I also called Mitch and Dan. Each said he wanted to be here. I figured they would. I've learned that when you've played for mortal stakes, you want to know why.

Charlotte reached under the coffee table and retrieved her well-worn copy of *Triple Threat*. "I knew I was taking a chance when I tried to hire you." She looked at me. "But I couldn't let that boy go to jail for something I knew he didn't do."

Molly said, "So you are confessing to your part in the murder."

"Oh yes. It's a great relief to do so. When I heard on the radio that morning that the boy . . . what's his name?"

"Freddy Meadows," I said.

"Yes. When I heard he was arrested, I was very distraught because I knew he didn't do it." She looked at me. "I was hoping that you would clear him of suspicion. I was also hoping that you would not catch Robert Estafan or connect him to me." She flipped through the pages of Lucas Anderson's book. "I'm not surprised that you did, though."

This was a different Charlotte Perry from the one I'd met in this room not so long ago. After that meeting, I thought she was demented. Now, I understood her behavior. I know from personal experience what grinding guilt can do to you.

Charlotte looked up from the book. "I know I don't deserve anything, but I would like to know how you figured it out."

"Me, too," Mitch said.

I looked at Molly. She shrugged and nodded.

I said, "A long time ago, Dan taught me to gather information. Something will eventually come together, even if the information seems insignificant at the time."

Charlotte said, "I remember that." She started flipping pages, then held the book up. "Here it is." It occurred to me then that Charlotte might be a bit demented after all. She had a strange fixation on *Triple Threat*.

My inclination was to retell the whole story, but I cut to the quick instead. "First, there was the ten thousand dollars that the sheriff found in Estafan's motorcycle. That's the exact amount of the checks you said Lawton sent every month for the past year. You said you hadn't cashed them. You even showed me a handful of them. But two were missing. The last two."

Charlotte sighed. "I didn't lie to you, you know."

"No, you didn't. You just showed me a bunch of checks and said you had few needs."

"Yes."

"This morning, Molly and I found out you'd cashed two of his checks. One after Mitch and I went to California. One before that—two days before Lawton was murdered.

"When Sheriff Cox told me about the money, a nice round sum, it seemed reasonable to think that either you or Lawton's sister Florina might be involved. Both of you received ten thousand dollars from him on a regular basis. Actually, she seemed more likely. She had admitted that she'd cashed the checks he'd sent her.

"But then Freddy Meadows said something that triggered some memories. Dorothy Sanford, the director of Park County DFACS had told me that Estafan had been on her caseload. I figured there was a good chance that he'd been in foster care so I called Dorothy and asked her to check her files. She said that five years ago Park County had asked their counterparts in Teal County to find a foster home for Estafan. She confirmed that your parents were the foster parents. He was here for three months." I moved to the piano.

"The murder weapon was a rare antique gun, and your parents had several antiques, like this rosewood piano."

"Yes," Charlotte said. "The Colt was one of my father's favorites."

I returned to the chair and sat. I leaned forward, clasped my hands, and rested my elbows on my knees. "Now, Ms. Perry. *I* need to know something. Why? Why did you hire Estafan to kill Lawton Fletcher?"

Charlotte Perry's stoical demeanor began to fade. A tear fell down her cheek. "I did it for my mother."

"You told me your mother loved Lawton."

Charlotte let the tear fall on her breast. "She did. But he didn't love her. He killed her."

"Lawton killed your mother?"

Charlotte banged *Triple Threat* on the coffee table. "Yes! When he first came here, he was eight years old and was an *awful* child." She shook her head. "Just plain awful. My mother and father gave him a loving home and the discipline he sorely needed. And how did he repay that? I'll tell you how. He went out to Hollywood and did *awful* things."

"What things?"

"Sex and drugs. It was all in the papers." Charlotte looked at me. When I didn't respond, she said, "Mother was mortified. He killed her two months after Daddy passed on."

"How?" I asked.

"We were at the grocery store. We passed by the magazine rack and there he was. On the front of a magazine, naked. He was turned sideways, but he was naked. Right there for everybody to see." Charlotte sobbed. She buried her face in her hands and said again, "Right there for everybody to see." Her crying intensified. *"He killed her!"* she screamed. Tears were flowing down her face. A minute later, the crying slowed and she began to sniff hard, her head jerking with every sniff.

I said, "You told me she had a heart attack."

Between jerks, Charlotte said, "Two hours after we got home. She kept talking about it. About the picture. Then she grabbed her chest and fell. She was dead when the ambulance arrived." She wiped her face with her hands, looked at me, and said quietly, "He killed my mother."

I wasn't going to argue with her about that. I said, "But he changed. You told me that."

With vehemence, she said, "It was a *cruel* change. Too late. Mama was dead. He acted like he didn't even know he'd killed her."

I looked at Dan. He rolled his eyes and shook his head slightly.

Charlotte continued, "And he was going to buy that town and live here. He said he wanted to live *here*. With *me*. In my mother's house." She hit an opened hand on the sofa. "I couldn't . . . I just *couldn't* allow that to happen. So I cashed one of Lawton's check and gave the money to Robert Estafan. I couldn't use Mama's money. She loved him."

I leaned back in my chair. From what Florina Harvey said, Fletcher hadn't told anybody but her that he was dying. He wanted her to know because his disease was inherited. Charlotte obviously didn't know he had a terminal disease. She didn't know his living here wouldn't have been for long. He obviously thought Charlotte would take care of him as his condition worsened.

Molly stood. "Ms. Perry, you're going to have to come with me."

"Yes," she said. "I know." She picked up *Triple Threat.* "May I take this?"

Molly nodded.

I was uneasy. A question remained unanswered. I said to Charlotte, "Have they sent Lawton's things from California?"

Charlotte nodded and pointed toward the back of the house. "It's out on the back porch. Just a box of stuff. I haven't looked at it."

"How about what was in his car?"

"It's out there, too."

"Do you mind if I look at it?"

"I don't mind. Just promise me you'll burn it when you're done . . . just like Lawton's burning in hell right now."

"Let's go," Molly said. To me, she said, "You'll lock up?"

"Yes," I said.

Dan, Mitch, and I stood at the door, watching Molly put Charlotte in her car. Dan said, "Diminished capacity would probably be a good bet for a defense."

"No doubt," I said, then looked at Dan. "How are you doing?"

"Fine, just fine."

Mitch said, "Tell her, Dan."

The three of us stood silently. Finally, I said, "Tell me what?"

Dan said, "Well . . . I haven't really decided yet."

"Yes you have," Mitch said.

Dan chuckled. "Tammi, I think my Freudian unconscious has been telling me something. I told you the other night that I've been feeling down."

"Yes," I said. "And you said something about your time in the army. Are you reupping?"

Dan laughed. "No. But I was in an intelligence unit in 'Nam.

Learned all sorts of things that I never thought I'd use again."

"Like picking any lock that's ever been made," Mitch said.

"Yeah, like that." Dan looked at me. "I thought that a change in venue might help, but it didn't. Going to Indiana just confirmed what I've been feeling. The fact is I'm tired of spending my days mediating fights among fourteen-year-olds. When it's not that, I'm dealing with kids in impossible situations. I know I can help them live through it, but I'm thinking of leaving that to the next generation and moving in another direction."

"What's that?" I asked.

"The most alive I've felt during the past few years has been during the Jarvis thing, and a year ago with Gilstrap, and now this." He rubbed the white spot on his black hair. "Of course, I came in late on this deal and about the only thing I did is allow myself to get captured."

"Dan—"

He raised his hand to stop me. "The fact is that there were some things in 'Nam that I enjoyed. The investigation part. Figuring out things. I've talked to Meg and she said I ought to do it. Her Aunt Rose left her a pretty good hunk of money and that'd get us by until I got established."

"Get established?."

"Private investigator. With the four-lane being completed to Atlanta next year, we could stay here and I could work where there'd be enough business to support us. I figure I'll finish out the school year, and work on selling myself until then."

I said, "I think that you need to do what you need to do. Maybe if we get the grant we're working on, we'll have money to hire an investigator when we need one."

Mitch said in a deep voice, "Name's Hawk. Call me when you need me, Spenser. That is, when you be in trouble and require rescuin'."

"Right, Mitch," Dan said. "Well, that's in the future and now I gotta get back to my teenagers."

"Me, too," Mitch said. "My salespersons. You wouldn't believe the stuff *I* have to deal with."

Dan took his arm. "Tell us about it later. Meanwhile, give me a ride to school in your battlewagon."

I couldn't hear clearly as they were walking away from Charlotte's house, but Mitch was saying something about the Beaver.

On Charlotte's back porch, I opened a box with a label indicating it had been sent by Fletcher's agent in California. There wasn't much in there and I'd already looked at most of it when Mitch and I were in Los Angeles.

But I wanted to go through it. The one thing left to know was why Lawton Fletcher wanted to buy Warrendale. I didn't *have* to know that, I just wanted to.

Chapter Forty-three

Jeff and I were sitting on his veranda that overlooked the rolling pastures and the hills beyond. When I'd called him from Charlotte Perry's house, he'd invited me for lunch. It was ready when I arrived.

We sat at a table covered by a linen tablecloth. I bit into the sandwich he had prepared. "This is wonderful."

He shrugged off the compliment. "It's easy. I first had it at the King and Prince on Saint Simons Island. It's shaved ham and Swiss. You put it on the bread and dip it in a beaten egg and grill it."

"I'll remember that. The best I can do is bologna with a lot of mayonnaise." He served the sandwich with grapes, strawberries, and a pineapple slice. I took a grape, chewed on it, and leaned back, regarding the magnificent landscape. "I don't know how you can leave this and go back to Miami."

He wiped his lips with a linen napkin and turned slightly to follow my gaze. "Like I said before, part of me doesn't want to go back." He turned his head to me again. "But, what I do is in Miami, and . . . there are a lot of hard memories here."

I nodded, and took another bite of the sandwich. "The stories you told . . . about your ancestors?"

"I don't want to be a part of that."

The song had been echoing in my mind since I heard it during the Fire-Baptists' Wednesday night prayer meeting. I said,

"You're worried about the power in your blood?"

He pursed his lips and nodded slightly. "I saw what happened to my brothers. As soon as they became responsible for running Warrendale, they turned out to be just like all the others that came before them."

"The difference is that you're thinking about it. You're aware of what power can do to a person. And you have the same kind of power in Miami. A landlord who befriends a tenant like Florina Harvey isn't likely to become Simon Legree just because he's in Warrendale."

"I'm not so sure about that. You heard the folks in town Saturday. They all call me 'Mr. Jeff,' for God's sake."

"Maybe you could structure it so your blood couldn't help but move you in the right direction."

"How?"

I told him what had happened. After the part about Charlotte Perry's arrest, I asked, "Have you wondered why Lawton Fletcher wanted to buy Warrendale?"

"Not until I started talking to you. I've heard the rumor that started after word got out about his interest in the town. He was going to make some kind of movie studio out of it. I thought that was stupid."

"It was. I think I know what he planned to do."

Jeff narrowed his eyes. "What?"

I reached down and retrieved a folder that was sitting next to my purse and placed it on the table. "I first saw this in Fletcher's apartment when Mitch and I were in California. I didn't pay much attention to it then. It didn't seem important."

"What is it?"

"It's a script for a movie. Its title is *New Dawn*. I read it this morning at Charlotte Perry's house. Fletcher's agent told Mitch and me that it was the only script Fletcher'd been interested in for over a year.

"It's about a kind of Boys Town. In some ways it reminded me of a book I read in high school called *Bless the Beasts and the Children*."

Jeff said, "I saw the movie on TV. One of those old movie channels, I think. I haven't read the book."

"*New Dawn* is about a place that takes care of homeless children. There's a lot of melodrama in it, but that's the basic idea." I turned the script toward Jeff and said, "Fletcher wrote this on the last page. That's what made me read it."

Jeff looked at the words:

> *Warrendale! Do it! Call Florina*
> *and find that guy's name! There's*
> *so little time—*

I pulled another piece of paper out of my purse. "This was found in Fletcher's car." Jeff looked at the drawing. "He planned to convert the mill to a gymnasium."

Jeff held the drawing and said, "You think he was planning to make Warrendale a Boys Town?"

"Something like that. But more like a foster town, I suspect. Someplace where kids could go so they wouldn't have to go from home to home, the way he and Florina did. Someplace that was always home." Remembering Charlotte's comment about Fletcher's interest in the Mexicans, I added, "Maybe a place that'd take care of the migrant children, too.

"In my job, I work closely with Family and Children's Services. I know what happens. Foster kids are like yo-yos. They're abused by their parents and are placed in a home, then they go back to their parents until it happens again, and it's back to another foster home. Over and over, forever and ever." I leaned toward Jeff. "That's not going to change. But imagine if there was a place, a whole town that was devoted to foster care. Not an institution—a big impersonal building—but a whole town. One where, when a kid yo-yos back, he's not going to another set of strangers, but to a place he knows. A whole extended family that welcomes him back with opened arms. In their homes, in the stores . . . everywhere." I patted the script of *New Dawn*. "That was Lawton Fletcher's dream."

Jeff pushed his chair away from the table and rubbed his forehead. "Rechannel the power," he said.

"Exactly," I said.

"I can't imagine how it would work."

"I can't either."

He rested his chin in the cusp between his thumb and fingers. "It's something to think about."

"Yes," I said.

Moments passed.

"I've got a reservation on Delta to go back to Miami tomorrow." He chewed on a strawberry. "I think I'll cancel it."

I nodded behind a smile and ate a strawberry too.

He said, "Do you have to get back to work?"

I thought about that. I'd been away from the office too much. Now that there was nothing left to do on this case, the guilt factor was multiplying.

Jeff said, "I was thinking about going to the river." He began wailing, right there on the porch.

I laughed.

I was decided.

To hell with guilt.

A soft knock sounded on my bedroom door. I'd just finished my bath and was on my bed, sitting against its headboard. "Come in," I said.

Misty came through the door. "Hey," she said.

"Hi."

"I haven't seen you in a while and, like, just wondered how it went with that guy? Was my dress all right?"

"Your dress was great. Sorry I messed it up. And the shoes."

"Oh, don't worry about that. Mom told me about some of the stuff that's been going on. You couldn't help it."

I scooted over on the bed and patted the space I'd left. "Sit down." After she sat, I said, "So, how's it going with you?"

"Okay, I guess. Joey asked me to go with him today."

"I thought you said your mom didn't allow boyfriends."

"She doesn't. Going out doesn't really mean 'going out.' Know what I mean?"

"I guess," I said doubtfully. "Anyway, this guy, do you like him?"

"Oh, he's all right. He just called and dumped me, though."

"Already?"

She shrugged. "That's the way it goes."

"It's good not to depend on a boy for your happiness, but I think you're sadder than you're saying. It's good to talk to somebody when you're sad."

"Yeah, well . . ." She picked up a book off my nightstand and opened it, but shut it quickly. "Sorry, I didn't know that was your diary."

"When you're older, you call it a journal. It's the same thing, though. Writing things down is a good way to get stuff off your chest, too."

"I guess. I always, like, forget to write in mine, though."

"I forget too," I told her.

Misty stood. "Well, I've got some math homework to do." She moved to the door. "Mama says I've got to make A's or I'm grounded. Even in math." She stopped and turned. "Do you think that's fair?"

"Without doubt. Especially in math."

Misty grimaced and left the room.

I was still holding the journal.

A lot had happened, and I had some things to resolve in my own mind. I decided to follow my own advice. I retrieved a pen from my nightstand drawer and opened the book.

Where to start?

From the beginning, I thought.

I wrote:

Something's happening.

My fear is diminishing. It hasn't gone away, but during the

*past few weeks there were times when I should have been afraid,
but wasn't. Not for long, anyway.*

*Anger has replaced the fear and that does scare me. If the
wrath keeps surfacing, someone who doesn't deserve it will be hurt
badly someday.*

That someone may be me.